Talking about It

Talking about It

Tim Parks

ET REMOTISSIMA PROPE

Published by Hesperus Press Limited
4 Rickett Street, London SW6 1RU
www.hesperuspress.com

Talking about It © Tim Parks, 2005
Tim Parks asserts his moral right to be identified as the author
of this work under the Copyright, Designs and Patents Act 1988.
First published by Hesperus Press Limited, 2005

Designed by Fraser Muggeridge studio
Typeset by William Chamberlain
Printed in Jordan by the Jordan National Press

ISBN: 1-84391-704-1

Contents

Talking about It

I

George and Michael became good friends one evening in early May. Till then they had only met through their wives, or just occasionally and casually at the lounge bar of 'The Mermaid', a smoky, unhealthy retreat more or less equidistant from their Holborn offices. Michael was an earnest, extrovert, nervous character, and tended to make friends quickly or not at all. He had little time for careful, reserved men of George's variety; true, the dapper George did possess a quick, sly wag's wit, but he would never expose himself, never confess anything, nor ever gossip about anyone else. And Michael, who lived in a whirl of chatter, self-disclosure and innocent denigration, found this rather dull.

However, with both these career executives fast approaching the day when people would refer to them as middle-aged, both constantly alerted by their wives to incipient weight problems, they had rather reluctantly been persuaded to kill the rush hour together one evening a week with a game of squash in a nearby club. Hence on this particular evening they met in 'The Mermaid' for a swift half after work, and then proceeded to walk through busy streets towards the club.

It was springtime, and for all the fumes the air smelt fresh and promising. The narrow streets were full of women – many of them well dressed, some attractive – jostling from office to tube. Michael, despite all the springs that had come and gone, all the endless days he had elbowed to and from one place of work or another, was extremely susceptible to such stimuli. What's more, he was presently going through a profound emotional crisis. So that as they walked into the club and found their way to the changing room, he couldn't help attempting another assault on George's reserve, and so enquired: 'Just between ourselves, you know old mate, what do you think about, well, I suppose you'd say platonic relationships? Are they, er, do you think they're really possible?'

The more compact, squarer man turned and arched thick eyebrows. 'We should manage,' he said lightly, 'if you can stop looking at my arse.'

It was precisely this kind of response that irritated the earnest, precipitous Michael. Not only did it bar the road to intimacy and the sort of frank, confidential back-and-forth he enjoyed, but it also made him feel rather inferior. He had to think more quickly than he usually would just to defend himself.

'The only thing I'll do with your arse is whip it on the squash court,' he got out after a moment. But it cost him a considerable effort, and then there was still the bleeding heart he hadn't managed to bare. For Michael was facing a crisis of tragic proportions.

On the squash court it was George, as it turned out, who won convincingly. The shorter man had a sly deftness of touch that bespoke confidence, aplomb and above all skill, so that if Michael did somehow manage to mount a serious challenge in one or two games, it was only because of the flustering fury with which he chased about the court, whamming the ball with grunting violence to elude perhaps by a hair's breadth, and then only very occasionally, George's masterful cover of the various angles. Humiliated, Michael almost wept with frustration; he shouted at himself when he made mistakes and commented unpleasantly on his opponent's luck when a ball landed exactly in the corner between floor and wall. In between rallies he moaned and moped and gasped for breath. At the same time he despised himself for this exhibition, so that afterwards, when the two office-bred men were out of the shower, sitting wrapped in towels on a bench, he begged the other's pardon for such a childish display.

George said equably not to worry – he liked winning, and the greater the margin, the more he liked it. He had been a prodigious batsman, he remarked, in his youth, which after all wasn't so long ago. 'A great stonewaller.' He mimed a couple of defensive strokes with an imaginary bat; then, as if to prove he had taken no offence, asked: 'Tell me about your friend, though, the one with the platonic problem.'

They ended up in 'The Mermaid' again. Michael, exhausted, overwrought, and suddenly sensing that this square, pale man might be one of those few people one could actually trust, drank heavily and told all: i.e. that despite having always believed in marriage and family and the traditional joys of bringing up children in a conventional environment, he had now gone and fallen hopelessly in love with a very young girl in Accounts; that he didn't know what to do about it; that his wife wasn't helping by being so unutterably dull and cussed these days, completely wrapped up in the children and her various domestic and community projects; that the girl in question obviously liked him very much, but being herself of the conventional variety, naturally imagined he was a no-no, what with his wedding ring and photo of Shirley on his desk, etc. etc.

Every time Michael used the pronoun 'I', George, across a wobbly table, frivolously corrected, 'Your friend, you mean,' articulating the words with extravagant pantomime softness through what Michael now noticed were thick and somehow sensuous lips, a curious dull red against the paleness of his face. 'Wouldn't like it to get about, would we?'

'But I've never been in such a mess,' Michael complained excitedly. 'I mean, it's horrible, you know, and wonderful at the same time.'

George asked sympathetically: 'And has your, er, dear friend always been faithful to his lady wife?'

Michael said Lord, yes, that was the whole point, nor had he ever wanted to be otherwise – they were great churchgoers for Heaven's sake, he believed in things – and in the end he felt that the best course would be if he somehow managed to go on being faithful, because if he didn't then the whole structure around which he had built his life would collapse. Wouldn't it? Hence the question about platonic relationships. It was just that…

'Your, er, bosom friend is afraid he may not be able to keep his filthy paws off that little ticket in Accounts.'

'Correct,' Michael admitted. He looked with some gratitude into George's solid, practical face, the lips pouting about a fresh cigarette now, eyes squinting as fingers snapped a lighter and applied the flame. 'What on earth shall I do?' he moaned, obviously determined to be advised.

George puffed, brows knitted in concentration. He drummed a little beat on the table with thick fingers. 'Fuck the wench,' he pronounced.

In the foyer to the tube station, reflecting that their two wives were the best of friends – indeed had encouraged them to pass these evenings together, Michael, with a shiver of fear, suddenly saw fit to plead: 'Not a word to anybody though, you know. Especially Margaret.'

'Nervous bugger your friend, isn't he?' George smiled broadly. He stopped by the two fluorescent-lit tunnels that would lead them off, one to the Piccadilly line, one to the Central. And to Michael's surprise this complacent, dapper man he had always found at once so dull and so sarcastic, rested a hand on his shoulder:

'OK, old mate,' he said, 'let you into a little secret of my own, if it'll put your heart at rest. Friend of yours truly's in exactly the same position. You know? Exactly. To a "T". Talk about it next week maybe.'

2

By mid-June a kind of ritual had been established. As follows: rendezvous Thursday evenings, six o'clock, in 'The Mermaid'; over swift half and on the way to the club only small talk permitted, i.e. chat about the kids, politics or business (George was very firm about these prohibitions and would quickly nip any confessionals from Michael in the bud); next, amidst rising tension, came the game (hard fought), after which (in an agony almost of delayed gratification) a long shower, drying and dressing; until finally, over two or three pints in 'The Mermaid', the two men would at last indulge in the carnival catharsis of detailed progress reports on their projected, then accomplished unfaithfulness.

It was an arrangement which made for some energetic if rather distracted squash, especially on Michael's part. Indeed, to anybody stopping to watch through the glass door of the court it must have seemed that the furious intent with which this tall, awkward man swung his racket had less to do with scoring points than with somehow willing the world, in the shape of that tiny ball, to be other than it was.

Quieter and more pragmatic, eminently more skilful, George continued to win, perhaps surrendering just an odd game here and there to Michael's *Sturm und Drang*.

And half an hour later in 'The Mermaid' it was inevitably the precipitous Michael who, perhaps still rather weak and out of breath, insisted on 'batting' first (the ironic terminology at George's insistence). So in mid-May he was explaining how he had finally managed to tell the girl (Carol she was called), finding her by the coffee machine outside the lift on the second floor, that she had 'seduced him utterly' (what a step that had been! – and one that owed much to George's encouragement); how the girl (heartbreakingly young, delightfully – how could he put it? – coltish, yes, coltish) had been rather amused and sceptical, but agreed to go out to dinner with him on his wife's next NCT night; how, on that fateful evening, he had slipped (glorious abandon) a hand round her waist outside an expensive Japanese restaurant he knew of old in Golders Green; how she had seemed worried at first, understandably so perhaps, then relaxed; how he had kissed her and kissed her, and she had responded readily, not to say ferociously, but then hadn't wanted him to 'come up for coffee' twenty minutes later in Islington.

'Too soon perhaps,' George commented.

Both men sucked their teeth.

'The problem is,' Michael insisted, 'she's such a decent girl. Very traditional. Upbringing, family,

outlook. You know? Though of course that's precisely why she's so exquisite too.'

'Yes, I can see that,' George remarked generously.
'Exactly what makes one want to get one's hands on
them.'

A week later, however, Michael would be tri-
umphantly recounting how he and the more-
amenable-than-expected Carol had made a mad
lunch-hour rush to her flat in Islington – cab both
ways, extortionate; how he had undressed her and
adored her body, which was truly the most adorable
body he had ever come across – not that he could
boast to having come across, or indeed inside, very
many; how they had then made the most exquisite,
the most extraordinary, though unfortunately hasty
love, during which she had confessed that he was
only her second lover and far more exciting than the
first (a tennis coach from Friern Barnet); how he
had extravagantly bought her a bottle of perfume
and box of chocolates while waiting for the cab
back to the office, where they had both arrived
together (for Christ's stupid sake!) and more than
an hour late, a give-away they could scarcely afford
to repeat.

George listened with his usual air of avuncular
sympathy, nodding, sighing and heartily congratu-
lating, until, fresh pint in fist, he would approach his
own innings with the air of one confident of topping
any performance that has come before or might
eventually come after. For Michael at this point it

was a considerable effort to settle down and play the part of the good listener.

Yes, his own lady, George explained – originally encountered at Swiss Cottage swimming pool, where he'd taken his boy for some sort of sports event one Saturday morning – was a twice-divorced mother of three whose alimony paid for a spacious flat on one of those Edwardian blocks on Gloucester Place. He'd spoken to her quite by chance in the little café area they had above the pool, and there had been this immediate, electric attraction – you know? – a shared awareness of possible adventure, something he honestly couldn't remember having felt for a very long time. She was a funny, witty, attractive, sexy woman. Who could beat it? Anyway, after much shadowboxing and various quick skirmishes in pubs and sandwich places (to check that she was really on for it), he had managed to arrange a morning meeting with a company client in Baker Street, from where it was only a five-minute walk to her place for lunch 'and lashings of dessert', as she had promised.

George rubbed his hands as one spoilt for choice over food too fine for words. Michael wriggled fretfully in his seat.

So he hurries over there, doesn't he, sweating in his suit what with the warm weather and the excitement, goes up in the lift, and then, horror of horrors, discovers she's got a lodger, something that hadn't actually been mentioned, a younger woman hanging around reading *The Guardian* in the living room.

'Shit,' Michael commented, relishing his friend's discomfort.

'Yes, a real bugger, prick-teaser's trap I thought, though rather attractive actually – the lodger I mean.'

Anyway, what? – he goes into the kitchen to stand behind her, Gloria that is, his lady, where she's sautéing something over the burners, and just lightly, oh very lightly, he rests his hands on her hips – 'you know, from behind' – the lodger being out of sight, though only three or four yards away. All rather nerve-racking. Well, Gloria immediately presses her lovely butt back into him. Then she whirls round and actually guides his hand to the hem of her skirt. And while he's registering, yes it *is* on, despite little Miss Lodger, while he's rapidly moving his greedy little fingers up her legs (where he finds she's got all the gear on, for Heaven's sake: stockings, suspender belt, garters, you name it), she's picked up, of all things, the knife she was using, sharp little vegetable knife by the sink, and with this incredible, knowing, corrupt, utterly sexy smile on her face, she starts tracing the point of the knife across his throat and at the same time thrusting her belly towards him.

'Good God!' Michael breathed in dubious appreciation, for this wasn't his scene at all, nor would he ever have expected to hear such sleaze from stuffy George.

'At which point the lodger walks in, doesn't she? And...'

George smiled tantalisingly, enjoying his listener's eagerness.

'And what?'

'What do you think?' he laughed. 'Low off the left-hand wall, with just the spin to kill it a whisker above the tin in the right-hand corner? Or the slow lob centre-court, or the fierce low drive hugging the left-hand wall?'

Michael vaguely registered that although his friend was confessing, he, Michael, did not seem to be getting that subtle ego reinforcement that comes from being confessed to. Perhaps George did not really need him. George was not a sufferer in search of sympathy. Rather it was as though he, Michael, had simply been admitted to a game the cannier man was playing. And indeed George was now proposing: 'Any bets? What do you think?'

'I don't know. Ledger was shocked and walked out. You felt stupid.'

'Got you again, I'm afraid.' George laughed. 'You see, I'm frantically pulling out my cunty fingers, aren't I, pursing my lips to whistle Humpty Dumpty or whatever, smoothing back my hair, you know, tra-la, how's things, when Gloria just laughs and says: "Would you mind looking after the lunch a bit, Hilary? Me and my friend here would like to retire for a minute." As if nothing could have been more natural.'

The teller looked to the listener for signs of appreciation. Low across the beer-slopped table he whispered: 'God, what a woman! Don't you think? What a woman!'

A few moments later Michael was enquiring: 'Contraceptives?'

'I had the old johnnies of course, but she said there was no need.'

'Previous lovers? Herpes? Aids?'

'God, you are a spoilsport, aren't you? The marvellous thing was...' and after describing at some length bedroom antics that left Michael quite breathless, George wound up reflectively: 'I suppose the truth is I've been making love in the old slippers, as it were, for so long now, I just couldn't believe it was happening, if you get what I mean.'

'Sense of guilt?' Michael tried, without conviction, having dwelt at some length on his own.

'Not a trace. Just wish I'd started earlier.'

3

The adventures were thus begun, and from week to week further progress was reported. Egging each other on, shriving each other, justifying each other with the argument that they were living at last, the two men became the closest friends. True, there continued to be some resentment on Michael's part that George did not appear to be suffering as much as he was, that he refused to see their affairs as *problems*, refused to acknowledge either the threat to their family lives or the desperate challenge to be happy with someone one truly loved; but for the moment such disgruntlement was no more than the smallest cloud on the horizon. The important thing for the moment was that they could talk to each other, experience the release and excitement of telling each other things they had never told anyone before. Such as, for example, that Michael had never loved his wife in so intense and generous a way as he now loved Carol, never adored his wife's body as he now adored (and combed for hidden pleasures) every inch of Carol's, never felt so humble and grateful, nor so simply and straightforwardly relaxed in anybody's company as in hers. She was such a good sport, so cheerful and easygoing. Everything about her was at once fantastically exciting and reassuring. Wonderfully girlish. Yes. The upshot being that he was now seriously thinking of leaving his wife. They got on so badly. They were so cold with each other. They were living a lie. It was even unchristian. Except of course that this prospect made him hopelessly unhappy with thinking about losing the children, and then how hurt Shirley would be. There were days when he seemed to be wildly exhilarated one moment and unutterably depressed the next, if not both things somehow at the same time.

George was ever sympathetic: 'You wish your wife would vaporise, don't you? Disappear. I know the feeling. Whoosh, gone. No argument, no unpleasantness. No this is mine, that's yours, what about access to the kids, who keeps the house, the car, what will our friends say, the parents, how can we explain it to Robert, will it upset his school-work? Horrible. Ugly. No, Spock, vaporise 'em, beam them elsewhere. Puff, gone, all problems resolved, deft little tap curling off the right-hand wall an inch from the corner – game, set and match.'

But despite such comradely support and declarations of shared unease, George's manner was philosophic rather than haunted, and still far too witty for Michael's romantic taste. It didn't seem to take into account the latter's desire to tear the world apart, to scream aloud in public, to abase himself in some way. And indeed only a moment later, fresh pint in hand, George would be taking up his innings unperturbed, as if nothing serious had been said or could be said about what for Michael was the central, the burning issue: that they couldn't go on like this, with this dishonest way of life, that something must be done.

So – George was rubbing his hands in delight – this business trip to Bristol. Right. He'd managed to arrange the meeting over two days. Very smart. Booked in at a hotel he knew in Clifton. Gloria got an ex-husband's mother over for the kids (these squalid details made him feel terribly contemporary). And they're driving down the M4, when she slips her hand into her skirt – get ready for it – slips her hand into her skirt, rubs a finger in her pussy, brings it out and pops it into his mouth with that sweet sex taste that drives him crazy.

'You're joking!'

'Then wriggles down her pants and actually starts to masturbate slowly while I'm trying to keep the old bus at seventy.'

Michael thrust his fist in a bag of pork scratchings. He felt at once annoyed and enthralled.

'Christ, and then a whole night of sheer pornography.' George shook his head from side to side as if in remembered disbelief. 'Sheer pornography. What that woman didn't do! What a find!'

Irritated, Michael asked: 'But aren't you sad sometimes that you can't be with her? All the time I mean.'

'Oh God yes. God yes.' Again George shook his head, pouting. 'I'd like to be there sodomising her every night.'

'Sorry,' Michael protested, 'but the way you talk one tends to get the feeling that it's all just sex for you. You know? As if it were some kind of new sport you'd discovered and that's the end of it. Not a really big emotional problem.'

George raised his eyebrows: 'Well, affairs do traditionally tend to highlight the physical side of things, don't they? What do you want me to tell you, that we looked into each other's eyes for half an hour? Which we did actually. No, of course, we've become excellent friends. She's a terrific lady. I mean, we have good chats when we go to the restaurant and so on, if that's what you want to know.'

'But listen' – Michael cast about for some way of getting at his friend, of bringing the hijacked bus of his confessions back to base – 'what I mean is, well, what's the general tone, inside your head, you know? How do you feel from day to day, going into the office and so on, and knowing, knowing that you can never spend more than the occasional night with this woman you're crazy about, that your relationship is frozen there – the odd night, good sex, maybe a nice meal and a bit of chat, nothing more?' And he added, 'I mean, I feel terrible about it, paralysed.'

George drained his lager, knitted the fatty wrinkles on his forehead. His black hair was greying to coaly curls around his ears. 'How do I feel? Day by day? Good question. Well, I suppose mildly bored. You know? Depressed. Excess of joy in one department tends to make the rest pale into tedium. But excited too. Constantly scheming where the next lay's coming from of course.'

'And that's all?'

'Not as depressed as I was before. That's the important thing. God, was I depressed before. Life had become such a wasteland.'

Michael would have liked to have talked more about such *Weltschmerz*, but George could never be kept on the subject very long, and all too soon was back to enthusing about that first full night with his mistress. Let's see. The point was not so much even the things Gloria did, you know, as the things she said, things his wife would never dream of saying: that she wanted him to fill her with cock and sperm, that she wanted to have him in her cunt, her bum, her mouth; that she wanted him to masturbate all over her breasts and smear the sperm over her face; that she wanted to be tied down and have him do everything he wanted with her.

Michael, who in his own innings of half an hour before had reported feeling a little squalid after some adolescent petting with Carol on a chair in the stockroom during yesterday's lunch break, groaned with what was at once excitement and anguish.

'God, I can't go on,' he suddenly butted in. 'No, I can't, I'm so in love. And I feel I'm drawing the poor girl into a relationship that can only hurt her, because I know I can't hurt Shirley – can't leave the kids, I just can't – and the kid's fallen in love with me; she burst into tears when we went out for a sandwich the other day, saying how awful it was to think I could never be hers. Then I live in fear that Shirley will find out. You know, I feel I should, I must stop before it's too late. God, it's like something beautiful's been born, something truly beautiful, and at the same time I know sooner or later I'll have to kill it. So probably the sooner the better.'

Interrupted in full flight, George watched the sufferer with a professional's frown, as though patiently waiting out some irritating pitch invasion. Then surprisingly he held out a pale fleshy hand across the table: 'Give me skin,' he said with his customary blend of sarcasm and parody.

Michael, miserable, took the hand.

A few moments later, coming back with the next pint, George remarked: 'Don't you feel, though, that this has opened up your whole life?'

'Oh yes,' Michael agreed.

'I mean, think of all the times you used to lie there in your bed thinking, "I'll probably never have another woman in my whole life. This is it for me from now on. Never suck different nipples. Never run my fingers between different buttocks." Or did you never do that?'

Michael agreed that he had. Rather frequently actually.

'And now here you are bonking a lush little twenty-year-old, and no slouch by the sounds of it.'

'Yes.'

'So you'd never regret this having happened, would you?'

'Oh, God no. Best thing that's happened to me in centuries. The only thing, come to think of it.'

'You'd agree I gave you the right advice that first night we talked.'

'Yes.'

'Want some more then? Advice?'

'OK.'

Both men smiled.

'Play it for all it's worth, Mikey. She gives you that sob stuff about never being able to have you because she senses it's what you want to hear. Gloria's just the same: "Oh, why didn't I meet you years ago? Why do you have to be married?" Moan, moan, etc. etc. Exactly the same. If I haven't mentioned it, it's because I thought you wouldn't be interested. It seems so obvious. Par for the course. But the fact is, you're not doing that lassie any harm at all. On the contrary, you're giving her a wealth of experience she will later no doubt deploy to the best advantage. She's in love with you now, but all too soon she'll grow out of it. She'll get bored with the situation and look around for something more convenient. What I'm saying is, you'll have to stop in the end, so for the moment you should play it for all it's worth. For all it's worth. Otherwise you'll never forgive yourself.'

And the two men wound up their session with a pleasantly detailed discussion as to whether, assuming one had, say, three hours at one's disposal, it was better to go for two orgasms, with the risk that one might not quite make it second time round, or to spin out the first one interminably with all the problems of control, possible mild disappointment, not to mention prostatic congestion that might entail. They swapped experiences. Until, on discovering that one was circumcised and the other not, it became apparent that they were making the mistake of comparing apples with oranges – or bananas with courgettes, as George suggested – and at nine-thirtyish they stood up to be on their way back to their wives.

4

Weeks passed. Events moved apace. In mid-July, with temperatures in the high eighties, Michael scored his first victory on the squash court, three games to two. He was radiant. George did not rant and curse, as Michael would when he lost, but he did appear somewhat disconsolate and definitely not in his usual form. In 'The Mermaid' that evening he quickly broke two more traditions, first speaking before they had got their pints and then ignoring the usual batting order.

'Made a terrible mistake,' he announced.

Michael was feeling rather splendid and magnanimous. 'What?'

'Terrible.'

'You've been found out?'

'Wrote her a letter, didn't I, not really dirty or anything, but sly, you know, allusion, innuendo, teasy stuff, how gratified I was that my application for use of her playground by my young friend John Thomas had been so warmly accepted; so many interesting games, not to mention the sandpit and waterchute. That sort of thing. Doodling during lunch break really.'

'So what happened?'

'Terrible mistake.' George groaned and put his head in his hands. 'I was in the office, wasn't I, so I stuffed the thing in an envelope, wrote the address on one of our company address labels and threw it in the basket with the evening post.'

'Where some suspicious sod went and opened it.'

'Getting warm, but no, actually it's more complicated. Problem was: first I didn't know the post code, second, like a complete idiot, Christ, I put Gloucester Road instead of Gloucester Place. Result, the thing comes back to the company, because of the return address on the label naturally, and I find it open on my desk this morning – I mean, spread right out, stapled to its envelope.' The greying man shook his head from side to side.

'The post girl had read it.'

'Must have, mustn't she m'dear, otherwise she wouldn't have known to put it on my frigging desk.'

'But only the signature.'

'I signed myself, "Georgie Porgie, your pudding and pie, kiss that girl and take her high."'

'Nice one.'

'Yes. Shit. So now anybody at the office might know. It's the receptionist who does the post, and she's such a bloody chatterbox. Oh God.'

'And any one of them might tell Margaret.'

'Correct. That is the worst-case scenario.'

The two men picked up their pints. George was smoking very heavily, but Michael seemed to be enjoying this development rather more than the usual detailed descriptions of fellatio, cunnilingus and the rest (on the previous occasion, he'd had to hear how Gloria had masturbated George to the most heart-stopping of orgasms in the back of a cab, provoking climax and swallowing the proceeds only seconds before their destination; while he, Michael, had had nothing to report but his routine Friday lunchtime at Carol's flat, the simple and poignant pleasures of which elicited only distracted avuncular smiles from George). So now he said grimly: 'Anyway, the wives are bound to find out in the end.'

'Oh Christ, I hope not,' George protested, but added morosely: 'Gloria thinks Mags knows already. Said she knew when her first husband started playing around, and the second knew when she did. She thinks partners realise these things intuitively, even if it's not conscious yet.' But then he laughed: 'Actually, I don't give a toss if she knows intuitively. The real bugger would be if she knew consciously and started causing ugly scenes and things. As long as we don't get to that point, the rest is plain sailing.'

With savoured bitterness, Michael told him: 'My own feeling is it might be a blessing in disguise – if Shirley found out I mean. Give me the push I need to split up and go and live with Carol.'

George frowned: 'In my case the disguise would be well-nigh perfect.' Then as if sniffing danger, he asked, 'Make a pact?'

'What?'

'If one of us is caught out, we absolutely mustn't rat on the other.'

'Oh, absolutely not.'

'You know, heat of the moment, make a stupid move and go and get your partner run out.'

'Never. I promise. Stay right in my crease.'

The two men drank and reflected for a while now on their forthcoming holidays. George was driving down to the Dordogne with wife and only son, Robert, an unremarkable boy in his early teens. Michael and Shirley were taking their three younger children to a beach in Cornwall. Both men were melancholy. Communications with their mistresses would be arduous, if not impossible. Confronted as never before with all the difficulties of conducting a long-term affair, the women would be able to stand back from their relationships and might well choose this moment to opt out.

'I've picked up a phonecard,' Michael suggested to his friend, 'for what it's worth.'

'Must be an equivalent in France, I suppose. Trouble is my French is so poor I wouldn't know how to ask for such a thing. Mags is the one who speaks when we're over there. I'm just a sleeping partner.'

They laughed at this remark, until George added dourly: 'Speaking of which, they're going to want sex of course.'

'What? Sorry?'

'The wives. They're going to want sex.'

'Oh right.'

'Something we haven't talked about yet. I mean, how are you scoring in that department?'

Michael was gloomy: 'Once a month maybe, if we're lucky. Used to be every other night of course.'

'Good God. Right up until you started with Carol?'

'No, no, way back.'

'Oh, way back, yes. Everybody's had their halcyon days at some point or other.'

'And yourself?'

George was phlegmatic: 'Well, not exactly a gold rush, you know, but then not quite the old retreat from Moscow yet either. Managed to cobble together something halfway decent last weekend I think it was. What's worrying me, though, is the thought that she'll be expecting that performance every night on hols, plus the whole romance bagatelle into the bargain.'

'And you don't feel up to it?'

'Just can't get excited, you know? Soggy erections, sudden loss of libido. Or maybe we'll manage something fairly respectable and then I'll feel terribly sad afterwards. About us. How we've changed. What all the fun and old photographs have come to. You know? And sadness is just the worst.'

At which Michael announced very firmly, even dramatically, that he couldn't, he wouldn't, he mustn't go on with such a situation. George had hit the nail on the head this time. Sadness was the worst. So no, he couldn't, wouldn't, mustn't spend the rest of his life pretending to make love to this crabby woman who didn't excite him at all and obviously wasn't much excited by him either. Didn't even really care for him. All she cared about, for Heaven's sake, was the kids, the church, the community. Well, he would put an end to it and go and live with the girl he was in love with. That was decided. Somehow or other the change must be made.

'You'd marry again then?' George narrowed his eyes in smoke drifting from at least the tenth cigarette.

'Yes, why not?' Michael was adamant. 'The thing with Shirley has always been this ridiculous antagonism. Even when things were at their best. Whereas Carol...'

George shook his head slowly, but made no comment as his friend now wound up the evening with the ritual hymn in praise of the splendid young Carol: her thick honey hair, the eagerness of her desire, her soft swollen lips. But on the way back to the station he remarked that it wouldn't surprise him if Gloria wasn't unfaithful while he was away. She was, after all, in her early forties and, for all her affection, obviously stacking in the last few orders before closing-time. Michael clapped his unhappy friend on the back. He was sure of Carol. Riding the Piccadilly line north to Turnpike Lane, he felt extraordinarily elated, more so than after any of their previous meetings, and on returning home he irritated his wife for the rest of the evening with accounts of his prowess on the squash court.

5

It was now some time before the two friends would see each other again, George taking his holiday in the first half of August, Michael in the second. And of course on getting back both men found so much to be caught up with at their respective offices that neither could reasonably contemplate a meeting until mid-September – which was when a very bubbly, revitalised George simply wiped Michael off the court: six games to love and with scores like 9–1, 9–3, even 9–0 – a rout.

'Now where did we leave off?' Settling in a comfy corner in 'The Mermaid', tonight's winner rubbed his hands together greedily as if at some long-awaited banquet where grace has at last been said and a troop of smart waiters are queuing with the food. 'You in to bat, or me?' He was back to his normal tone of apparently parodying one didn't quite know whom, some facile sports presenter perhaps, and it was this comedian's tone, this laconic, never serious humour which somehow substituted, when George was talkative, for his reserve when he was not – and which always disorientated Michael. It attracted him, it irritated him, it excited him. Above all, it made him jealous.

'You go,' Michael conceded despondently, having apologised for the usual ranting when he lost. It was just so much more disappointing after last time's win.

George brushed him aside. Squash scores were neither here nor there. 'Two fronts to report on,' he set off brightly. 'First, batted a quite brilliant rearguard action in France. You know? Sensible, defensive strokes, cautious prod at anything suspect, lovemaking on maybe five occasions, no attempts for the boundary or anything like that, tactical play, just hoping to hang on until stumps were drawn, as it were. Halfway through the second week, exactly what I needed, rain stopped play. That is, it pissed down. Paper forecast more of the same, sightseeing absolutely miserable, so we drove home early. Silly Robert desperate to see the World Cup on telly too. Odious sport, but there you are, played right into my hand. Anyway, all in all it was what you would call a professional performance, I think. Old Mags perfectly satisfied. Even felt rather affectionate towards the dear girl. Poignancy and the like. I mean, her not demanding more than was on offer. Very sensible and endearing. Oh, sorry, should have mentioned, just one glorious, quite glorious six in the middle of all that stonewalling. Burnt up a hundred-franc phonecard in a single call, Gloria just talking me through the most amazing, really extra-ordinary filth you can imagine. "Now I'm letting my hair fall over your tight scrotum, now I'm licking all down the back of your thick cock." You know, on and on for half an hour. Glorious.'

'You're crowing,' Michael objected, but couldn't help feeling excited.

'Well, you don't know what I got back to, do you? Before which, another pint is in order if I'm not mistaken.'

Michael did the honours. 'Trouble about the letter?' he enquired hopefully on returning to his seat.

George frowned. 'Oh, that.' He laughed. 'Yes, funny but that letter turned out to be one of your blessings in disguise I've never believed in. Actually,

I rather recommend it: billet-doux to non-existent address with sender's details on envelope to guarantee discovery back at work. Girls in the office have been looking at me with fresh interest. Yes, getting all kinds of winks and smiles: "How do you do, Mr Bryson?" "You're looking a little tired this morning, Mr Bryson, had a hard night?" "That's a dashing haircut you've got yourself, Mr Bryson." Lovely. All the world loves a lover, I suppose.'

'Nothing filtered back to Margaret?' Michael wanted to know.

'No, no, no. And why should it? I was thinking, it would take a real bastard to actually want to go and tell your wife. I mean, nobody knows her personally or anything, do they? Yes, it's quite fun at the office now. Opened up vistas.'

Michael took comfort in the fact that his wife often remarked that George, with his square pale face, frizzy greying hair and thick lips, was a very ugly man, and she could never understand why her friend Margaret had married him, except of course that he was witty and kind.

'No, listen, got back, MD calls me into his office before I'm barely through the door, says I'll have to substitute for this bloke in Sales who's been headhunted by one of our competitors and go out to this fair in Germany which is always a big deal for us.' George beamed. 'Only I managed to get Gloria to come along, didn't I? Four fucking nights.' He drummed out a little rhythm on the table.

'You absolute sod!' Michael breathed.

'Want the details?'

Although George had obviously meant this enquiry to be merely rhetorical – part of his general tease – it was in fact a pertinent question. The frank descriptions of sex in their earlier meetings had excited Michael and spurred him on where otherwise he might have left off. He had even found himself trying to copy with Carol what George had been so rapidly learning from the well-travelled Gloria. So that for example, on one recent occasion he had slipped his finger between the girl's legs and afterwards into her mouth, to then share the taste of her in a long kiss, something he would never have dreamt of doing with his wife. But right now, with the way simply everything had gone wrong for him since they last met, the idea of having to sit through yet another of George's eulogies to pornography was distinctly oppressive.

The other man, however, was already well launched. Indeed it often seemed that his impulse to retell these experiences was as great as, if not greater than, the desire that had presumably inspired them in the first place. 'So,' he was saying, 'there I am lying on the bed drinking that marvellous beer they have there, goes down like cream you know, and Gloria – she's wearing real dagger high heels and one of those silly Tyrolean hats with the feather – insists that I simply give her a long string of orders: do this, do that, you know, so as to gratify absolutely every fantasy I've ever had. Those were her words, every fantasy you've ever had. What a woman! So, what do I do, I talk her out of her clothes – soft music on the radio in the background – just getting her to keep her bra and pants on (usual de-rigueur porno cami-knicks and garter belt), then tell her to pull the strip of her pants to one side and start rubbing her pussy with the phone receiver. Jesus. She...'

Michael became so excited he said: 'Shirley found out.'

'What?'

'Shirley's found out.'

George had the dazed expression of somebody woken from a dream. 'But, for Heaven's sake, why didn't you tell me before? You should have batted first.'

Michael quickly explained: he too had had a stroke of luck, as it were, though this was before his holiday. Shirley had taken the kids to his parents' place in Swanage for a week. During which time he had had Carol in his house, though getting her in and out without the neighbours seeing had been a regular nightmare and rather taken the shine off things. Wonderful week though. So tender, so bittersweet. Night after night. 'Until Shirley comes home and finds a bloody earring under one of the sofa cushions.'

George winced and narrowed his eyes, as if upon hearing something in extremely bad taste.

'And wants to know how come I've taken the trouble to wash the sheets.'

'Putting two and two together.'

'And kicking up hell.'

George waited a moment before remarking softly: 'Your blessing in disguise.'

'Yes, and I refused to accept it.' Michael was rueful and at the same time angry with himself, as when he made mistakes at squash. 'I mean, the moment came and I just couldn't take the plunge. You know? I realised I couldn't do it, couldn't face it – knew what shot to play, but froze. I went and denied everything.'

'Ah.'

'Yes, what a fool. If only because I'm sure she didn't believe me. What a total total fool!'

'You're too hard on yourself. Difficult decision to take from one moment to the next.'

'And the thing is, I feel so guilty towards Carol, as if I'd let her down.'

George said he couldn't quite see that. Michael hesitated. 'You see, to top it all, we've got a pregnancy scare on.'

'You do seem to be in hot water.'

The thing was – Michael filled in the details – this week of bliss had coincided with the first few days after her period. And of course one got so incredibly excited. Didn't one? That was the thing about sex. You got so excited you lost all sense of proportion, absolutely. Anyhow, it had somehow seemed so important to do it with nothing on. She'd wanted it. He'd wanted it. Because at the crucial moment one was willing to take any kind of risk. 'And now it's a good six weeks later and...'

'Hold tight,' George said. 'I'll get a couple of shorts. What's yours?'

When he returned, Michael remarked: 'So you can just imagine what kind of holiday I had after that.'

'Right.'

'With Shirley tearful and lovey-dovey wanting to punish me and win me back, and saying how she'd given me three beautiful children at the expense of figure and sanity and was probably headed for an early grave, etc. etc., and me all along denying everything and wondering if Carol was pregnant.'

'Yes, not much fun to be had there.'

'Worst fortnight of my entire life.'

'I can believe it.' George spent a couple of moments consoling his friend, then lightly remarked on his own good fortune in finding a woman who'd had the old tubes cut after an extra-uterine pregnancy. 'What a woman though!' he breathed, and Michael realised, with a sense of shock almost, that the other man was steering remorselessly back to those nights of erotic splendour in that Frankfurt hotel. Which could only leave him, Michael, feeling ignored and misunderstood. His misery had barely been articulated, he felt; it hadn't been given its due; all he had done was simply to say he was suffering, and the other man had, yes, acknowledged it, nothing more, and then went blithely on to gloat over his brothel-style smut. It was obscene.

Unhappy and resentful – his life, he thought, in a terminal mess now – Michael kept his head down over his beer, only half-bothering to follow the many and varied erotic contortions his friend was talking him through. 'Chin up,' George finally conceded at the tube station. 'May as well be hung for a sheep as a lamb, what?' And the two set off along their diverging fluorescent-lit tunnels.

6

The following Monday George called Michael at his office and in a soft voice suggested that for at least the next couple of weeks, rather than play squash, they should just cover for each other and go their separate ways. 'Know what I mean? Otherwise it's going to be hard to keep up the old impetus, so to speak. Gloria's got her kids into some theatre workshop or something that evening. And if you're still having trouble with Shirley, here's your cast-iron alibi.'

Michael, in a state of near-intolerable depression, could not find it in him to tell George that on her return from holiday in Majorca, Carol, only that very morning, had sweetly and sadly informed him that she wanted to call it a day. It was not, she said, that she didn't love him, but that the situation was unbearable. It made them both extremely moody and unhappy. Waiting for her period had been a nightmare. The affair was over.

'Wet your towel in the loos,' George was saying, 'and wrap your kit inside so it gets nice and steamy.

You know? And when you take a shower at her place, remember to wash your hair.'

Thus Thursday evening found Michael alone and very close (it seemed to him) to suicide in the lounge bar of 'The Mermaid', drinking lager over a copy of *The Standard* which was explaining in two two-page spreads how a man whom neighbours described as 'perfectly normal' had killed fifteen people, firing an automatic weapon from a gallery into a crowded swimming pool. Such folly did not seem as inexplicable to Michael this evening as the newspapers would have it.

Ordering a second pint, he thought of George. The man liked to speak of an underlying sadness, but this was obviously rubbish. He knew nothing of the grief that he, Michael, was experiencing. 'I have heard the key turn in the lock,' Michael said out loud, repeating something vaguely remembered from somewhere. He lit a cigarette. And an extraordinary wave of bitterness swept over him: the way that man managed to be perfectly relaxed with his home life and then go out and thoroughly enjoy himself with this other woman who was plainly a whore and pervert of the worst variety! Then crow about it as he did too! The way he seemed to treat life as a game – squash, cricket, whatever – with him deftly tucking balls away to right and left. Never never baring his heart. Never truly suffering. Always smug. Clearly George wasn't capable of real love, wasn't capable of deep emotion, was just an empty little bastard with a hugely inflated opinion of himself. And this was why he was having such a smooth ride of it while Michael's finer feelings – his passion for his mistress, his desire to maintain a decent family life and not to deprive his children of their father – tended to plunge him into states of mental wretchedness so intense and crippling it seemed impossible that they would not eventually lead to some appalling explosion of violence, or more likely the classic psychosomatic process of self-destruction. Yes, quite probably, he would all too soon be dying of cancer or some such thing, brought on by the terrible conflict in his soul.

At which despondent thought, Michael rose on impulse from the synthetic pink velvet finish of his seat and, far earlier than he should have, set off home. 'George cancelled,' he announced briefly, and spent the entire evening rolling around on the living-room carpet playing dutiful father with his children.

'Clockwork,' George said brightly on the phone the following Monday morning. 'God am I going to have a lot to tell you when we have time to do some talking.'

'Great,' Michael agreed nervously. But couldn't understand it. He knew their two wives, best of friends, talked daily about them. He could thus be fairly sure that George's Margaret was now aware of the discrepancies in their stories. Of course he was ashamed of himself. Yet felt justified too somehow. Anyway, what was done was done. There could be no undoing it. So the most he had been expecting from George was an incredulous, irate call in response to which he had already decided he would simply hang up. Instead his friend was enquiring: 'Pregnancy scare over, is it?'

'Yes,' Michael managed.

'Goody-oh. Wet towel trick again this week then.' And George rang off.

October had arrived, and there was a definitely autumnal feel about the air that next Thursday evening as Michael stepped out of his office to wander aimlessly about the busy streets. His life, he thought, was so irretrievably wrapped up, settled, a closed book, and he so irretrievably incapable of being happy with it. Seeing a phone box, he pushed in and, using a phonecard in surely premature Christmas livery, called Carol. She was gentle and kind; she spoke with a catch in her faintly cockney voice, suggesting tears; she asked after his children and said how moved she had been by the pictures of them all over his house that week she was there. But she didn't want him to come to her flat. She had suffered so much when they had decided to split up; to backtrack now would just make her feel stupid. She'd have to go through it all again.

Michael called George's home number. When Mags answered, he waited while she asked who it was, breathed mysteriously for a moment, then hung up.

Stepping out of the phone box, he brushed against a very attractive black girl waiting to go in. As he excused himself, the girl smiled what could only be described as an alluring smile. People pushed by as they will. Michael turned away. There were voices and the jostle and grind of traffic; and so many girls, their scissoring slim legs, their flapping skirts tightening to the swaying fullness of thigh and arse. So much opportunity. Michael wandered up and down New Oxford Street with his briefcase and squash kit, uncertain how to pass the time. Why not approach one? If the family situation made it impossible to maintain an affair with a nice girl he loved for any length of time, why not begin a long series of casual encounters? At least it would be less heartbreaking. He watched a small, well-stacked brunette mince vainly by. The problem being of course that he wouldn't know how to approach such women. It had been possible with Carol because he had truly fallen in love with her, and because the office gave one all the time in the world for falling in love and then finding some way to express it. But just to go up to some woman in the street, or in a pub, or café, as George had done, such a thing was unthinkable for Michael. He was an extrovert, yes, but only when he was sincere. He didn't know how to play games, which was where he and George were so different of course.

He thought of George. At the moment no doubt he would be tying his woman down on her bed with thongs of leather or letting her lower her arse onto his face on the sofa, or having himself pissed over in the bath. With bitterness in his heart, shame vying with self-righteousness and that ever-obscure feeling of justification, Michael again went home to his family, again calmly announced that George had cancelled. Later, after *Newsnight* and a variety show he always liked to watch for the dancers, he was kept awake by the most extraordinary series of erotic fantasies, many of them borrowed from George's descriptions of his antics in Frankfurt. Vaguely, in the last moments of consciousness, Michael wondered if such a development wasn't just the echo of that key he had heard turn in its lock the week before when Carol had said enough.

George called as always on the Monday. Michael simply couldn't understand it when the man again spoke as if nothing had happened. Was everybody stupid? Or George invulnerable, impervious in some way? Why hadn't the wives blown his cover? 'Family all right?' he enquired cautiously.

'Oh them!' George laughed. 'Or rather her! Couple of tales to tell there, and no mistake.' Then in a lower voice:

'Mind if we actually play this week?'

Michael hesitated.

'Sorry, I mean, look, if you've already got something arranged, you know, far be it from George Bryson to thwart a lover's plans.'

'No-o-o,' Michael got out. But was nervous. What was the man up to? Trying to lure him to some meeting so he could accuse him, shout at him, even beat him up?

'I mean, I could go and see Gloria,' George was laughing. 'Just that, well, you'll think I'm crazy, but the fact is, I miss talking about it. You know? Sometimes it seems you haven't really savoured what you've done properly until you've told someone about it.'

'I wouldn't go that far,' Michael said carefully. 'Anyway, doesn't matter. You're on.' He put the phone down and stared at it.

7

It was raining heavily Thursday evening, and, in a sombre autumn twilight butchered by the stabbing glare of city neon, the two men turned a corner into stiff wind whipping sleet in their faces. Girls passing by were no more than flurrying shapes in the staring half-light fighting to hold on to umbrellas. Neither man paid any attention.

'In for another winter of gales,' George remarked. 'At least they're exhilarating.' And indeed both felt unusually fresh and healthy as they stepped into the warmth of the club and changed for the game.

They began to play. At the end of the second game, which Michael lost, as he had lost the first, by a considerable margin, George remarked that at least he had cooled down and was keeping his head.

'I am going through a period of such intense self-loathing,' Michael said truthfully, 'that I came this evening determined to lose in sensible fashion.'

George eyed him with his comedian's wry frown, uncertain how to take this. After which Michael proceeded to win the third and fourth games by a hair's breadth, only to lose the decider a resounding 9–1.

In 'The Mermaid', almost empty on this wind-blown evening, the men sat opposite each other in subdued mateyness. 'You to bat?' George enquired. He was genuinely intrigued by his partner's change of mood.

'Toss for it,' Michael said cautiously, still concerned about what might come out.

'Oh, that adds an element of fun,' George said gamely, and pulled out a fifty-pence piece. 'Even authenticity.'

In the event, Michael won the toss and put his friend in to bat. 'Sticky wicket,' he explained.

George sighed, looked frankly across the table at the sanguine, nervous man who had so recently betrayed him, smiled broadly. 'Enthralling news,' he said. 'You're going to be enthralled. Promise.'

Michael ducked his head to light a cigarette.

'First, Mags has found out.'

'But…'

George raised a hand to prevent interruption from an obviously alarmed Michael: 'Don't know how. Just don't know. Wouldn't tell me. Said she didn't want to descend to the squalid details.'

'But you denied everything,' Michael said, with an urgency he could only hope would be misinterpreted.

'Called her bluff. You know. Probably it was just a shot in the dark.'

'Was going to,' George agreed. 'That was the contingency plan of course.' He frowned. 'Just that for some reason I found myself coming right out and telling her yes, it was true.' Again he held up his hand and cocked his head to one side in parodied rebuke: 'No interruptions please. A lot to get through this evening. Let me keep up the scoring rate. Yes. I said: "Mags, I'm sorry, I really am, but whatever you suspect, it's true." Frankly, the most courageous moment of my life, I think – I mean, just going right out there and attacking a full toss like that.'

'Caught her by surprise,' Michael agreed. 'Especially since she probably didn't know anything at all.'

George eyed his friend with fleeting puzzlement. 'Perhaps. I don't know. Anyway, the truly amazing thing was the reaction.' And he went on to explain how, contrary to all expectation, dear sensible Mags had been quite decent about it, said she understood perfectly, had been tempted herself on various occasions, and thus couldn't really blame him. Obviously it was sad. There was no passion in their relationship any more, but it was a relief at least to admit it frankly to each other. Robert would be an adult and off to university in just a few years' time and then perhaps if he, George, wanted to, they could split up. In the meantime, as far as she was concerned, he was free to do whatever the hell he liked, so long as he was discreet about it and didn't catch anything.

'What do you think?' George drummed his little beat on the table as if to accompany the production of some particularly white and fluffy rabbit from a particularly black, battered and unpromising hat.

'Extraordinary,' Michael agreed, staring at the other man.

'Not your scene, I know, old chap, you being so idealistic and wanting to live with the woman you love, and so on – and I do sympathise. But it suits me down to the ground.'

'Almost a good job she found out.'

'Yes.' Again George's eyes were narrow across the table top. 'Yes, you could say that. I feel so relaxed. Which of course brings me to the second half of the story.' He paused and did his pantomime shaking of the head: 'What a woman, Mike! What a woman!'

A couple more pints were brought in now, and Michael dutifully settled down to listen to half an hour of smut. Feeling he had been let off the hook for his atrocious behaviour towards the in-the-end pleasant and harmless George, he was determined to be jealous no more, just as he had been determined to lose well at squash. He would turn over a new leaf. So he shut his eyes and listened, tried to enjoy it the way one might enjoy perhaps, in spare moments at the hairdresser's, the letters and true stories in *Playboy* or *Penthouse*.

The thing was, George was explaining, the quite miraculous way they had stepped up their dirty talk. My God. Bringing in a whole cast of other figures.

Imagining threesomes, foursomes, orgies; sucking and fucking; oral and anal. And when they went to a restaurant, or even were just walking down the street, she'd say, 'What about that little number? Why don't we get her to play with us?' and begin to describe how he would undress the girl and sit her astride his cock while she was astride his face. Endless, oh quite endless fantasising of this kind. Until, one night, they were sitting on the sofa watching TV with Hilary, the lodger, when Gloria began to whisper in his ear for him to put his hand on her knee and so...

Michael listened to all this, and as he listened he thought of his spacious semi-detached off Turnpike Lane, dripping now in the rainy dark, but yellowy warm inside; he thought of his petite, but slightly flabby, irritable wife whose interest in sex was at best desultory; he thought of his three tiresome, time-consuming, splendid children, and then of dear Carol and the simple traditional lovemaking they had made in her room – the friendly, poignant intimacy – then he thought how, running deep beneath that adventure with Carol – yes, deep deep in some dark stream that frothed fast along the rocky bottom of a plummeting psychic gorge – bubbled the very same fantasies George was now so gloriously living out, but which in himself, Michael suspected, would never be liberated, perhaps in the end because he didn't want them to be.

'Hope I didn't, er, bore you?' George finished brightly.

'No, no. I closed my eyes so I could concentrate harder.'

'Curious thing is how loving it is, you know – I mean, the cruder it sounds, the more tender it is somehow. Mmm. Hard to understand. Anyway, you to bat old man. How have you been spending your time?'

'Dropped Carol and am presently having it off with a black woman,' Michael said brutally. George spluttered into his beer and had to sit up sharply.

'That's why I was a bit reluctant to come tonight actually. Still, didn't want to let you down.'

For once the other man had what looked like straightforward, naked curiosity on his face. He gazed. Michael was gratified. And coolly at first, but ever more convincingly, he began to elaborate his story. He had met her outside a phone box the other week. She needed to make a call urgently and only had a twenty-pound note. He offered her his phone-card and so had to wait while she made her call. He could see her face through the glass in neon light, shiny and intense, the great round red-brown lips. She gesticulated and spoke excitedly, one hand pulling hard at ironed black hair with a faint magenta tint in it. Coming out she had admitted she'd made a long-distance call and spent almost two pounds. She'd meant to be quicker. Still, if he hung on a moment perhaps they could find somewhere to get change. She wasn't in a hurry now. He'd said in that case two quid sounded very like the price of a couple of drinks to him. She'd laughed. 'And I thought you were just being generous,' she said.

He'd brought her in here, to 'The Mermaid'. 'Do you always gesticulate so much when you speak on the phone?' he'd enquired with a smile. She'd said quite the contrary, but she'd been dumping her boyfriend, and the urgency was, she'd felt if she didn't do it now, that very minute, she never would. She hated men, she said. She hated the way they were so fucking presumptuous and invasive and jealous, checking up on everything you did, as if they owned you.

'Oh, we're not all that bad,' Michael said he'd said, adding: 'She was sitting right where you are now as it happens.'

George wriggled on his seat.

Anyway, Tracy – because that was her name – had said, well, perhaps she was exaggerating a bit, she didn't hate all men. 'In fact you seem rather nice,' she'd laughed, 'giving me your phonecard and all.' And he, Michael, had pointed out that since he was married he could hardly be terribly invasive with her, could he?

'Oh, very discreet way of breaking cover,' George remarked appreciatively. 'Real spin on that one.'

Michael raised his hand in a parody of his friend's protests against interruption. 'Lot to get through tonight,' he said. But his mood was of one who suddenly realises he has it in him to stage a remarkable comeback. Except he must be careful.

Anyway, he'd been supposed to be going to Carol's of course, it being last Thursday evening, but the upshot of all this friendly (and it had to be said promising) chatter was that he'd phoned her to say it was off – logistical problems ('first time the wife's ever come in useful, I think') – and taken a very expensive taxi to Tracy's place in Holloway. 'On the way home, fortunately,' he remarked, as it were by the by.

'Mind if I rein in a couple of shorts to celebrate this?' George interrupted, marginally delaying gratification. 'Won't be a moment.' And together with the drinks, he brought back two fat cigars, lit in expectant silence.

'It was the smell of her skin did it for me,' Michael finally picked up, puffing slowly on the thick wad of tobacco. 'Sort of acrid and animal, but so... oh God, so exciting. She was living in this seedy first-floor flat with two other girls' – he hesitated – 'fortunately out on our arrival. You know the scene: stale biscuity smell, crappy rented furnishings, drapes over damp on the wallpaper, subsidence making everything look slightly wonky, big stereo and TV, cigarette stains on second-hand carpet the wrong shape for the room, struggling pot plants, clothes overflowing from half-closed drawers...'

'Underwear of course,' George interrupted hopefully, cigar waggling in his mouth as he spoke. 'Lacy?'

'Please.' Michael was stern. 'Don't trivialise. So she asks me if I'd like anything to eat, and I say I'm not hungry.'

'Except for a bit of the other.'

'Oh, for God's sake, I'm not so crude as to say that kind of thing. Anyway, all of a sudden, and I really don't remember how this was achieved – I mean, I think it was a look which just sort of pulled us together – all of a sudden there we are locked in the first serious kiss on this springless old sofa. And what lips, really, Heavens, deep and wide, as if I was somehow being sucked into some fantastically erotic animal world, you know, just eaten.'

'All right!' George breathed, letting cigar ash fall on his good office jacket. Michael noticed in passing that the other man's dark curls were thinning seriously about the temples.

'Just eaten,' he repeated, 'kept coming and coming at me, never experienced anything quite like it. Like her mouth was all over my face.'

'And you adjourned to the bedroom.'

'Slowly does it, old mate,' Michael protested, and laid a restraining hand on his friend's arm. Then added teasingly, 'Now, let me see.'

After which, and for perhaps ten or twenty minutes, this amateur performer flew as it were by the seat of his pants, constantly racking his brain to come up with any details, images and exploits his friend George might have left uncovered these last three months of their relationship. It was hard work, but rewarding, and Michael felt inspired this evening. He was going to make it. Indeed he had rarely enjoyed himself so much.

'There was the routine introductory fuck of course,'

he explained, offering a sop to realism, 'just to get things going, you know, and then, well, the most amazing, just amazing explosion of erotic energy I've ever experienced.' Michael sucked on his cigar. Tantalisingly, he described her tiny bedroom: the thick yellow quilt on a traditional double bed wedged between basin and wardrobe, the walls amateurishly painted a throbbing wine-dark over that sort of embossed wallpaper, posters of black rock stars, a little rack by the window she hung her undies and things on, through which came yellow light from the street. (George tapped an urgent rhythm on the table.) And he described her clothes, the purple silk synthetic blouse on perfectly square shoulders, the black pinafore minidress, the underwear cut high and gloss-white on big hips. ('Yes,' George said.) Until, drawing more heavily on his cigar, he dwelt minutely on the curiously different shape – when she undressed for him – of her stiff breasts, on the cherry chocolate rubberiness of outlandishly large nipples, the football round of her buttocks which somehow made sodomy so much more attractive, the unexpectedly soft furriness of matted jet pubic hair against his tongue and lips, and the mysterious transformation of taut ebony skin into the hot, maroony, wet meatiness of her...

'Well, game, set and match to you,' George admitted some fifteen minutes later, as they finally stood up to go. He shook his head. 'What can I say? Take my hat off to you. Lecher of Honour Award. Really.

Phew. An innings that will go down in the annals, so to speak. Inspire our youth and so on. What talent!'

Both men laughed, though with the sudden return to reality involved in picking up one's kit and buttoning up one's coat they must have felt just a slight nervousness at the forces being unleashed between them, for they had drawn terribly close, as if having spoken some spell together. 'Yeah, I can see us at sixty,' George tried to snigger it off, 'buggering little Arab boys and being sucked off by Amazons.'

'If not extraterrestrials.'

Again they laughed. But that feeling of strangeness was still there.

8

Then, stepping out of the cosy comfort of 'The Mermaid', these two men discovered there was a gale blowing across England such as neither had ever experienced before. Yes, the usual safe, half-deserted tedium of Holborn at nine o'clock of a Thursday evening had been transformed into a vast blowy dark, full of the clatter of rolling cans and bottles, of flying litter frenziedly clutching at your coat and feet, boxes scraping and banging against your shins. They started to walk. The street lamps were out. The rain came torrentially in great flapping squalls. Across the street an elderly woman held on to her rags in a doorway, cursing toothlessly. Michael caught the distracted stare of her eyes. Water simply poured into his collar, wind pressured his shoulders from behind, until it came naturally to him to grasp for his friend's support, and in response George immediately saw fit to put his arm round Michael's back and grip him tightly. Bowing before prodigious gusts, the two men thus picked their way around a window box that had come down, muddying their feet amongst plants twitching wildly in their scattered pots. At the corner, a great shiny black rubbish bag spun erratically a long High Holborn, spewing filth of every kind. Faint through the screaming wind came the puny call of a siren. The two men forced their way, arm in arm, towards the station, dodging, at one point, a small newsagent's advertising stand which came banging along the wall of the Bank of Scotland. Until at last there was the safe quiet of the tube.

'Meet again next week,' George said by the inevitable tunnels that would separate them, 'forces of nature permitting, of course. Can't say how enchanted I was by this evening's chat, by the way.' Michael smiled. Briefly the two men embraced, held each other cheek to cheek for a moment, like Europeans almost, then set off.

Michael hurried to his platform, but with public transport in the state it was and a fallen tree blocking the car park at Turnpike Lane it would be past midnight before he finally made it home. He stood in the porch fiddling for his keys, drenched and weather-beaten after hanging on to railings all along

Hornsey Park Road. In a near panic with everything the television had been announcing in the way of death and destruction, his wife ran to open up for him. The door flew back before the wind. The squash player stumbled in. Uncharacteristically, Shirley hugged her husband and wept into his sodden coat. Something crashed to the floor. 'I've been so nasty to you,' she wailed. 'So stupid of me. I thought, if you were killed...'

'Crazy thing was,' Michael was saying brightly a few minutes later when they'd fought the door shut and picked up the shards of an expensive decorative plate, 'I mean, we were just sitting there in the pub having a heart-to-heart – I suppose you've heard about this awful business with George and Mags splitting up – and nobody told us about it. You know? Could have been a bloody nuclear war going on. Didn't hear anything at all. When we walked out, it was like we were on a different planet.'

Rushing to the fridge, Shirley insisted on opening a bottle of bubbly that had been bought for their wedding anniversary some months before and then never got drunk with all the squabbling and sulking that had been going on.

'To us, Mike,' she told her husband over the foaming bottle. 'Now, why don't you pop upstairs and take a shower and get warm, and I'll make some cheesy snacks and light a candle.'

Such was Shirley's endearingly naive manner of sending signals to her storm-torn husband.

Later that night, having acquitted himself as well as could be expected, Michael dreamt an unusually vivid though apparently meaningless dream. He was going on holiday with his wife, his mother, the children. They had booked in at their hotel late in the afternoon, and immediately he wanted to go to the sea, partly to show the others he had chosen a nice place, partly to take his first exhilarating dip. His wife, now back in her characteristic role of spoilsport, had refused to come, but Michael had taken the others. However, on approaching the beach they found the sea thundering in in long angry white rollers whipped and frothed by the wind as they came pounding on sand and rocks. The children, frightened, turned back. Michael insisted he knew another path that led down to a small secluded bay where they could definitely swim. For a moment it seemed he might persuade his mother to come, but in the event she turned back with the children.

The dream became more obscure here. The sky was low, he somehow couldn't see more than a few yards in any direction, and the scene was constantly changing. Still, what he remembered next morning was that he had picked his way through gorse and brambles down to this tiny cove he somehow knew, but only to hear, as he rounded the last twist in the path, a voice through a megaphone announcing that the water was too polluted to swim in. Even more disappointing, as the beach came into view he found that the few square yards of sand there were, were densely packed with holidaymakers playing bingo, the numbers for which were being read out with traditional brashness by the same man with the megaphone who had warned of the pollution. Standing in a small kiosk to one side, he was surrounded by a rabble of distinctly unbeautiful bathers trying to buy Coca-Cola and hot dogs and the like, and speaking in regional accents. Annoyed, Michael pushed through the crowd and interrupted the man conducting the bingo to ask if the sea, quite calm here, really was so polluted. 'One of them nasty pipes, pumping out sewage,' the man explained, upon which Michael recognised him as the barman in 'The Mermaid'. 'About a hundred yards out. Probably if you stayed near the shore... But why risk it, mate?' And indeed on turning to the sea again Michael found it had grown suddenly dark and uninviting. A lurid claret-red sunset on the horizon was being rapidly eclipsed by billowing storm clouds, and the water, though still, was black and breezy. So quite apart from the pollution, the dreamer thought, with a lucid daytime common sense and resignation, there was always the danger that if one swam out any distance one might be hit by lightning; upon which reflection, with towel under his arm, he hurried back to his hotel and his wife.

Lying in bed the following morning, Michael could make neither head nor tail of this dream. Why had it been so vivid and memorable? All he knew, as he got up to look after a whimpering child, was that he felt better than he had done for some time – more collected, more cheerful.

Going through to the living room, he found Shirley, chubbily neat in her pyjamas, staring out at the garden where the old apple tree had come down, crushing part of the fence.

'A disaster,' she breathed, 'the radio said millions of pounds of damage.'

'Nothing a couple of months won't put right,' he said brightly.

An hour later, in the tube, briefcase on his knee, Michael again found himself trying to analyse that dream, until at last he dismissed it as just another testimony to the ultimate irrelevance of everything but the real world in which one lived. He thought then about the previous night, how satisfying it had been, what a good friend George was, and how well he felt in himself this morning. The problem would be, he reflected, to think up something week after week that was at once believable and astonishing. But it was a prospect that left him quite excited. He felt that perhaps life could be made to work this way.

Changing Address

When in Italy, one learns Italian, one becomes Italian, but the process is not always an easy one, nor always welcome. Susan came from New Zealand; the breakup of her first marriage had sent her fleeing to London, the breakup of her second on a holiday to Italy that had lasted seven years. Now she was talking to a builder about the price of an apartment he had permission to renovate in a dilapidated part of town just across the river from the old centre.

'Plus a mortgage,' he was saying.

'Oh, so that's not the price?'

'That's what you have to pay, then there's the mortgage.'

'How much for?'

'It depends.'

She wondered for a moment if it was she being stupid. The young man was tall and not unhandsome, in a rough-and-ready kind of way. But there was a smirk on his face. He said: 'I might adjust the amount you have to pay in cash. It depends on you.'

'In cash? I can't draw that much in cash.'

From his slim height he smiled rather wryly down on her primness and shrugged his shoulders.

'Anyway, what is the price in the end? The global price,' she added, inadvertently using a favourite Italian expression.

'You can get a mortgage for 50% of the declared value of the property,' he told her. 'Always given you have the right income.'

'You don't mean the whole thing costs double what you said?'

'50% of the declared value,' he repeated patiently. 'We can decide on that at the last minute. Let's say 25% of the real price.'

'But…'

'Up to you,' he said. Loose-limbed, he shifted his balance to stand on a beetle marching across chipped and broken tiles. The room was a chaos of demolition. He grinned again. 'We can discuss little details like that when you've decided whether you want to buy or not. Obviously I'll have to look through my papers, do a few sums.'

'About a hundred million,' she told Dwight that evening. 'Sibylline bastard.'

'That's out then,' Dwight said, obviously relieved to find the decision so easy. At forty he was still a nervous boy. 'I mean, I don't mind being swindled myself, quite the contrary, I'm used to it, I even take a certain masochistic pleasure in it, but I'm not paying one price and declaring another so that some corrupt wheeler-dealer can get richer and fatter than he already is.'

Over the next few weeks Susan went to talk to other builders and proprietors in the attractive old area destined for renovation. She climbed broken staircases and made phone calls. But the story was always the same. Either you bought this way or you didn't buy at all.

'After all, we don't declare the money we get from private lessons,' she reflected.

Dwight was working on one of his little sculptures.

'They'd never believe how little we ask,' he said.

In their different ways Dwight and Susan were both children of the Sixties revolution. Some twenty years ago, albeit on opposite sides of the globe, both had been sitting on the floor late into the night smoking dope and talking music and revolution. With the Seventies and her first marriage, Susan had become a feminist and later a committed socialist. In England she had been an active member of a pro-abortion group. She believed in a state where the rich would pay, and through the nose, to relieve the sufferings of the poor – and though she had never thought of herself, relatively speaking, as rich, she was ready enough to pay her taxes, so long as the structure was fair: in Italy, however, it patently wasn't, and hence the problem really didn't present itself. She was a forthright, serious, attractive woman with a great capacity for turning up the wrong man. She had an endearing way of constantly batting large lashes over wide, pale-blue eyes, a tic which made her seem vulnerable, perhaps because associated with short-sightedness. But when she spoke, she could be quite sharp, even authoritative, a girl who knew how to look after herself. She kept up with films, read a lot of contemporary fiction, and on occasion liked to think of herself as resembling one of the worthier minor characters in a Christina Stead novel, a modern woman.

Her companion Dwight was more diffident and unpredictable. His face was still scarred with the acne of twenty years before, and he wore bluish tinted spectacles. 'To let them all know about my persecution complex,' he would remark with a humour so dry and deadpan it might not have been humour at all. 'What do you want from a Jew anyway, sanity or something?' He had had several nervous breakdowns in his teens and early twenties, seen various shrinks and always attributed all the blame to his middle-class Scarsdale parents. Miraculously he had avoided the draft by swallowing about half of everything that was in the family medicine cabinet the morning of his check-up. His father was a hypochondriac.

Later Dwight would wonder if he hadn't missed out on something in Vietnam, his rites of passage, perhaps even manhood. He dropped out of university twice and changed majors and colleges three times before finally coming away from Missouri State with a piece of paper that declared him a BA in Art History. He felt he had a vocation for art without ever believing he might be an artist. The result was an endless series of little 'sculptures' made out of each day's trash. He made no claims for them. 'Therapeutic creativity,' he said. 'I guess that must have been God's excuse too.'

When angry with the world and the liberties it was all too obviously taking with him, Dwight was prone to react with petty vandalism or theft. In the State of Connecticut, where his parents had moved in the mid-Seventies, he had accumulated a considerable criminal record for unlawful trespass and shoplifting (mainly of items for which he could have no conceivable use). Dwight was at once rather proud of this tangible demonstration of his rebellion and at the same time nervous that the Italian authorities would somehow find out about it and kick him out. For although he frequently claimed to hate Italy for its so self-satisfied bourgeois materialism, its fat provincial complacency, the truth was he'd never been on an even keel for so long. And recently Susan had begun to infect him with her obsession with security.

They had met at a weekend Buddhist retreat in the pretty hills to the north of the city. In fact there were a surprising number of Anglophile vagrants among the fifty or so people attending. 'After an acceptable spiritual substitute for our lost social revolution,' Dwight remarked to the blonde girl on his right, and Susan was attracted to his wryness, his straight-faced, more-than-half-meant self-mockery. 'Got to keep believing we're not like the yups,' he said. 'Don't you think?'

'I use a diaphragm,' she told him a few nights later, 'but you have to put it in and take it out afterwards, OK? That's part of the bargain. I'm not going to do all the messy stuff all on my own.'

'And when I have trouble enough just getting it up,' he complained.

Whatever their ideal visions of their lives might once have been, these two expatriates had long since lost them; disappointing relationships, psychoanalysis, unsatisfactory jobs, humiliating skirmishes into politics and groups liberal, feminist and religious had seen to that. Their thirties had proved a rough ride. In the end both in their own ways had emerged with an external robustness, one might almost say a personality. Cloaking inner fragility? It was hard to tell. Susan sometimes liked to say jokingly that she felt like a bit of flotsam thrown up on a foreign beach and waiting for the next spring tide to wash her away. She said it brightly. But at thirty-nine she found herself crying out for precisely the kind of things she had most readily despised years ago in the heady days of soft drugs, political activism and easy self-sufficiency: for what she wanted most in the world now was a home that would be her own, her retreat, her rock, her security against an uncertain future and an old age she was at last beginning to believe in, a home that no one could evict her from, as she had so frequently been evicted from London squats or the kind of rented accommodation offered to foreigners in Italy precisely because it was so much easier to send them away. What she needed, deeply and psychologically, she confessed to Dwight, was some tangible sign that she had arrived somewhere, that her wanderings were over, that her twenties and thirties had at last added up to something.

'Let's buy a place,' she said. 'We could do it together.'

But Dwight said he'd had enough of Italy, he was going back to New York. He'd only come really because he couldn't face another term with Reagan.

'To do what?' she countered. She sat in a dressing gown typing up a paper for a Warwick University Masters in Linguistics correspondence course, supposedly the key to some cushy minor post in the lower echelons of the local university. Dwight was hanging a mobile of his own making from a paper lightshade. Four little piggies flapped their wings.

'Where, for example,' she asked, 'would you get the money you can pick up just giving lessons here?'

'I miss the street noise,' he said, 'the racial tension.'

About once a week Dwight went to argue with the local police about the fact that they wouldn't give him a work permit and never renewed his *permesso di soggiorno* for more than three months. Although it was clear that his going to bother them could only draw their attention to his anomalous situation, Dwight never missed a week and never failed to get involved in a shouting match with some *maresciallo* or other.

'Perhaps subconsciously you want to be thrown out,' Susan suggested.

'You think you need to tell me that? An old hand at suffering like me?'

'If you really needed a work permit to work, I could understand it,' she said. 'But you patently don't, so why bother. Come on, learn to be more Italian.

Be nice to the bureaucrats. Tell them you're here for tourism, get your *permesso* and we go on working just the same. We're doing fine, aren't we?'

And they were. For the extraordinary truth was that Dwight and Susan were getting rich, they were raking it in, rolling in it, working flat out and making millions (albeit of lire). And perhaps this was the real reason why they didn't go back home, and this more than anything else explained Susan's growing obsession with security: she simply couldn't face the idea of losing the good fortune, the material wealth she had so suddenly and surprisingly come across.

For both of them, as for so many others, it had happened quite by accident. Passing through the city, you liked it. Directionless, with time on your hands, worlds of it actually, you thought you might stay, the only problem being that without friends or parents to put you up, you'd have to find work. And so you did the obvious thing, gave English lessons, put notices in the shops, in the local paper, talked to people you met; thus discovering, in the space of just a few weeks, that you had uncovered a gold mine; without exception the Italian middle classes wanted to learn English and were willing to pay for it. Indeed, the higher the price the more satisfied they seemed to be that they were approaching their studies with proper seriousness. It wasn't clear why this should be so, nor what purpose English really served them, but what did that matter? You worked, and having discovered the work yourself, rather than simply accepting a job description and a salary, you got a little excited by your success and looked for new openings, new areas. So Dwight was paid handsomely for teaching a group of student nurses at the local hospital, Susan even more so for instilling 'I do, I don't' into the sales force of a welding-equipment manufacturer. Then in summer there were the guided tours of the city for a company bringing over elderly Americans interested in art (Dwight's degree at last coming in handy); there was the university professor who sent them students who'd failed their exams, the public relations office which gave them translations... And all without paying a lira in tax.

'That's their fault,' Dwight remarked, 'if they won't give me a work permit and let me be legal. I know I'm Jewish, but otherwise I'm white enough. Obviously they think our money stinks.'

'I'd be happier if we were paying a bit of tax,' Susan suggested cautiously: sometimes she gave fairly generous amounts to aid organisations operating in Ethiopia.

'At least,' Dwight said, 'we have a reason for not paying, which is more than can be said for most Italians.'

'I don't want to be forced to be corrupt,' Susan repeated, but the following week was saying: 'I hadn't actually realised that when you bought a house you had to pay 2% VAT. It's a lot of money, when you think of the sums involved. That's why everybody's so willing to play along and declare less than they paid. Savings for everybody, not just the builder.'

At present Dwight and Susan lived in separate rooms, cramped and squalid places they had rented, they imagined temporarily, on arrival in the city. 'A draft dodger doesn't deserve any better,' Dwight would laugh. Anyway his sense of identity and personal pride was very much wrapped up in cleaning teeth over the kitchen sink and using stacks of milk crates for tables. 'Don't try to put me somewhere yuppie now,' he protested when she went off looking for a place that might make him change his mind. 'Think of the trauma.' But of course Susan would never be able to buy an apartment on her own. And she had set her heart on it now. So one way or another she finally brought him round.

They handed over the first deposit in a derelict room on the fourth floor of a three-hundred-year-old ramshackle *palazzo*: twenty-five million lire in cash. The young builder, the same she had described as a sibylline bastard two months before, was seated on a pile of bricks. Accepting the money, then offering cigarettes from a golden case, he announced: '*Signori*, a house, you'll understand, is like, well, like an overcoat.' He sighed as someone who still seeks to put conviction into words life has obliged him to repeat a thousand times: 'You can buy one off the peg, like the worker getting his flat in a ten-storey subsidised block, and find it doesn't really fit; or you can have it tailor-made for you, tailor-renovated. By an expert.' He gestured grandly to the rubble around them. 'I am at your command.'

Dwight and Susan thus discovered that they themselves were to plan the renovation, the price of which was to be fixed separately from that of the property itself. Faintly smirking, not deigning to count them, the builder tucked the wad of fancy banknotes into the back pocket of his overalls. 'Just tell me what you want. I'll need the plans by the end of the month.'

Walking home, Susan said: 'For God's sake, and all we've got is a receipt scribbled on the back of a piece of packing paper. We must be mad.'

'That's the last he's ever seeing in cash from us,' she insisted. 'Absolutely the last.'

Dwight said: 'We must remember to tell him not to use fibreglass padding for insulation: they're thinking of banning it in the U.S.A. Cancerogenous.'

He said: 'The crucial thing will be to exploit the light on the south side.'

And he said: 'Too bad there's so much traffic in the area. They should really restrict it now they're doing the place up. We should join the local Green Party.' He sounded pleased with himself for once, and determined.

But that night he woke in a cold sweat. He shook Susan and spoke in a low voice. He said try as he might he couldn't see himself here in this small Italian town when he was fifty or sixty, he couldn't see himself padding out to the bar for a grappa in his slippers like the other old men and talking football and checking the deaths column in the local paper. He just couldn't see it. It was unthinkable.

Unusually for the tough woman she'd become, Susan burst into tears. 'You can't start saying that now,' she protested. 'Not after shelling out twenty-five million.'

'I've always imagined myself,' Dwight said, 'in some New York institution for the elderly being ignored by burly black orderlies. I'd feel at home with that. I'd know where I was.'

But his dry humour didn't cheer her up. Coming back from the bathroom she said grimly: 'I just hope that guy's honest. You'd never give anyone that much money without a contract in New Zealand.'

The following week Susan announced that she was having problems with her bowels. For some reason or other, she had to go and shit every ten minutes. 'Too bad we're not on the health service here.'

Dwight had heard that they never actually asked for your number if you just went along.

'Not that I'd trust them anyway,' she said, and went to a herb specialist at a health food store.

The builder was called Angelo. He asked: 'Did you do these plans, or did you have an architect do them?'

'Guilty,' Dwight told him.

Angelo laughed, but said nothing. He continued to study the two large sheets of paper. 'Don't say I didn't warn you.'

'What?'

'Where does the boiler go? And the radiators? What's the flooring going to be: tiles, wood?' He looked at the diffident, tall, curly-haired American with his blue-tinted glasses and bad skin, his constant expression of mild surprise. 'I'll bring the guys in next week,' he said. 'But you'll have to put in another fifteen million before we can do anything.'

'But you said...'

'We can't start work without even the money to buy the materials. What you paid for before was a deposit on the property, not on the renovation. By the way, which way are these doors supposed to open?' He smiled again at the plans; he had very bright, attractive, even merry blue eyes. It was the way they shifted that was worrying. 'Nice apartment this. You've got yourself a bargain here, you know. I like the way you've rearranged the space too. The money next Monday then.' When Dwight protested about paying in cash again, Angelo said: 'Savings book made out to "The Bearer", if you like. It's all the same to me.'

Stepping out into the narrow street, Dwight ran the point of his door-key hard along the wing of a BMW he hoped must be Angelo's. He didn't look down, but the sound was certainly satisfying. At home he made a small coffin out of matchboxes.

Susan rang the bank. Her Italian was better. Somebody, she explained, had asked her for a savings book made out to 'The Bearer'. No, for a deposit on an apartment. What was the procedure?

'It's illegal,' she told Dwight, putting the phone down. 'They say you can't use it as a method of payment. It's only for use in the family or for bosses who need their secretaries to be able to pick up cash and so on. Definitely not for payments. Because untrace-able.'

Dwight laughed. Susan was indignant. Coming out of the bathroom a few minutes later, she said: 'I'm sorry, but I don't see why I have to start doing things that are illegal just so that some slimy builder can pay his workers on the side.'

At which point Angelo rang. One of the main beams in the sitting room was rotten, he had just discovered, and would need a steel girder put in it. 'Make it twenty million.' And did they want an air vent in the kitchen or didn't they?

'So decide,' Susan said. She had her hands on her hips, as if it were Dwight she were defying. 'Do we pay him the way he wants, or don't we?'

'Please,' Dwight protested. 'Remember you're talk-ing to a guy who wet his bed till he was fifteen.'

In the supermarket that evening, picking up the basics after seven numbing hours' teaching, he pocket-ed a bottle-opener he had no use for and a can of tuna. It was the first time he had ever stolen in Italy. Perhaps, if they caught him, they'd send him back home.

Susan's bowel problem was worsening, but she didn't believe in modern medicine. It didn't treat the body as a whole. It had no place for the mystery of being. So when the doctor she paid to see advised her to have her colon filled with a radioactive tracer fluid so that a good X-ray could be taken, she declined. It would merely fuck her up worse than before, and to no end. 'If you're not ill after a diagnosis like that,' she told Dwight, 'you never will be.' Anyway, it would cost a fortune paying privately. So she went to Milan to see an acupuncturist who cost no less. On the train going, the toilets were so bad she had to get off at Brescia and make a dash for the *diurno*. Coming out, the train was gone and she was late. The acupuncturist thought her problem was most probably psychosomatic and advised a strict diet, no fruit and less work. Coming back, she spent the entire journey adding and subtracting seven- and eight-digit numbers on the 'X' page of her address book.

Angelo said the way they had rearranged the internal walls, the window in the main bedroom was the old lavatory window, which was too small. Why not enlarge it? Dwight agreed, except that he had heard that you weren't supposed to change the façades of the buildings in this area. Anyway, they couldn't afford it right now. Maybe some time later. But Angelo explained that now was a unique moment for doing something like this, because the government was presently offering its Building Misdemeanours Pardon. 'Pay a nominal sum and they let you off. You still have two months to make an application.'

'Only for violations prior to 1986,' Dwight said quickly. While waiting for a nuclear war, he listened regularly to the news.

Angelo was neither impressed by the other's knowledge, nor perturbed by the problem: 'Who's to say
when the violation was made? They don't really care
what you do. It's just a way of raising money, getting
people to pay a bit to be in the clear.'

'But if the change had been made in 1986 we
wouldn't have been proprietors then.'

The builder shrugged his shoulders. These were
details. 'Just go and see a solicitor and get him to
draw up your request for pardon. Perfectly routine.
When you buy a house you want it to be how you
want it, don't you?'

Coming away from this discussion, Dwight was of
the opinion that the whole question had been left up
in the air until he had spoken to Susan about it. And
as he expected, she was against. A bedroom was for
sleeping in, or making love in, and only a minimum
amount of natural daylight was required. Then, after
her sums on the train, she was seriously worried
about money now, and worried too that her worries
were the source of her bowel problem, worried above
all that she was turning out to be the kind of person
who had worries which turned into bowel problems.
She had always imagined herself such a tough cookie,
after two divorces and all. So she didn't want to take
on anything else that could become a further source
of worry and ill health, not just for the moment.
Because of course if they became seriously ill and
couldn't work, nobody was about to pay them for
doing nothing, were they? They had no insurance, no

dole, no pension. And then they wouldn't be able to pay the mortgage. She worried about that too.

'For God's sake, what have we let ourselves in for?' she wailed, batting big eyelashes. 'And we haven't even looked at the furniture yet. What are we going to do when we get in there? Camp? My God.' Chasing security, it somehow seemed to have slipped even further beyond their grasp. Quite apart from which, the relatively easy life they had enjoyed prior to the BIG DECISION, the weekends in the pleasant gardens of the Buddhist centre, the bike rides, the regular trips to the vegetarian restaurant, to concerts, to surrounding areas of cultural interest – all this had had to give way to the need to do more and more lessons so as to be able to pay, pay, pay for what they had so rashly bought. They were constantly tense, weary, nervous.

'You know,' Dwight said, 'that the University of Frisby South Dakota is offering courses in psycho-monetary disorder?' He ate a fried egg direct from the pan. 'Still, it takes a Jew to get himself properly crucified.'

'Just forget the window,' Susan snapped apropos of nothing. 'Forget it, OK? You can just imagine the bureaucracy involved in asking for this pardon. The forms you'd have to fill in. And it's all so underhand. Having to worry about it. Forget it.'

But when Dwight went round to see Angelo, the wall had already been knocked out and a worker was banging in a new plinth. 'Had to move fast,' the builder explained; there was always something condescending about his explanations, as if the customer couldn't really be expected to understand. 'You don't want the cement still wet when the inspectors come round.'

'But you said they didn't really care what we did.'

'It's always the small guy gets caught,' Angelo said. 'The big fish always get away. Don't breathe a word.'

If the BMW wasn't his, it must be the Volvo, Dwight thought, feeling for his keys as he stepped out into the poker glare of the sun. How come everybody round here had such expensive cars anyway?

'Italy…' Susan said later that evening, 'you never know where you are.' She had just discovered that the handles were not included in the price of the doors they'd ordered, though they featured prominently on the photo in the brochure.

For his part, Dwight had just found that there was a 2% tax at source on mortgages, though they hadn't told him about this until after the papers were signed. Another two million and more. In comparison with which the handle business was a joke.

'Fifty fucking thousand a shot,' she told him. 'It sounds serious enough to me. They're such sneaks!'

'I only came here so I could feel a total outcast,' he said phlegmatically. 'My anger levels were getting pretty low in Connecticut. Anyway, there's not much chance of any real anti-Semitism stateside.'

Susan blinked hard; she was eating a plate of plain cold boiled rice to keep her sphincter tight. Her short blond hair framed an obviously ageing face which she would never try to redeem with make-up. She leafed again through the brochure.

'It's worse than being married.'

'Maybe I'll try that next time.'

'Not with me, you won't.'

They looked at each other, both sensing how what there had been of the carefree and light-hearted in their lives was lost now. They took no pleasure in each other's company. Dwight said: 'Actually I was thinking of somebody rather older, black maybe, Palestinian, handicapped, obese. Whoever would have a guy...'

But Susan interrupted, 'You just wish you could beat them at their own game.'

'Who? Come again.'

'The Italians. Beat them at their own game. Know what I mean?'

'Oh, them.'

The following morning, by post, Dwight received notification that his presence was urgently requested down at the police station. 'Perhaps they're going to tattoo my number on at last. I can't wait.'

Susan, however, was seriously worried that it might be about the window, or their working illegally, or some of the false declarations the builder had suggested they make to the bank for the mortgage, and almost immediately she had to go to the john. 'It's so humiliating!' she screamed. And she said: 'They'll chuck us out and we'll never get our forty million back off that swindler. I can just see the smirk on his face.'

When Dwight was at the door, she said: 'For God's sake, though, at least this time, put a jacket and tie on, please. You know how they respond to that kind of crap.'

Lanky, diffident, very Jewish, he went out in a thin flowery tie and shabby black blazer. Thanks to pressure from the friendly bureaucrat who'd given him the job teaching the nurses in the hospital, it turned out that the police were conceding a work permit. A puffy, sympathetic man with pantomime moustaches smiled avuncularly: 'Welcome to the Italian labour market.' He offered a squeezy hand. 'Best of luck!'

'But you can't start paying taxes now,' Susan cried, 'when we'd already made all our calculations. It's outrageous.'

Angelo was getting on far faster than they had expected. The ceiling had been fixed, the internal walls knocked down and rearranged. 'Got another job to start in a month or so,' he said, 'much bigger deal than this.' Curiously, even in dungarees with his hair full of plaster, his smile was always that of the well-dressed successful man. Dwight and Susan found themselves having to decide from one moment to the next on the colour of the tiles, the position of all the plugs, the light switches, the telephone outlets…

'But who needs more than one?' Dwight asked, perplexed. 'It wasn't in the plan.'

Having prided themselves on muddling through in badly furnished accommodation for the best part of their lives, they both – and particularly Dwight – felt a certain embarrassment at the luxury of plugs and switches in such abundance, and tended to go for the cheapest solution. Poking his nose into the bathroom and seeing a cord switch hanging from the wall over the bath, Dwight immediately hurried back to the kitchen to speak to Angelo.

'Standard fixture,' Angelo told him. 'For calling for help when you're in the bath.'

Dwight felt that for a guy who'd never come any nearer to harm in the tub than contemplating suicide, there was hardly much need for an alarm bell. Added to which he hadn't been consulted on its installation.

The builder sighed. He leant both elbows on a window sill. Then, still leaning and sighing with quite blatant theatricality, he turned to look at the American. For a good thirty seconds. 'Listen, Signor Berkowitz, what you have to think about with property is the selling price, *va bene*? Given that you've bought now, you want the selling price to be as high as possible. *Non è vero*? Now, a little detail like the bathroom alarm bell only costs you sixty or seventy thousand, once you've got the walls stripped, but when it comes to selling the place it contributes to an air of luxury that can raise the price by millions. Especially if the interested party is elderly. And the facts of life are that it's usually the old folks who have the money.'

'So why not have a whole series of geriatric appliances installed?' Dwight demanded. 'Why not a crane over the bath, never mind a switch? What about walk-rails along the walls? Listen, we haven't even bought the place yet, so we're hardly thinking of selling it. Forget the selling price.'

Angelo smiled indulgently. 'I've got experience in these things' – his voice was caring, paternal – 'and I'm telling you to think ahead, OK? Trust me,' he added, as Italians invariably would.

But for some reason Dwight found himself digging his heels in over that bit of cord dangling from the bathroom wall. Hadn't Angelo himself offered them a tailor-made job? Well, they hadn't asked for that cord and they didn't want it. Recycling the other man's metaphor, he said: 'It's like somebody sticking tassels on your coat you don't want, and then asking you to pay for them into the bargain.'

'But the difference between a house and a coat,' Angelo explained complacently, for only an idiot would have thought of such a comparison, 'is that you don't have to think of selling your coat second-hand when you buy it.'

'I've bought plenty of second-hand coats,' Dwight came back, but found he had lost his way. Anyhow, what did he want the man to do? Take out the alarm, adding even more expense? Or did he just want to prove him wrong? Always a sign of vulnerability. As it was, he said nothing, but vowed to come round at least once a day from now on to keep a check on what Angelo was up to.

And thus caught the plumber in the act of fixing a radiator under the living-room window.

'I specifically said not under the windows,' he told Angelo over the phone.

'Radiators always go under the windows. It's the most convenient place. Otherwise you reduce the wall space available for furniture.'

'Yes, but the fact is that it's my house and I asked for them not to be by the windows. Nobody has them under the windows in America,' he lied. 'All the heat goes out through the glass.'

'But we've put in double-glazing all round.'

'The simple fact is I asked for them to be elsewhere.'

There was a considerable silence before Angelo said: 'OK, you're the boss. God knows how much it's going to cost, though.' And he said: 'By the way, aren't we about due for another instalment? Say twenty million next week. Or no, throw in an extra five if I have to get the plumber back.'

The radiators stayed where they were.

Susan's bowel problem got better, and then worse again when they received the first anonymous letter about the altered window. She went to see a Japanese faith healer who was visiting the Buddhist centre for a week. Well over eighty, he was a delightfully active, obviously charismatic, scrawny little man. She didn't tell him her exact problem, and as a diagnosis he simply ran his hands lightly over her fully clothed body stretched out on a table. His knuckly fingers crackled over her tights, his small, bony, pointed face brightly concentrated. Then, apparently sure what the problem was, he proceeded to blow on her from top to toe. For the sake of hygiene he did this through the filter of a wet bidet towel, but with great determination, huffing and puffing for upwards of a quarter of an hour, so that she began to wonder, under the steam of warm breath, how his ancient lungs could take it. 'A question of transferring energy and stimulating natural health,' he explained in broken pantomime English, and he advised her not to eat so much fruit, since it was 'polluting her system'. 'I not eat fruit since thirty years, and am very well,' he beamed. At no point had they mentioned her bowels, and of course she hadn't eaten fruit since the acupuncturist, yet she felt confident somehow the problem was gone. And had her first john-free afternoon for what seemed like a lifetime.

'You realise I haven't done a sculpture in months,' Dwight told her on one of the rare occasions these days they had a few moments to spend together. He had just come back from the lawyer about the pardon.

'I dream a mixture of grammar soup, police investigations and floor measurements,' she acknowledged.

'Humdrum middle-class stuff,' Dwight said. And he said: 'I never meant to live like this, you know. Really. Sometimes I hate myself.'

She said: 'But what can you do? When you've got money you have to spend it.'

'Plus a lot you haven't got,' Dwight said. 'Still, at least we're not having a baby.'

'Touch wood.'

He said: 'One of the advantages of putting in the diaphragm yourself is that you know it's there.'

The condo *palazzo* they had bought into was arranged in four sections around a dingy central courtyard. Their apartment was on the top floor overlooking the street, and since this section of the building was higher than the other three, their kitchen and bedroom windows at the back looked directly down over the tiled roof of one of the perpendicular sections barely a metre below. It was from this roof, just a week or two before they were due to exchange contracts, that a long thin chimney suddenly sprouted. Dwight arrived on a fine spring morning to bring Angelo his next twenty million and saw the thing belching wood-smoke straight into his apartment.

Dwight took a very deep breath. For a moment it seemed a choice between bursting into tears and kicking out at the wall. His normal reaction would have been the latter. Except that this time the newly plastered wall was his own.

'So now you know who sent the anonymous letters,' Angelo said with his wry smirky smile. 'You can't get at him because he knows about you and the window.'

When Dwight flopped into an armchair later and looked hopelessly at Susan, she said: 'But this is completely different. I mean, slightly altering the façade is one thing, but this is a question of hygiene, of public health. We can't live in a place with smoke going straight into our window over the food we're cooking.'

'A reminder of Dachau,' Dwight muttered, casting about for humour. 'Like Angelo said, we can't complain because he knows about our trick with the window.'

'But surely you can't get away with something that's a health hazard. I mean, that's going to stay a health hazard.'

Dwight said: 'We must be in Italy.'

On her way to the loo, Susan was shouting, 'And I'm already late for Technosald, for Christ's sake, I'm going to die.'

A few days later Dwight spent an afternoon looking for the offending proprietor. The name on the door was Bragastini, but nobody was ever in. He rang the bells of other doors in the *palazzo* until he got the chance to explain his problem. Bragastini, he was told, was a tenant, but he had left more than a year ago. Giordano Bragastini. Dwight rang the three Giordano Bragastinis in the phone book and found the wife. The apartment, at least when they were there, had officially been owned by Ligozzi, but he had been dead more than a decade. The real owner was the niece, Ranalli. And she gave Dwight the number. Ranalli, however, denied ever having owned the apartment. To the best of her knowledge, her uncle Ligozzi had sold it six months ago. To Ballicella.

Fulvio Ballicella was gruff and aggressive. Yes, he had bought the apartment, for his son. Of course his son wouldn't have put up a chimney illegally. It had always been there. If he – Signor Berkowitz was it? – hadn't noticed it before, it was because it was easy not to notice such things, and if he insisted on discussing it, why didn't he just knock on the door and discuss it with his son.

Because Ballicella junior was never in, because the apartment appeared to be unlived-in for the moment. The chimney had only smoked that one time.

'Then it can't be bothering you very much, can it?'

'But it will be bothering me when he does move in.'

Not to worry, Ballicella said, his son wouldn't be moving in until he got married.

And when was that?

'I'm sorry, but I really don't see why I have to discuss my son's private life with every stranger calling on the phone.'

And so on.

Returning home, without anything special in mind, Dwight wandered into a supermarket, and finding, which was not unusual, a plastic bag in his pocket, began to shove in one item for every item he put in his supermarket trolley. A kind of principle. He took ketchup, which he hadn't touched in years, ten eggs, an expensive chunk of parmesan, an almond cake, a fistful of steaks. Then at the checkout he realised he was being watched. The easy alternative would have been to lower the plastic bag to the floor and simply leave it there, deny any knowledge. But Dwight was in a cold rage. He had spent all the money he had, all the money Susan had, on this apartment; they were both working fifty immensely tedious, energy-sapping hours a week to pay for it; he had given everything, in a way even sacrificed his principles, his identity and certainly his lifestyle for this hundred square metres of city, and now these lawless Italians were going to make the place unlivable, going to smother him in pollution. He would have been better off in Manhattan.

So, as the till-girl rang up his legitimate items, he packed them away in a legitimate bag and then, even before she could ask for the money, ran, made a wild dash for it, banging through swing doors, whirling the two bags like maces amidst a crowd of shoppers. The detective, caught unawares, prepared only for the firm hand on the unsuspecting elbow, hurried after, shouting. Dwight foolishly shouted, in English, for him to fuck off, then managed to lose himself among passers-by and traffic: an American Jew, lanky, curly-headed, panting, flailing his bags, running hard in a foreign city.

Susan cleaned the egg off the steaks and wiped the ketchup bottle.

'You seem to have chosen all the things I'm not supposed to eat. You might have a minimum of consideration.'

And she said: 'A real man would know what to do about that chimney.'

'Real feminist tough talk.'

'But for Christ's sake, it's a man's world here, and you just run around pissing in your pants and ripping things off from supermarkets, which is about as much good as a little boy making faces behind the teacher's back. It doesn't achieve anything, only makes things worse if you're caught. How the hell am I supposed to pay for the house if they put you in prison?'

'I always felt my virility went out the window with my foreskin.' He watched her as she busied about the kitchen corner of her room, her thin hands rapidly moving and removing objects with no obvious purpose. 'Anyway, what do you expect me to do? Hold a knife to somebody's throat? Angelo's? Ballicella's? I'd have brought my six-shooter with me if they'd have let me through customs.'

She went on with her tension-releasing movements at the sink.

'Come on, what do you expect me to do?'

For the first time in their relationship, she turned and shrieked at him. 'Just do any fucking thing that works, before I have to start wearing diapers.' Her face was contorted, her eyes red and small. 'All right?'

'But what?'

Holding her stomach she tottered a few paces across the room and fell back into a chair. The anger had already gone out of her. After a moment she said: 'There must be something.' She got up and started for the john. Dwight watched her: slim, ageing, vulnerable, attractive. 'Something Italian,' she muttered.

Dwight went to his first condominium meeting. Susan was feeling too ill. Ballicella junior was there, dressed entirely in '*bon ton* Benetton', a dark sulky boy with a long jaw and heavy sensuous lips. The administrator, stout and bald, had a tan surprising in May and a hurried, low-voiced way of speaking which more than anything else conveyed the impression that he didn't want those present to actually listen. Dwight chose the first pause to launch into a long complaint about the health hazards of the chimney that had appeared so near his window. But whenever he spoke in public, and particularly when he was angry, his Italian went to pieces. The words felt like so much gravel in his mouth. The vowels slurred, the endings disappeared altogether. He could sense the others sniggering. He knew they thought his tinted glasses were ridiculous. He thought them ridiculous himself, but would never wear anything else. Angrier, he made even more mistakes; he heard his voice degenerating into an incoherent whine. He shouted, 'That chimney has to go!' Ballicella shrugged his stylish shoulders. He could hardly be responsible for something the owner before him had done. Could he? Everybody knew the chimney had been there for ages. The six or seven other property owners sat expressionless. It wasn't their problem.

'But the cement's fresh, for Christ's sake.' After a short, tense silence, smiling condescendingly, the administrator said that actually he'd had a few men up on the roof recently for repairs. Maybe they'd done some pointing. Foolishly, scorching about the ears, Dwight walked out...

...And worked all night on one of his little creations. He cut the pieces from the cardboard of Susan's rice packets. He used paste, tape and colours on first one model then another, till he had it just right. In fact he hadn't enjoyed himself so much for some long time, albeit in a rather vicious, uncool kind of way.

A few days later Ballicella junior would thus receive in the post what at first appeared to be a perfectly innocent greetings card with the word '*auguri*' written flamboyantly across the front, the kind of thing a man soon to be married might expect. On opening the card, however, a red-tiled roof popped up as in a book for children, and above the roof a chimney. A thin piece of thread around that carefully painted cardboard chimney, with its black spume of smoke, was tied in such a way as to form a delicate noose, and when the card was opened, just as the roof popped up, so, by force of gravity, the naked tortured figure whose head was strangled in this noose fell to his ugly dangling death a few centimetres below the card, red tongue protruding, mouth open in a wide howl, penis – as rumour would have it – obscenely erect. On the back of the card, in words and letters crudely snipped from newspaper and telephone directory, was glued the message:

EMANUELE UMBERTO LIGOZZI. DIED MARCH 7TH,
1978. VICOLO OROLOGIO 6 (APARTMENT 5) SOLD
TO FULVIO BALLICELLA, FATHER OF RENATO LUIGI,
JANUARY 20TH 1988. BY EMANUELE UMBERTO
LIGOZZI. VALUE OF EVADED SUCCESSION TAXES
EVENLY DIVIDED BETWEEN LEGAL HEIR, ROBERTA
RANALLI, AND PURCHASER, FULVIO BALLICELLA.
OR NO? (COPY SENT TO ROBERTA RANALLI)

Dwight came down with the flu. 'I've been sickening
for it all my life,' he said. 'The usual anticlimax.'
Susan was out teaching and hunting for furniture.
Only now did it occur to her that, apart from real
antiques, there was no second-hand market in Italy.
Nothing to be had cheap. However were they going
to furnish the place? And in a fever almost as high as
Dwight's, she thought about the depth of cupboards,
the length of sofas, the way doors opened, the quality
of this wood and durability of that, weighing
everything against the dregs of their bank balances,
the eventual size of mortgage repayments. She was
acutely aware, as she hurried from one shop to
another, looked through one catalogue then the next,
that she had never meant to get so deeply involved
in these material, bourgeois and inherently mean
aspects of life. She was aware of betraying her
militant past, not to mention that spiritual side she
had hoped to cultivate when she turned to Buddhism.
She felt nervous and unhappy with herself. On the
other hand what a shame it would be, now they

had spent so much on the place and on doing it up, if they didn't go the whole hog and furnish it decently. She was too old to sit on cold floors and keep her clothes in boxes. What would be the point of white walls, marble window sills and beech skirting boards, if they then just went and filled the place with junk?

Except that everything cost so much. So much. And in the middle of conversations with overdressed, over-made-up, overenthusiastic sales-ladies praising the ease with which an armchair's covers might be removed, the practicality of a double kitchen sink in stainless steel, Susan would look at her watch and break off in mid-sentence to scuttle away to a lesson to earn the money she had already counted in her calculations. By now she knew every loo available to her from one side of town to the other.

'It's finished,' Angelo said. 'We can exchange contracts Friday. I've already made an appointment with the solicitor. Three o'clock. Via San Nicolò 2. That'll give you clearance for the mortgage.'

On the phone the builder's voice was so firm and sure and matter-of-fact he might have been announcing an airline departure. 'You owe me a further seventy-three million,' he added, as if to say, 'Gate 15, boarding card at the ready.'

But Dwight had learnt enough by now to ignore this. Sitting on his bed, speaking through a fever that seemed more inspirational than debilitating, he asked:

'You fixed the door that was catching on the tile going into the bedroom?'

'Sure.'

'And checked out the thermostat?'

'Sure.'

'The damp by the living-room window?'

'A leak from the frame. We sealed it off. Should be able to put another coat of paint on in a couple of weeks.'

'All ready then.'

'Yes.'

Dwight paused before apparently complaining: 'God knows how long it'll be before the mortgage comes through.'

Angelo was complacent. 'Six weeks, usually, after the exchange of contracts. That's why we want to get through the formalities fast. Then when it arrives I give you the keys and you can move in.'

'Oh, I'm in no hurry,' Dwight said.

'As you will.'

'No, I mean over the exchange of contracts business.' Dwight managed to sound as if he was bored, yawning almost. 'Let's delay it.'

'But...' For the first time Angelo seemed faintly concerned; he hesitated, as if he had missed the thread somewhere. Dwight waited, adrenalin pumping through the steamy heat of the virus.

More formal than usual, Angelo said: 'But isn't it in your own best interest, Signor Berkowitz, to get it all sorted out as soon as possible? You've already paid nearly a hundred million. You want to realise your investment, don't you? Enjoy the benefits. Stop paying rent elsewhere.'

Again Dwight paused. Pauses were so fruitful on the telephone. Plus he could use the time to think, to remember his lines. Then he said bitterly: 'Not with a chimney pumping smoke through my windows all over my new furniture.'

'Look, don't be so neurotic.' Angelo's voice had an edge. 'He's not going to be using his fireplace every day, is he?'

'Only all winter.'

'But in winter you'll have your windows closed.'

'And my view obscured.' And Dwight said: 'It's a question of health. And principle. I've decided to see a lawyer about it.'

There was another long pause now, though it was unlikely that Angelo was leaving it there on purpose. Sounds of a deep sigh, then the builder said flatly: 'You'll never get anything done with a lawyer. Maybe in America, but not here. Lawyers take for ever... I can't wait that long. You owe me seventy-three million.'

Dwight said nothing.

'Anyway, he's got you over a barrel with that window you altered. False request for pardon. It's a criminal offence.'

Dwight said: 'I'm quite willing to face that, if I can get rid of the chimney.' And he added casually: 'Though I suppose you may be implicated in the window business too.'

'You ordered it,' Angelo said quickly. 'Not me. I'm just the builder.'

'But the property is still officially yours, right? Or your company's.' And not allowing Angelo to interrupt, with a complete change of tone Dwight enquired, as if merely curious about a technicality: 'Anyway, how easy would it be to knock that thing down?'

'The chimney?' On his own ground again, Angelo could allow himself his customary knowing snigger: 'A tap with a sledgehammer.'

'I'd exchange contracts tomorrow if that chimney went.'

Angelo laughed broadly now, genuinely amused. If threatening to withhold payment was cowardly, proposing to take up arms was admirable. However stupid. 'But he'd build it again. Or start throwing bricks through your double glazing or something. Forget it.'

'That would be my problem, wouldn't it?'

Angelo hesitated. 'He might even go right away and report the whole affair with the window and then we'd…'

But now, all at once and quite automatically, Dwight interrupted with exactly the right thing: 'Look Angelo,' he said, using the man's name for the first time, 'please, just trust me. Trust me. I can promise you there won't be any problem. Whatsoever.'

'Well…'

'We know each other by now,' Dwight added, having found the vein. 'We're old friends you and me. You know I won't let you down.'

'I'm not sure.' But already Angelo seemed more relaxed, at home even. For his part, Dwight had a delicious sense of fine dovetailing, a sudden and curious communion of minds across hissing phone wires. He had never felt so confidently foreign.

'I suppose...' Angelo began, and again Dwight cut in perfectly: 'While you're about it' – he was consciously giving orders now – 'you may as well cement the thing over properly, make a tidy job of it, and relay the tiles, which are still in a pile in the far left corner of the courtyard. Under that piece of tarpaulin. I'll pay you the cost of your man, plus any materials.' Then, in a single breath, he finished, 'I'll see you Friday at three then, at the solicitor's.' And he hung up.

Susan was exhilarated on her return, having just bought a sofa and two armchairs with Armani-designed covers. She found she felt better when she had made an attractive purchase – brighter, more satisfied. Even if she had wildly overspent.

'But the credit terms were so good.' She heard herself saying a sentence she had always previously heard from other mouths. Or was it from a TV commercial?

'How much have we got left?' Dwight wanted to know. 'In the bank, now?'

'I'm overdrawn.' She fiddled through the stubs of a chequebook. 'And there's two hundred and fifty thou in yours. Barely enough for a couple of weeks' shopping.'

Dwight went out, bought a case of French champagne and asked for it to be delivered Friday morning to Ballicella junior, together with a card that read: 'Congratulations on your wedding. I do hope we can be good neighbours.'

At the solicitor's office they declared and swore that they had paid ninety million lire which constituted the total price of the house. Then, in a separate document, they declared and swore that even if in the previous document they had declared and sworn otherwise, they were now declaring and swearing that in fact they still owed Angelo Tosi and Company the sum of seventy-three million, which would be paid by a mortgage just as soon as it arrived. Only Susan raised half an eyebrow at this rigmarole, but quickly lowered it. 'And our copy?' she asked. 'Of the house purchase, I mean,' for the solicitor was handing her only the declaration of their indebtedness.

'When the mortgage comes through,' he told her. 'A normal precaution. I shall be with you when the bank gives you the cheque and you hand it to me.'

To Dwight afterwards she began: 'In New Zealand…' but then didn't bother going on.

Six weeks later, after the mortgage had arrived, they moved in. Now he had the last of his money, Angelo became congratulatory, helpful, even generous. He lent them his van for the move, insisted on opening a bottle of good Prosecco the evening of their first night there, wandered loose-limbed and handsome about the living room, proudly pointing out the finer details of his work, offering his services for any minor adjustments that still might have to be made. From the supercilious condescension of the practical man who knows better, he had transformed his behaviour into that of the excited and respectful young boy. 'Honoured to have worked for two foreign *professori*,' he said at one point. 'The people I usually work with are so provincial, so small-minded. Not often you get a chance to deal with people who've got taste.'

Sitting on their Armani-covered sofa in a daze of wine and physical exhaustion after hours and hours of carting boxes up and down stairs, Dwight and Susan were wondering when on earth the builder would go away and leave them alone; when there came a knock on the door.

Dwight stood up to answer, drawing back the heavy, fire-proof, axe-proof front door he hadn't asked for in his plans.

'May I?' It was young Ballicella. He wore another complete set of *bon ton* Benetton in green and orange. And someone was hovering in the hallway behind him – not, Dwight immediately registered, a henchman come to smash up the apartment, but a slim little woman with tiny pointed features and carefully applied make-up.

Afraid of how her unpredictable companion might behave, Susan sprang to her feet and somehow managed hellos while holding back a fierce impulse to go to the bathroom. 'Our builder,' she said, introducing

Angelo. But Angelo didn't need any introduction; he strutted across the room, warm and affable: 'Ciao Renato. What do you think? Nice job, eh? Excellent investment buying into a piece of real estate like this. You can both feel pleased with yourselves.'

'Oh, hello Angelo,' Ballicella said. 'You here, are you?' The two smiled very warmly at each other. Politely, with a hint of a bow even, Ballicella asked Susan: 'May I have a look around?'

Too surprised by these developments even to take them in, Susan said of course. And Ballicella and his spouse began to compliment. Very nice the way the sitting room made an L like that. Laying the wooden flooring at an angle was very attractive. Angelo was a real magician when it came to renovation. The best in town. Beautiful furnishing too. Beautifully chosen. Yes, weren't things expensive. Until, in the kitchen, going to the window to look down on the neat array of tiles where the offending chimney had been, Ballicella said over his shoulder to Angelo: 'You know, you're just the man I was planning to speak to actually. You see,' and he turned to include Dwight now, 'Grazia and I are barbecue fanatics. Fanatics. What would you say to putting up a good brick barbecue in common, maybe in one corner of the courtyard. Somewhere where we can really cook a good meal in the open. Maybe eat together sometimes.'

The little woman smiled sweetly. 'I love smoking trout over an open fire.'

Dwight and Susan could only stare.

'Our friend here could do the work.'

Angelo said: 'Illegal I'm afraid, the courtyard's protected. Three hundred years old.' But he said it as one recalling a hitch rather than announcing a full-blown obstacle.

'Still, if everybody's agreed...' Ballicella said. 'I've already spoken to the others.'

'Where would the chimney go?' Dwight demanded, with a definite edge of belligerence. For a moment he thought he might say he was a vegetarian. Except of course they would then sing the praises of polenta and grilled aubergines.

Angelo opened the kitchen window and studied the dusk-lit courtyard and surrounding roofs. 'If you put it,' he said, 'in the far corner on the right, outside your apartment, Renato, run the waste pipe up in brick in the angle of the wall where there are no windows, then take it to the crest of the roof and maybe up another metre or so, it won't bother anybody. Will it?' He turned and beamed. Likewise Ballicella. Waiting for Dwight's response.

In bed, lightly touching, for they hadn't made love in months, Susan said: 'I can't believe it's ours.'

Dwight said: 'I can't believe we're going to pay a 15% mortgage.'

Susan said: 'I can't believe Angelo didn't cheat us. I was sure we were going to lose everything.' She added: 'A question of trust, I suppose. You have to trust people.'

Dwight said: 'I can't believe we're not going to be arrested. False declarations. Illegal payments. Abuse of protected property. Threats. Anonymous letters. Trespass. Wilful damage. And I still haven't paid a lira in tax.'

Susan giggled. He hadn't heard her giggle for some long time. It sounded very attractive. 'Run-of-the-mill,' she laughed. 'What I still can't believe is those fabulous credit terms for the furniture. That was a coup.'

They lay a while in silence before drifting off into a dreamless sleep.

Lice

While Greg and Hannah Lawrence were out of the country procuring a brother for their daughter Emily, Granny Joan ran into trouble with their best friends, the Reardons. It was the long summer vacation. The heat was unusually oppressive. Since she had various tests to do at the hospital, Granny Joan left little Emily with the Reardons, who had four children, of whom the second, Catherine, was Emily's age. She picked the child up again shortly after lunch, and was grateful for an offer of coffee and biscuits. But that evening Catherine's parents discovered that their daughter had lice. While Douglas rushed out to buy a disinfectant shampoo for all four of their children, his wife Susan phoned Granny Joan and the elderly woman dutifully went to inspect the ten-year-old Emily's head. Emily resisted. Her hair was a thick mat of blond curls. Granny's fingers were rough and bony.

'I can't see any,' Granny Joan reported.

Discussing the matter late into the night, Douglas and Susan Reardon decided that it would be unwise to let the two girls play together again until Emily's parents returned and the situation could be sorted out. As an only child Emily had been terribly spoilt, Susan Reardon thought. Her grandmother didn't seem to want to make the effort that was required in these circumstances. 'Why can't I go to Catherine's?' Emily wept. 'Why won't you take me there?' It made for a difficult three weeks for Granny Joan. Fortunately the Lawrences' large apartment was air-conditioned. Granny Joan abandoned the two rooms that her son and daughter-in-law had bought for her on the floor above, and while Emily watched interminable videos the older woman stared out of floor-to-ceiling windows onto the river below. Reduced by the drought to less than half its normal volume, it flowed sombre and muddy under Victory Bridge. The old lady had been born on the banks of the same river, but fifty miles downstream, in the farming country of the delta, where the heat haze was never so suffocating.

'What do you want for supper, sweetie?' she asked her granddaughter.

'Can't we go out for a burger?' Emily begged.

The Lawrences were in Laos. Through an agency they had negotiated the adoption of a two-year-old orphan boy. The transaction was expensive. A token month's residency was required to satisfy some international agreement. As a close friend and colleague too at the city's general hospital, Douglas Reardon imagined that the Lawrences had been physically unable to have a second child, and so had finally decided for adoption in order to complete their family. Susan Reardon wasn't so sure. 'It's because they don't want to take the time off work to have a child,' she said. Susan had given up her career for her four children. 'And because Hannah's so obsessed about her figure,' of course. Susan sensed that her husband was attracted to the beautiful Hannah, who could still wear the kind of short tops and low-cut pants that exposed your belly. For his part, it wasn't that Douglas felt he had married the wrong woman, but he did wish that his wife had kept her girlish figure. Sometimes this busy father would slip into a dreamy, rather sullen mood.

When the Lawrences got back, they were appalled to hear from Emily how seldom she had been out during these four weeks of vacation, how often she had eaten burgers. Then Susan Reardon phoned. And yes, the child did have lice! She would have to be kept segregated from her new brother. 'You must make sure they don't play together,' Granny Joan was instructed, 'at least until we're sure Emily has a clean bill of health.'

On her husband's death two years ago, Granny Joan had been very promptly saved from a life of widowed loneliness in her small village on the delta. She was brought to the city and given two rooms in this luxury renovation overlooking the river. So it made perfect sense that in return for this generosity she would babysit Emily and, of course, any future child her son and his wife might have.

Hannah discussed the little boy's diet with the elderly lady. He wasn't used to milk products. Unfortunately both parents would have to be back at their hospital jobs even before they had got over their jet lag. But they were used to this kind of sacrifice and didn't complain. Granny Joan said she felt she could manage. At least, she thought, she could now retire to her own little sitting room when Greg or Hannah got home in the evening. It was rare that they both had night duty at the same time. Crossing, in three or four steps, the small smart space that was now her home, or at least her sleeping quarters, Granny Joan stood for a few moments at the window in the half-light that filtered through the blinds. But this side of the building looked down into a busy street. To get a view of the river, she had to lift the blinds, go out onto the tiny balcony, stand in the far right-hand corner and peer round the frosted glass that screened off the neighbouring balcony. Every night it seemed to Granny Joan that the band of water flowing under Victory Bridge was now narrower and greyer than the night before. 'If this drought continues,' the country woman thought, 'the river will disappear altogether. The crops will be ruined.' The thought made her extremely anxious.

Lice are not easy to get rid of. Susan Reardon kept finding that however much shampoo she used, the creatures' eggs always survived, and in a few days Catherine was back at square one. She discussed the matter on the phone with Hannah. Emily's hair was so thick! The disinfectant stung so badly. She fought you when you tried to put it on. She wailed that the fine comb you needed to remove the eggs pulled her hair and hurt so much. 'God knows where Granny took her to get them,' Hannah said. 'The trouble is, these older people are still back in the Forties, when everybody played around in the dirt and didn't give a damn.' Susan couldn't agree more. Greg's mother was hopelessly lax.

'As soon as this nightmare is over,' Hannah sighed, 'we can all get together and have a party to celebrate Andrew's arrival.' They had decided to call their adopted son Andrew because his Laotian name was unpronounceable.

'I know I couldn't spell it if you paid me,' Hannah laughed.

'How's Emily taken it?' Susan enquired.

'Taken what?'

'Having a little brother, of course.'

'Oh, she's delighted,' Hannah said. 'Only it's such a pity the two of them can't play together. No, I mean because of the lice. When will it end? And I'm run off my feet at the hospital after being away so long. With the responsibilities I have it was really pushing it a bit.'

Then young Andrew got lice too. Returning from a night on the casualty ward, Greg spotted the little flecks when he bent down to kiss the foreign boy's polished black hair. Hannah had already left for work.

'I didn't want to tittle-tattle,' Granny Joan admitted, 'but yesterday morning I came in from the balcony and caught Emily leaning right into the playpen shaking her curls over the poor thing.'

'I did not!' Emily protested.

'You sleep,' Granny Joan told her son firmly. 'You've been up all night. I can handle the kids.'

'Well, you don't seem to be making a very good job of it so far,' Greg muttered sourly. He was exhausted.

From the bedroom he called his wife, who ran the hospital's radiology unit. 'At least now the two of them can play together,' he said apologetically. But Hannah was upset. She felt let down. You brought an orphan back from the third world and what was the first thing that happened? He got lice. Lice! Granny knocked softly on the bedroom door. 'Would you like anything special for when you wake up, dear? I'm off shopping.' Greg wondered if his mother had been eavesdropping on his phone conversation.

Despite the heat, it was important to get the children out of the apartment so that the man of the family could sleep. Granny Joan appreciated that this was her duty. Her son and his wife worked so hard. A doctor suffering from fatigue is a danger to his patients. Out in the street, pushing the little boy's buggy, the old lady wondered if she wasn't getting some curious looks from passers-by. The child's face was a smooth ochre brown with shining black eyes. The few words he knew were in another language, and he twisted in frustration against the buggy's safety harness. Emily pulled faces at him. It seemed strange to Granny Joan that this boy with Asian eyes would be the one to pass on the name that her husband had given her so many years ago. Walter had complained bitterly when the first immigrants began to arrive. All his predictions had come true.

On Victory Bridge, Granny Joan and the children stopped to look through the railings. Even in its shrunken state this was still a powerful river, and since it dropped here over a ledge of rocks and boulders, a cool breeze came off the water.

'A rat!' Emily cried. 'Oh Granny, a rat! How yuck!'

'Where? Where?' Granny Joan couldn't see.

'There, look, there! Are you blind?' the girl shrieked. In fact, the mud bank was little more than a grey blur to the elderly lady. The scales on her eyes must harden, it seemed, before they could be removed. Emily climbed onto the railing to get a better view.

'Oh, my dear, you mustn't.' Granny's bony fingers grabbed her smock. At the same instant, Andrew finally worked out how to release the belt buckle on the buggy. He tottered to his feet on the busy pavement with the traffic thundering by in a haze of fumes and heat shimmer.

Greg awoke to the hum of the air-conditioner. He was looking forward to tennis with Doug Reardon in the hopefully cooler early evening. 'Food in the fridge', said a note on the kitchen table in his mother's shaky writing. There was a plate of cold beef, salad, boiled potatoes. The children were thankfully quiet. Greg turned on the radio. Perhaps Mum had taken them out again. Listening to some more alarmism about the drought, the heatwave, global warming, he reflected that, on the contrary, all was well with the world. They had got the boy back safe and sound from the other side of the globe. They had a family. Emily had a companion. And as a result, his ageing, depressive mother now had a purpose in life. 'We have saved a child from poverty,' Greg told himself. It couldn't be a bad thing. He went to dig out his tennis kit and heard Emily's shrill voice coming from the sitting room. 'Lice,' she was repeating in a mocking voice. 'Lice, lice lice!' Then she started a little chant: 'Lousy lice! Lousy lice! Andy Pandy lousy lice!' He found the girl standing over the playpen mouthing at the little boy, who was trying to repeat her. Greg burst out laughing.

A few minutes later, he called his friend Doug, who had just got into his car at the hospital.

'Problem, Doug, I haven't got anybody for the kids. Granny must have forgotten. She's gone out.'

'Take 'em over to Susan!' Doug said cheerfully.

'And the lice?'

'Oh, she'll sort something out. A mother of four is never without resources!'

When Greg arrived, Susan was secretly pleased that the old lady was showing signs of unreliability. It seemed unfair to her how easily the Lawrences had combined kids and work.

'She must have gone to church or something,' Greg apologised. 'Or window shopping.'

'I'll put shower-caps on their heads,' Susan said brightly. 'Oh, but what a pretty boy you are, Andrew! What an utter sweetheart!' Entirely careless of the lice problem, she lifted the boy in her arms and hugged him tight and tweaked his small brown nose. Susan was a born mother.

Greg and Doug played hard, whacking the ball back and forth on the synthetic surface, sweating profusely in the sullen heat. They were both good-looking men in early middle age with vigorous bodies, good jobs, healthy principles, plenty of money. After showering, they drank some iced juice in the club's air-conditioned bar, despaired of their hospital's many inadequacies, passed comments on a couple of young women, laughed, said goodbye. But only a few hours later they were speaking again.

'Doug?'

'Greg, for Christ's sake, what time is it?' Doug Reardon had fallen asleep in his youngest child's bed. It had taken him a while to find the cordless. Greg asked him if he could come out and meet him at once, urgently. That wine bar on the corner of Victory Bridge, he said. Doug imagined a marriage crisis. He was excited. Hannah was such a pretty woman. He explained the situation to Susan, dressed quickly and drove across town to meet his friend. Greg was already sitting at a table outside.

'My mother hasn't come back,' he announced.

'Oh.' Doug sat down. Now he felt rather irritated. His friend had called him out at almost midnight when he knew he had to be on the ward at eight.

'I'm terribly worried,' Greg insisted.

'Take it easy.' Doug ordered a coffee. 'Tell me.'

Granny Joan was nowhere to be found. She hadn't come back. The children thought they had last seen her around four o'clock. Emily was watching some kids thing on TV.

'And she has no friends here,' Greg said.

'You told me she goes to church,' Doug remembered. 'Crazy prayer meetings or something.'

Greg admitted that his mother had given up most of the evangelical stuff when she moved from the country into town. It had been a relief actually. He couldn't remember when she'd last gone to church. A pretty waitress brought them coffee, and even at this hour the air in the city streets was still and warm. There was music from a distant window.

'Some kind of loss of memory,' Doug thought, 'a mild stroke, a touch of Alzheimer's?'

Greg explained that he had phoned their colleague Austin on emergency, and that there had been no such admission. No one jumping off buildings either.

'Well there's a relief,' Doug half-laughed, then asked: 'What is it, Greg?' Something, he realised, hadn't been said. His friend, who operated on cancer patients on a daily basis, seemed to be having difficulty coping with the situation.

'There was an odd note on the table. In her little apartment.'

'Yes?'

'It just said: "I want to go home".'

Doug could not see the problem.

'So that's what she'll have done. That's your answer.'

'But there's no home to go back to. The old place was sold to pay for the apartment here.' Visible a hundred yards along the further bank, Victory Mansions was certainly a luxury development in a prime location. Even for the Lawrences the purchase had been a major investment.

'So she's staying with friends, or at a hotel or something.'

Greg admitted he didn't have any phone numbers for Granny's friends back in the country. She never seemed to call anyone. 'In any event,' he protested, 'why wouldn't she have told us?'

'Afraid you'll be upset about her not looking after the kids,' Doug said.

Indeed this was a huge problem. If Granny didn't turn up, he or Hannah would have to miss work tomorrow. So soon after their long vacation.

'Take 'em over to Susan,' Doug said, then added, 'for the one day, you know. In an emergency.'

Greg wasn't listening. 'No, but the point is she's always been so totally reliable. I mean, it's so out of character. She's never spoken about going back.'

'Everybody can be allowed one aberration in their life,' Doug said. 'It's been a hell of a summer. You should hear how Susan's mother's been behaving, rearranging her furniture in the middle of the night. Somebody even complained to the police.'

The men had finished their coffee. For a moment they sat in silence in the warm night with the sound of the occasional car, somebody playing jazz. Both were pensive now, anxious. Doug wanted to get home to bed, yet the woman's disappearance was troubling. 'If she had just taken a bus down to the country,' Greg said decisively, 'she would have written, "I've gone home." Wouldn't she? Not, "I want to go home." She would have said for how long. She's a practical person. Always has been.'

'She's getting old…' Doug began. Then he said: 'Greg, what is it? There's something on your mind. Why did you get me out here?'

'I think we should search the river bank,' Greg said.

Partly because the proposition seemed so strange and melodramatic, Doug agreed to do this, but said he must phone home first. Susan was at once on the edge of hysteria. First the lice, now this! The men got to their feet.

'Oh, it's just a horrible hunch,' Greg began to excuse himself. 'I think the heat's been getting to her, the problem with her cataracts.'

'No problem,' Doug assured him. 'I'm your man.' The truth was that suicides in the river were fairly frequent in this city. And since both these doctors were obliged from time to time to do nights in casualty, they knew well enough that while men tended to choose the gun or the rope, women preferred the water.

'We've all been bothered by the heat,' Doug reassured his friend. 'And so many older people have cataracts. It'll be all right, you'll see.' But all the same they set off to look.

Travelling downstream, Victory Bridge was the last of the town's main crossing points. There followed a half mile or so of residential suburbia, then the open fields. First they walked along the cycle path by the parapet, constantly looking down. Under bright reflection from the street lamps, the river slid darkly between banks of shale and mud. There was a stale smell. When you focused carefully, you could see that the occasional flecks of white by the bank were nothing sinister, just tattered plastic bags snagged on the bushes the last time the river had been high.

'I can't believe we're doing this,' Greg said. He seemed extremely agitated. Then his friend insisted they call the police. The river was long. It meandered back and forth for miles. 'We can't do this on our own.' They called from Greg's mobile in the parking lot where the cycle track ended. A proper search would have to wait for morning, the desk sergeant thought. Such things required a lot of men. And good light.

'You'll probably find she's just fallen asleep on a bench somewhere, sir. There's been a lot of that in this weather.'

'But where would a body normally wash up?' Greg demanded. Doug was shaking his head. It was past two o'clock.

'By the dam,' the policeman said promptly.

They walked back to Victory Bridge, picked up Doug's car and drove down to the dam, where Greg found Granny Joan in a mill of bottles and litter to the right of the flow where the dam wall met the bank. With the drought, the sluices were all but closed, so that everything was turning slowly on itself in sluggish circles. Greg had to walk through deep mud and then wade into the filthy water to his thighs to get at her. Her bun had come loose, and the grey hair was tangled round her face. The mouth, when it fell open, was full of silt. Before he got her ashore, an ambulance was already on the scene, siren blaring. In the blue light that flashed out across the water, Greg saw his mother's blind eyes; they were surprisingly alert and bright. 'I shall never have the strength to forgive you,' he said. He cursed. 'Never.'

The Room

This afternoon she didn't go straight to the room. Instead, she mooched for half an hour, first in a music shop, then looking through posters in a place that mainly sold bric-a-brac for tourists. She imagined the posters on the wall opposite her bed, each one changing the colour and flavour of her life. Then she imagined buying one for the room. Apparently this was a strange thought, for she stood there frowning at a boldly painted naive image of man, woman and child against a postmodern backdrop. What sense would there be in hanging this in the room?

And she decided not to buy fruit today. Today would be different. Perhaps this was what had been disturbing her. Sameness. Or, more specifically, lack of progress. Looking at her watch, seeing she was going to be late, she very deliberately did not quicken her pace. And this perhaps was a far greater change than anything that might be worked by the purchase of a poster or the non-purchase of fruit.

Life. Walking past dreary boarding houses in Earls Court, this young woman was very beautiful, though she herself did not believe so. Her camellia-coloured skin had the faintest soft freckling below wide, plum-dark eyes. She walked too quickly in flat shoes and loose, casual clothes, hiding everything, one among so many on these pavements. Essentially she was a happy person.

Arriving at the famous 69 (trust him to remark on its appropriateness), she let herself in, discreetly obeying all the rules they had established: a light but not hurried pace along threadbare carpeting, softly down the stairs with the creak where they turned, almost silent insertion of the key.

She opened an old brown London door onto the familiar stale smell.

The room. It was untidy, for today was Monday and the others who came at the weekend always left it like that. There was the bed to be made up, a bit of clearing away to be done. These were tasks she would normally tackle brightly, lowering shabby drape curtains over the legs of passers-by, lighting the spots, finding music on the radio. Today she swung her shoulder bag onto an armchair that no charity shop would accept and lay down on the bare mattress. The mattress, in sharp contrast to everything else, was new. Sweet Dreams it was called. Nobody, as far as she knew, had ever slept on it.

And how odd that today, of all days, with her feeling the way she did, he was late. She remembered a recent conversation. Since he taught statistics, since she had studied with him, it was not unusual for them to talk about chance, probability, coincidence, though usually jokingly. ('Assuming a man comes once in every bout of lovemaking and a woman twice, and given a mean copulative frequency of the population as a whole, pensioners, infants and war-wounded included, of once a month, what is the probability that the total number of achieved, non-masturbatory orgasms, of a randomly selected sample, will etc. etc.' They used to laugh about this kind of thing.) But it must have been last week he had said quite seriously that he had noticed that when he was feeling different sometimes different things happened; a curiously inarticulate proposition, coming from him, as she had swiftly, joyfully pointed out. And yet he honestly had noticed it, as if there were such a thing as premonition after all. But not in the classic sense. More a sort of extraordinary subterranean process by which one's feelings were already attuned to an eventuality before it happened. So intriguing if one could think of a way of analysing it statistically: frequency, circumstances. Yet he himself could hardly offer one concrete example. Something was going on, but so elusive.

Lying on the superior sprung surface manufactured by Sweet Dreams Ltd, the only significant investment in this shabbily furnished room, Alice observed that she was not crying, nor especially sad. Yet, by that curious process he had spoken of, she realised that she was already prepared for what would happen. She knew they would not make love today. Nor ever again perhaps. Those terrible words.

Then she was just thinking of where she, Alice Norton, had come from, where she might be going to, and what place this room might have in her life between those two distant points, when the scratching of a key in the door appeared to belie her melancholy. He was here. Immediately she was on her feet, pulling the clean bed linen out of the bag by the dresser. Bustle, bustle. Spread the sheets, pull on the pillow slips, mix a drink perhaps, if the others had left any. They would only have an hour or so at max. Glasses. Those bastards hadn't even washed the glasses.

'Sorry,' a woman's voice spoke behind her.

She turned in shock. For Heaven's sake, could this be the wife?

The woman by the door was older, a shade thick about the middle, but very fashionably dressed in skirt, silk blouse, a light jacket around her shoulders. Her face was at once authoritative and friendly, the skin only faintly tired about cheeks, the corners of the mouth.

'I'm sorry,' she repeated with a full, strong voice. 'I really didn't mean to disturb. Just that I left my watch here I think. I'd hate to lose it.'

They looked at each other. Alice understood and relaxed.

She must be Jonathan's friend's woman, the other couple who used the room. She smiled broadly, almost burst out laughing, the release from tension generating a sense of hilarity – naughty children getting away with things. So when the other woman had found her watch on the floor by the bed, she suggested: 'Why don't you stay and have a cup of tea till he gets here? It's so odd actually seeing you after all this time. You must be Christine, right?'

Smiling, somewhat wry, the woman agreed. They sat at the table with its sticky wooden surface below light filtering through the curtains: it was early afternoon.

'Oh, by the way,' Alice began, 'now I've got the opportunity, can I make a complaint? You never clean up properly. I mean, the dishes and crumbs on the carpet and stuff. Even the loo's dirty sometimes. I don't want to be a bore, but it is rather a drag us having to do it on Monday.'

The woman was straightforward, unembarrassed: 'I'm sorry. You're right. Jack's always in such a hurry. You know. He tells his wife he's playing football, so he only has a couple of hours, and if I stayed on behind I'd have to get the tube and bus home, and there's my boy waiting for me. We always mean to clean up,' she added, 'but Jack's so impulsive. We end up making love right to the last minute. We only have the once-a-week, you know.'

'Jonathan's incredibly orderly,' Alice said. 'He always says we should leave it tidy for you.'

For a moment both women, one old enough to be the other's mother, laughed. The afternoon ticked by in this small, quiet, run-down room in London which two lovers had rented to pleasure their mistresses. Alice looked at her watch: 'He's disgustingly late, he's never been late before.' She laughed again. 'We should really get them to put a phone in here to make communications a bit easier. Perhaps with an answering machine, you know, so that when you arrive you could check to see if the other had left a message.' Then, barely pausing and only realising the truth of her words as she spoke them, this beautiful young woman said: 'Though I was meaning to tell him it was over today.' No sooner was it out than she felt that dazed surprise that comes with the realisation of the glaringly obvious. So this was what had been on her mind.

'What? Why?'

'Oh, I don't know.' Alice stood up and ploughed a hand into the jet-black hair he raved so much about. 'It's become such a ritual. OK, he loves me, he really does. He's so passionate about me and everything and we make love so well. I've never made love like with him. I'm so happy with him. But in the end there's his wife, there's his children. He's never going to leave them. If it were just his wife he says he'd leave her, and I believe he would. The letters he writes me. The way he is with me. I'm sure he would. But not the kids. I've seen him with them. We went out for the day once with his boy. He'll never leave them. They're so lovely.'

Sipping her tea, the older woman asked: 'How old are you?'

'Twenty-one.'

'And Jonathan?'

'Thirty-four.'

'Like Jack.' She smiled. 'I'm forty-one.' Then she merely added: 'I wonder if he'll be able to afford to keep the room on his own if you two drop out.

Perhaps we'll have to sort out some other arrangement.'

For a few moments neither spoke, apparently stilled by the dustiness of this small sad space usually so alive for both of them with the intensities of erotic pleasure.

Straight-backed, dignified, a definite air of careful preservation about her, Christine sipped her tea. Alice paced about the room. Then the girl said: 'Oh, shit,' and plumped herself down on the edge of the Sweet Dreams mattress. 'At the beginning it was so wonderful. We even managed to go on holiday together. To Paris. And of course I half-believed that something might come of it. You know how you do. Just that now it's such a ritual. We come here. We mix a drink, put the radio on. We make love, gloriously. We smoke, we eat grapes or kiwis. We talk about the same old things. And we can never be seen out together, because all my friends know him as the Statistics Prof, and of course all his friends know his wife. So we can never grow together or become anything different or hope for anything.' Very determinedly she finished: 'Well, I get my degree next month and that's it. I'll break it off. Start a new life.'

To hear her speak, she gave the impression of talking to one who didn't believe her. But the older woman nodded her comprehension: 'I've never met him, but Jack told me something about him, that he'd leave home and live with you, but for the kids.' She shrugged her shoulders in an expression that told the younger woman: '*C'est la vie.*' It wasn't perhaps quite the sort of elder-sisterly comfort Alice had been expecting, and now she asked almost abrasively: 'And Jack?'

'What?'

'Your one. Is he planning to leave his wife?'

'Good Heavens, no.'

'So he has children too. They seem to be a universal curse. Or an excuse.'

'No, he doesn't actually. The wife wants kids, but it seems they haven't been able to have them.'

'So he could leave her tomorrow, if he wanted! He has no excuse at all!'

'I suppose he feels sorry for her. If he left her now, she'd be nearly forty with no kids, nothing. She's older than him.'

'But feeling sorry for someone's hardly a good reason for staying with them, is it?' Alice was growing indignant.

'No, but probably he's not that unhappy with her or the whole arrangement anyway.' She laughed quite cheerfully: 'He always says: "Inertia will pull me through in the end."'

Still chuckling, this older woman, who Alice now found time to notice was heavily though tastefully made up, began to hunt for and eventually found a packet of cigarettes in her handbag.

'But you, wouldn't you be better off with someone who could give you everything? You know, if you're already forty-one, you...'

'Oh, he has a fine line in dirty talk. I like that. He's good company, lusty in bed. He knows how to give me what I want.'

'But that's an awful thing to say.'

Her tea finished, the mature woman held up a hand, then ducked a little out of habit to light her cigarette. She tossed her hair back with simple, stylish self-assurance: 'Sweetheart, I was actually married for fifteen years. I have a twelve-year-old son. After? …What, about ten years, first Phil, my husband, and then I were unfaithful, and after a while we both found out. But we never split up. I don't know why. It wasn't just Joey, my boy. More a feeling that, well, that life went that way, that that was the direction. We were set in our ways. You know?' And now she added, as if inconsequentially: 'A couple of years later he died in a car crash.'

'I'm sorry.'

'Oh, you don't have to be. All I'm saying is that one learns, I suppose, to separate passion, sex, from the mainstream of your life.'

Taking this in, Alice said intelligently: 'I think that's awfully sad.'

'Well, maybe at first.'

Alice stood up again and went to look in a foggy mirror which showed her full length and tomboyish in jeans and yellow T-shirt. Her movements as she swayed there, then swung away on one heel, were so much those of a girl doing some sport, rather than a woman who knows how to wear clothes and hold her body. Which curiously made her seem vulnerable in her very vitality.

With sudden fervour, she said: 'Well, I don't accept it. I won't. I'm going to tell him: either he leaves his wife, or it's over.'

'You're not of an age to accept it.'

'I hate it,' Alice snapped, raising her voice and rounding on her lover's friend's lover, 'I absolutely hate it when people try to circumvent any proper argument by simply saying I'm too young. As if the old couldn't talk to the young. It's terrible.'

'It is terrible,' the other equably agreed with one raised eyebrow. For a moment the two women stared at each other, then Alice laughed bitterly: 'Anyway, he'll understand. He's idealistic too. I mean, he suffers this separation of his love life from his family life, coming here to this squalid little shit-hole to fuck, never being able to go out together in company. He's always saying, either he'd like to fall in love with his wife again or somehow substitute me for her. Only the problem is she'd get the kids. Which is understandable of course, though I'd be perfectly willing to look after them, and from what he says she's not a very good mother either.' The girl hesitated, emotion had brought quite bright spots of colour to her cheeks: 'All I'm saying is, he understands perfectly well that the situation's not ideal. He'd never ask me to accept it permanently.'

For all reply the older woman pulled a mirror from her handbag and scrutinised her face as one who is preparing to leave.

'Whereas this Jack of yours is just in it for fun and fucks, I gather.'

But this deliberate provocation drew only a broad smile that the mature woman exchanged with herself in her compact.

'Oh, I'm sorry,' Alice said. 'What a stupid little girl I'm being.'

'Not at all. You're perfectly right. He's in it for sex, fun, excitement, to relieve the boredom of his happy marriage. I'm in it for the same reasons, to relieve the boredom of my pleasantly humdrum existence with son and sister. What's the fuss? Neither of us really want to change anything, I shouldn't imagine. And if this Jonathan's got any sense,' she added, 'nor would he.'

'Well, I think that's awful. It may be OK as a temporary arrangement, but as something permanent it's dishonest. To others and to yourself.'

The older woman put her mirror back in her bag and began to edge out from behind the table, dusting cigarette ash from her jacket sleeve. And again Alice had that impression of careful, cosmetic preservation. 'Dishonest,' she repeated, almost in tears now.

'I can understand why you would think so.'

'I mean, there must be happy marriages, relationships, which have no need of outside entertainment, which contain everything.'

After a moment's pause, straightening her jacket, the older woman looked up and said: 'Yes, I think you're right. There must be. Certainly that would be the best thing.'

'Well, I think Jonathan and I could do it. I really do. And that's why I'm going to tell him it's over. To force him into action. One thing or the other.'

There was a challenge in Alice's voice. Checking her watch, Christine said: 'Do you know that old joke about asking an Irishman the way somewhere, and he scratches his head and says, "Oh, if I wanted to go there I wouldn't start from here."'

Alice said yes. She'd heard it before. 'So?'

'So, if I wanted to go where you do, love, I wouldn't start from where you are now. That's all.' To which the younger woman came back with a student's sharpness: 'I don't care how rough the ground is, you can always draw a line between two geographical coordinates.' But then quite suddenly she burst into tears. Throwing herself face down on the bed, she sobbed so fiercely her sharp shoulder blades seemed to leap up inside her T-shirt. The other woman came over to sit by her side, though without touching her. She asked: 'Do you love him, then?'

The girl moaned, 'Terribly. I only think of him. All day every day.'

'And he tells you he loves you?'

'But he does, I know he does.'

'That's not exactly the point.' And then she said: 'Look, if he was supposed to be here an hour ago, he's obviously not coming now. Why don't we nip out together and grab a sandwich or an ice cream or something? Cheer you up. Then I'll have to get back to work.' When the girl went on crying, this fashionable, carefully dressed, middle-aged woman put a hand on her back and caressed her lightly. Speaking softly, she said: 'Alice, Alice, why don't you think of him as just a good lay? No, no, listen, I don't mean in a crude way at all. I mean as something you enjoy, someone you like to be with, an adventure that satisfies one part of you. But not the centre of your plans, your work, your home. You know? You've done a degree, haven't you, you're starting out in life, you don't want to look after his children, iron his shirts. OK, you love him, but there's no need to wrestle with words like temporary and permanent. Let things take their course.' Half-laughing, but still soft, she added, 'London's teeming with rooms like this, you know, teeming, but they're never really part of anybody's home, are they? Come on. That's the way to see it.'

'No! No! No!' the girl suddenly shrieked, loud and quite frighteningly, as if some spirit threatened with exorcism were clutching at her throat. 'No! No! No! I won't!'

The older woman was clearly shocked by the wild energy of this refusal, for she immediately jumped up and backwards, as if scorched or genuinely shaken, as when a memory is too sudden and searing to allow of any defence. She stood staring at the girl, struggling to regain composure.

'Oh, I'm sorry,' Alice said, calming as suddenly as she had lost control a moment before. 'I don't know what's come over me today, I'm such a misery. I don't usually cry. I'll just wash my face a minute, then I'd love to come out with you.'

She got up and padded to the tiny bathroom where they had often joked that you could perfectly well shower sitting on the loo, if you wanted; and so at last she found his note.

Taped to the mirror. Obviously he had supposed she would, as always, make straight for the bathroom to prepare herself, not imagining that her mood might mysteriously have attuned itself to this event beforehand in the very way he had himself observed. She had not gone to the bathroom because she had known there would be no sex today. And she had told herself she was fed up with sameness because in some remote part of herself she had known things would never be the same again. The note said:

> Dearest, my dearest Alice,
> I know this is no way to announce things. I do know. It's cowardly. It's mean. But I can't face telling you in person. I would simply burst out in howls and sobs. I love you so dearly. Our times together have been so precious. But I feel constantly pulled in two directions, the object of some vicious tug of war. God knows we've talked about it often enough, and as you yourself suggested once, seeing you makes it impossible for me to act normally at home and

*be a good husband and father. At the same time
I know now that I will never have the courage
to leave my family for you, and am plagued by
guilt at the thought that I am wasting your life,
your marvellous capacity for love and tenderness.*

*Oh, Alice, my beauty, my dark eyes, my
endless little giggler, I think of you so constantly,
of your extraordinary capacity to be cheerful
and make others so. I think of how happy, how
light-hearted I have always been with you, and
the idea that all this must end is torture.*

Please, please remember me with affection.

Your truly loving,

Jonathan

With turning on the taps then to wash her face, Alice
did not hear the sound of the room's main door
opening, but, catching just the vaguest tremble when
it slammed shut on its spring as it always would, she
imagined that the older woman must have decided to
leave alone. So, with towel in hand, she slipped
quickly out of the bathroom to catch up with her, not
wanting to be left without company at this unhappy
moment; and was thus able to cover her face a
moment with the red cloth to hide the inevitable
shock when she saw what she saw.

'Jack,' the woman who called herself Christine
cried. 'Jack. This is Alice, Jonathan's girl.'

There he was.

And in an extraordinary act of generosity, or perhaps contempt, and anyway with that apparent gaiety he had always most appreciated in her, and most misunderstood, she managed to ask, appearing from her towel and even offering a hand: 'Oh, have you forgotten something too? What a day!'

'My diary,' he invented, as promptly as he must often have been obliged to with his wife.

'Is this a page from it?' The paper was in her hand.

But his eyes were imploring. What? Forgiveness? Or more?

Clearly his only reason for arriving was to take back what he had said in that note. He had changed his mind.

'I'll leave the field to you then,' she said very practically, 'since Jonathan's obviously not coming.' For indeed the other woman was at this moment kicking off her high heels as she rapidly made up the bed. He stared at her, but nothing more. Almost expressionless. She felt his eyes follow her out.

And emerging a few moments later into a grey afternoon light, walking by the curtains drawn over their pleasure (so dusty from this side), finding the note still crumpled in her hand, it occurred to Alice very lucidly that perhaps he had been entirely sincere in what he said there. Why not? She was worth so much more than the older woman, she had so much further to go. Let them keep their squalid room.

Keeping Distance

They were both studying to be doctors, so they had that in common. And then the ages were right – right, that is, for his preconception of how ages in a couple should be a difference of three years in his favour – and while she would always have objected in any discussion of the issue to the notion that in the ideal couple the girl should be younger, she nevertheless enjoyed the idea of having an older man (or rather boy: he was only twenty-four) to slip under her thumb.

The same could have been said of their respective heights.

Then the place was right, too: Selva di Val Gardena, he skiing with friends, spending his father's money, she working temporarily in a distant relative's hotel – every day bright and clear, the crisp exhilarating thrust of the Dolomites silenced by snow, the chattering of winter holidaymakers barely denting the mystery. You felt different here: cleaner and more passionate.

He was recovering from having been left by his first love: after five years together, Paola had walked out on him in August and married another man in November. She, on the contrary, had never had a real love, only encounters.

And then there was the excitement of each other's foreignness. He was Italian, she German. Why is it that a foreign lover is always considered a greater prize, a greater adventure? Giuseppe and Hilda made love only hours after having come across each other in a discothèque attached to a pizzeria.

She took all the initiative, for he was still sulking and, having had no other girls but that fatal first love, was shy with women, despite his one-of-the-boys, heavy-drinking, loud-laughing manner with his friends. Quite simply she took him to her bed, and in doing so fell in love with him. For his part, he was most impressed with her physical prowess, with the suddenness of her devotion. He was a man who loved to be loved. Unfortunately, her face was not especially attractive: the nose was too big and wide, the lips too thin, the skin unhealthy somehow. Only the bright blue eyes saved the situation – the bright honest smile displaying well-kept teeth – plus, when it came to introducing her to his friends, her slim but well-endowed and very modern body.

Giuseppe on the other hand was almost unbelievably handsome. In every department. She loved him and loved him. For the first time in her life she was swooning.

They spoke to each other in halting English. Which separated them from their friends. They giggled over misunderstandings. When they spoke about medical matters, though, they found they had a large vocabulary in common and, being her senior, he had the pleasure of explaining things she didn't know about, at great length. In fact he was rather a bore at times, but she lapped it up: there was his face to look at, the fine intelligent forehead and Roman nose, there were his incredibly square shoulders. They both felt pleased to be improving their English, although there was no one to correct them when they made mistakes.

In the mountains everybody wore jeans or ski pants, thick woollen sweaters, quilted jackets. But when, having finished at the hotel, she travelled down to Verona for a week before returning for the next university term, it came as something of a disappointment for Guiseppe. He was an elegant dresser. In a very Italian way he followed fashions. In his imitation Armani sweater and generously cut autumn-coloured wool trousers he walked with an idle strut perfectly adapted for the *passeggiata*. In bright winter weather in Via Mazzini, he cut a figure. But Hilda wore the same jeans, boots, sweaters and quilted jacket she had worn in Val Gardena, and her gait had a hurried A-to-B purpose about it which didn't do much for the huge attribute her body was.

Just when he was beginning to get seriously annoyed with this – and annoyed with the way that, despite her lavish bedtime love and eager if inexpert cooking, she would argue quite belligerently against the notion that women should be sex objects and that money spent on attractive clothes was well spent – just when he was getting seriously irritated (with the fuss she made over finding an old *Playboy*, for example), it was time for her to go home. They were both sad. It had been such a passionate affair, and love had been made such an impressive and unprecedented number of times. They both promised letters, phone calls, visits. She told him very frankly she loved him. He mumbled something in his halting English into her hair, which privately, he thought, she would have done well to have washed more often. Perhaps permed.

She lived in Munich, five hours on the train from Verona, four hundred kilometres, sixty thousand lire, eighty-eight marks. It was not an impossible distance, but expensive for young people living on student incomes, or, in his case, no real income at all. Between degree and specialisation she had six years to go. He was nearing the end of his degree, but then there was his military service to get through, and the prospect of no jobs in Italian hospitals. It all made the relationship such a safe one, as his long affair with Paola had not been. And at Easter Giuseppe thought of himself as travelling up to Germany for a much-needed holiday and a week's solid sex.

Hilda greeted him in Italian. The progress she had made in just four months was astonishing, and likewise astonishing was the love she lavished on him. Nor did her lack of dress sense seem so important in Munich, where everybody dashed about under umbrellas between supermarket and bus stop without any regard for style. She held his arm tight and talked about the coming summer. He felt the slim suppleness of her lively body against him.

On Easter Sunday she took him to her family home to the north of the city, where he was welcomed with open arms by mother, father and brother. A young doctor and so handsome. Their kindness was doubly welcome, since Giuseppe's own parents lived and worked abroad, and it was some time since he had had the chance to experience the warm bath of parental care, parental cooking. Tuned in to modern mores, the Meiers allowed Giuseppe and Hilda to share a room for the night as if already married. This gave a curious touch of respectability, permanence, general acknowledgement to something Giuseppe had so far only thought of as an affair. When he ran out of money, as he regularly would, Hilda lent him five hundred of the marks she had saved from her holiday job, though she did say a few words about not spending so much on clothes. He said if only an Italian medical degree were acceptable in Germany, he would be able to come up permanently in a year or so, after his military service, and do his specialisation in a German hospital. She said, 'That's wonderful,' as if somehow this plan might be feasible.

He did his military service in Naples, and every time he had a few days' leave they met in Verona, seven hundred kilometres north for him, four hundred kilometres south for her. There was a train from Rome that left him on a cold deserted platform at 2 a.m., where he stretched out on a bench under his combat jacket till she got in at 3.30, and they took a taxi back to his room together. It was very romantic kissing in the back of that taxi. The railway people should put a plaque up for them at the station, he said, or name one of the trains after them, the amount of money they'd spent. And it was very erotic making love just a couple of days every couple of months. Each occasion became a rediscovery, a first time almost. She said she loved him so much. She said if only the Italian universities would accept the exams she'd already done in Germany, she could come down here to finish her degree while he did his specialisation. 'That's true,' he said. 'My Italian's good enough now,' she said. 'I know,' he said, 'it is.' 'Except I can't throw away my degree now, can I?' And he agreed she couldn't.

They had no time to form a circle of friends in common. Which made her indifferent skin and worse dress sense easier to take. There was no one for him to lose face with. In fact, he felt a great deal of affection for her. At times he thought of himself as being in love. Certainly the word was being used often enough. And at the barracks, where he was assistant to the military doctor, he spoke frequently of his German girlfriend and said she had the best pointed tits anybody could imagine.

On returning to Verona, he took up residence in his room again and began his specialisation in urology. Which occupied a good sixty hours a week. He watched older people dying of cancer, young people shocked by their first serious illness. He was kind, efficient, but unmoved – in short, well suited to the job. He had no official salary or scholarship – such was the way in Italy – but after a few months they let him do the occasional night duty for a modest sum, and then there were his father's erratic cheques from Algeria. He got by and, spreading his borrowing among everybody he knew, even managed to keep a battered Fiat 127 on the road. But he was hungry for money now, for new clothes, a decent flat, a real car. What had he studied seven years for, if not for money? And when Hilda came down, or he went up there, it was so embarrassing to have to scrounge. He kept a close record of his debt to her, which, after two years now, was something over two million lire.

Hilda chided, but always gave. Her evening waitressing financed two summer weeks in Yugoslavia. Two very happy weeks: the sun brought healthy colour to her face, and in her bikini one could forget the dowdiness of her clothes. Roasting on the beach, she thought it would be a good idea if they could both get jobs in the South Tyrol, the German-speaking part of Italy. Except that Giuseppe's German had made no progress whatsoever. And her degree still wouldn't be recognised, he pointed out. Satisfied that this course of action was well and truly out of the question, they went back to the campsite and made love quite passionately on sleeping bags in their tent using contraceptives she had paid for. In the balmy dark later they discussed the latest advances in cancer research and a theory Giuseppe was developing about prostate problems. Who knew what progress medical science mightn't make during their lifetime? They were both more than satisfied with their chosen profession.

Back in Germany, Hilda completed her degree the following year with excellent results. Offered a paid post to specialise in Frankfurt, she agonised for a month or two, but in the end felt she would be a fool not to accept, and went north. The four hundred kilometres became seven hundred.

She rented a room in a nicer suburb, and put her few belongings in it. She wasn't avid for special comforts or clothes, as Giuseppe was. Being a 'Green', she was quite content to use the bus rather than buy a car, though she could have afforded one now. Naturally gregarious, if a little bossy, she was very soon part of a new circle of friends, but took no lovers. She wore a ring on her third finger and referred to it as an engagement ring. The only decorations in her room were photographs of Giuseppe, who inevitably came up for long weekends those months when she didn't go down.

This went on for seven years. But it was curious how much of the freshness and simplicity of their first encounters they managed to retain, curious how young they still were. Distance seemed to have frozen time, so that if there was no progress (whatever that might mean), still there was very little loss either. He or she would arrive. Coffee would be made and then love. The mood was one of holiday, a well-deserved break. Saturday and Sunday they would eat in restaurants, walk in parks. There were cinemas, discothèques. The weekends, as ever, gave them no time to gather acquaintances about them. No social fabric underpinned their partnership. He hadn't seen her parents since that Easter almost a decade ago. She had never seen his. So they sat, sipping granita on sultry Verona nights in the central square, or walking arm in arm under an umbrella to stare in Frankfurt's shop windows running with October rain. Both salaried doctors now, their staple conversation was their patients, hospital organisation, Germany versus Italy, modern medicine. They never tired of it. They could talk way into the small hours, discussing difficult diagnoses. Of course her pasty skin and lack of dress sense still bothered Giuseppe occasionally, but then he was only with her for the weekend, of which a good fifty per cent was spent indoors, and a great deal of that in bed. She still chided him for his wasteful ways with money, but then their resources weren't in common, his loans had been paid back, and no mention had been made of saving jointly for a house, since the geographical location of such a house was unimaginable. What they both still enjoyed very much was their lovemaking, a feeling of physical tenderness they had for each other. And if either masturbated or ever had the occasional adventure during the four or five weeks that separated one visit from the next, this was never talked about.

Until, at thirty-one, Hilda decided – or perhaps it would be more accurate to say discovered – she wanted a child. It was a disquieting discovery, the more so because entirely unexpected. She had thought of herself as a girl in love with her lover Giuseppe – that was one vision; she had thought of herself as a responsible career woman taking her rightful place in society at the hospital – that was another; but she had not thought of herself as a mother. The first two visions were remarkably easy to sustain. She divided her life into work (feminine assertion in what had once been a male preserve) and holiday (Giuseppe, restaurants, bars, summer beaches). There was no conflict here; on the contrary, all was perfect complement. But it was difficult to imagine integrating these two visions, or perhaps it would mean sacrificing them, in that third and new vision, a life that would accommodate motherhood. And yet she did want a child. It had to do somehow with a new consciousness of her life as a whole, as a human creature, of its finiteness, its inevitable span, its trajectory you might say. And this wasn't just a negative discovery, a sense of time running out, although that came into it; it was also a positive feeling of coming to fruition, of being in her prime. This, she sensed dimly – in a way that had nothing to do with politics, profession or love – this should be a moment, *the* moment, of plenitude. Now. And she wanted a child. Otherwise, and she had never really seen this before, her existence would simply go on being for ever what it already was, without any shift of gear or change of rhythm or further depth or richness, without somehow being properly harnessed up to life.

Although never bringing the issue to full consciousness, for her professional mind had so much to be busy with, Hilda was aware of two choices. There was, for example, a slightly older doctor in paediatrics, shy, retiring, a little watery, but very intelligent, who had made it clear in one way or another over the last three years or so that he would like to form a relationship with her, if only he could pluck up the courage, if only she were available. A little effort, she knew, a little encouragement, and she could marry him within the year. Or some other local man. Why not? Three months' maternity leave at some point and back to work. A crèche was available for the children of hospital staff.

Or there was Giuseppe. And complete incompatibility with her professional German life.

Again without weighing up the pros and cons, she was aware, over a period of some months, of a decision-making process going on. Until, at short notice, just as that winter was turning into spring, Giuseppe cancelled a weekend visit in order to attend, he said, a conference in Naples, on urodynamics. Her acute feeling of let-down, her sense of desolation cutting alone into the cake she had baked for him, her inkling of jealousy (why had he left it to the last moment to tell her? How was she to know whether there really was a conference in

Naples or not?), brought her to a sudden decision: or so it seemed, for now she was sorting through possible ways to broach the subject, now she was definitely fearing how he would respond, as if quite suddenly he was her only hope. It would have to be him.

As it turned out, Giuseppe surprised and actually rather unnerved her with his ready consent, his willingness to make plans, immediately. She wondered if he wasn't being a little naive. For as it was she who would have to bear the child, so it would have to be she who left her job, who went down to live with him, became dependent on him. Did responsibility sit so lightly on his shoulders? Did he really know what he was letting himself in for? And if he was so ready to agree to the idea now, why hadn't he suggested it before himself? It wasn't a notion that required a great deal of imagination to dream up, marrying your girlfriend of ten years' standing.

It was a curious weekend this, in that it just wouldn't live up to its apparent momentousness as the turning point of their lives. Perhaps because, with all those years of relaxing holiday breaks behind them, of cinema, restaurant, lovemaking, of fascinating case histories recounted in bed, they had never learnt the knack of declaring themselves, or even arguing. How much did they really know about each other, about living together? Sunday afternoon, after 'yes' had been said, had a flat, dull, unreal feel to it.

In answer to her questions, he explained – but unconvincingly – that he'd never felt he had the right to encourage her to leave such a good job, nor, obviously, could he ever have dreamt of leaving his and so becoming dependent on her. But now that she was actually offering to make the sacrifice, to come down and be with him, of course he was delighted. He didn't want to go on living on his own for ever. It was tiresome sometimes. And then he fancied himself as a father. It was time life took a turn. Lying beside him, she was profoundly dissatisfied with this, as if somehow he'd let her down, though when you thought about it, what he'd said was perfectly reasonable. And although they had decided now – or said they had – that if a child was to be born it had better be born as soon as possible, nevertheless they used their contraceptives as usual that night, as if it might be unthinkable after all these years, or even obscene, that his naked flesh should at last penetrate hers. They used their contraceptives, all was as it always had been, apparently, yet even so – and they both sensed it – there was something deliberate, something cautious and rather self-conscious about their lovemaking tonight. The embrace had lost its old holiday feel of sheer pleasure and weekend relief between tenderly consenting adults. Their minds were elsewhere.

He found a bigger flat to rent. More decisively, she gave up her job, her world, and travelled south. After some difficulty satisfying the authorities' hunger for documents, they were married in the registry office set up romantically, if rather ominously, in the ancient *palazzo* that was believed to have housed Juliet's tomb.

After all those years of care with contraceptives, the queues in night-duty chemists, the occasional painful renunciation, it now transpired that getting pregnant was by no means automatic. As doctors, of course, they should have known this. Indeed for doctors they were somewhat naive. Unless perhaps a strong groundswell of naivety is a positive quality in those who daily have to exercise an imprecise profession in the face of calamity. Either way, nothing happened. Lovemaking took on a distasteful, inhibiting significance, but produced no fruit. Installed on the sixth floor of an apartment block within sight of the hospital, Hilda struggled to fill her unemployed time, cleaning, studying, improving her Italian, giving German lessons and doing the odd translation. She was a resourceful woman. But inevitably there were mornings, afternoons, evenings when time hung heavy. The more so because Giuseppe didn't always return promptly at the end of his periods of duty. For years he had been going regularly to a gym, God knows what would happen to his body if he stopped now. And then there was the paper he was writing in collaboration for post-operative kidney patients. Hours had to be spent sifting through data together, assessing case histories. For the first time in her life, Hilda caught herself staring blankly out of windows.

And more effort was required with the time they did spend together. There was no weekend sense of occasion now. Nor did he, from one morning to the following evening, gather much in the way of news. Routine set in. When he wasn't watching television, Giuseppe liked to go out with old friends, meet in a bar, eat in a trattoria, parade up and down the fashionable Via Mazzini. But gregarious and sociable as Hilda was, she found such excursions tedious. His friends were frivolous, overdressed, the women over-made-up, the men interested in football, if they were interested in anything at all. Back in Frankfurt the staples of her social conversation had been politics, arms reduction, the environment; she had been a serious talker; now she smiled wearily as Giuseppe retold the endless dirty jokes he picked up on the ward, guffawing loudly as one punchline followed another. And it occurred to her that she had never really heard her handsome lover talking at length to anybody but herself, never had the opportunity to observe him in a group, where, she now discovered, he acted rather like one of those big complacent dogs who are forever expecting a pat on the head from everybody and frequently launch into fits of barking out of sheer excitement with their own thorough-bred, beautiful, well-brushed selves.

For his part, Giuseppe was privately wondering how it had come about that he had married some-body who was so much not his ideal of what a woman should be. So unfeminine, with such poor dress sense, and never a trace of make-up on her face. Had it been just the excitement of her foreignness, of all that travelling to and fro, the train juddering to a halt at various borders (he missed it now), of saying to people, 'my German girlfriend,' and adding in certain company, 'with the best pointed tits in the world' (though what was the point if she insisted on hiding them in these baggy old sweaters)? It was not that they had stopped caring for each other, not that all tenderness had already gone, just that these two people found themselves soon bored, soon disappointed.

And when they got home, lovemaking was not as voluptuous and eager as it had been on all those weekends always so carefully arranged so as not to coincide with her menstruations. Indeed, perhaps love would not have been made at all, were it not for this child she had set her heart on having, this child whose arrival had become a matter of faith now; otherwise the move south, the marriage, the sacrifice of her job, her life, would all have been an unfortunate and expensive mistake.

But Hilda was not an unintelligent woman, and life now was giving her plenty of time to think. So she came to appreciate over the passing months that all this had probably been fairly predictable, perhaps in fact she had herself foreseen it, or at least had a pretty good inkling; it was just that she had stifled her doubts with that overwhelming determination to have a child. Yet was such a determination wise?

Wasn't this urgency to become a mother something she should have fought against, perhaps, some mental unbalance brought about by changing hormone patterns? Should she have defended the carefree state of mind that was her younger self, the chemical equilibrium she had been so happy with? And shouldn't she have resisted that peculiar sense of fate that had invaded her, that intuition of what life was for, or rather of the subjection of her own life to the great natural cycle?

When winter set in and his paper was written and sent off, Giuseppe watched a great deal more television; adventure films and sports were his favourites, it turned out. A lot of their time together passed without words, not in the silence of resolution and serenity, but against the background of a nagging tension, of something unresolved, unsettled between them, which they were becoming less rather than more capable of talking about. So that Hilda had practically decided to call the whole thing a day before it became a lifetime, had already telephoned the hospital administration in Frankfurt about the possibility of getting her job back, when at last she skipped her period.

What great and genuine excitement! What hours spent lying in the dark in almost mystical communion with her body! What sheepish grins and thoughtfulness from Giuseppe, getting home more promptly, bringing flowers, fruit, as if she had suddenly become an invalid! When in fact she had never felt better in her life. And so elated, looking at baby clothes, calculating dates, choosing names. What festivity!

For about two weeks. Until routine began to set in again – it was, after all, the best part of nine months till the child would be born – and to set in rather worse than before. Why was this? Why, after a fortnight's intense excitement, did life suddenly seem so depressing, so unutterably dull? Why this sudden and dramatic deflation? Was it just winter beginning to make itself felt, the first fogs creeping across the Bassa Padana into the southern suburbs of the city, so that, nose pressed against the damp window pane, Hilda could barely make out the glow of lamps in the street below? Was it to do with the seething hormonal redeployment she had now unleashed on herself, her moods an insignificant by-product of this inexorable creative process that was so much bigger – she knew that – than either herself or Giuseppe? Or was it, more simply, her awareness that with pregnancy, far more than with marriage, a trap had sprung and closed? The phone call to Frankfurt, the departure note she had already prepared in her mind, these must be things of the past; her life was here now, in this two-bedroom flat on the sixth floor, watching the fog, looking for sensible ways to fill time, battling with a sense of waste. How many years would they live here? How many hours would she spend by this window? Why, now this baby was on the way, was she experiencing such a tremendous sense of desolation? As if she had lost far more in leaving her job, her language, her homeland, than a baby could ever replace. Had lost herself perhaps.

Always businesslike in the past, equable, sensible in her work, playful in her play, well balanced, admirably capable in every department, Hilda now began to lose her self-control. And more particularly she began to lose the attitude of reasonable amenability she had always imagined to be an indivisible part of herself. Why should she get in the shopping and cook for him? Why should she trail into town to eat crusty pizza and listen to him retelling jokes she had heard a thousand times? She refused. She went to the cinema on her own, sat at home and read novels. She had no idea why she was acting as she was, was only aware that there was an element of self-destruction involved, which at once made her feel helpless and yet afforded a grim sense of satisfaction.

Giuseppe was lost. Basically carefree himself, he simply couldn't understand what he saw as wilful unpleasantness. And in someone who had always been so friendly, so devoted. He was nonplussed. He didn't possess great powers of intuition, perhaps because it was so very long since he had lived in such close proximity to anyone else. Most of all, he didn't appreciate how much his affection for Hilda had depended on her devotion to him. Naturally inclined to be generous, so long as it didn't cost him too much, he oscillated between kind attempts to cheer her up, treats, anecdotes, and angry slammings of the door when she only became more prickly than before. After all, he was tired when he got home, he deserved a little respect, deserved to be able to put his feet up in front of the TV if he wanted. She sneered at him in a German he didn't understand. He stared at her unwashed hair lank around pale cheeks. And he saw now that she had always thought of him as less intelligent than herself. She despised him, despised his habits, despised his friends. And forgetting – as one does – the ten years of happy weekends, the lightness, the affection, the tenderness, he began to feel resentful. He began to feel he had been used. Simply to fulfil her female craving for motherhood. Because nobody else would have her. Wisely so. Except that he, like a fool, had allowed himself to be drawn in without even thinking about it. Why hadn't he thought about it?

His life before Hilda came to live with him – which he had frequently found rather dull and dissatisfying at the time, eagerly looking forward to their week-ends together – now appeared to him in all the glory of its happy blend of achievement and potential. He'd had his hard-earnt job at the hospital, he'd had his weekends with her for emotional and sexual fulfilment, he'd had his friends, his gym, his volley-ball, and perhaps most of all he'd had the sense that anything could happen, that he could do anything, embark on any project, sleep with any woman, because his future was not a settled thing, but something he had perfect freedom to decide on day by day. And in contrast now, he thought, he might never sleep with any other woman again. This was it, permanence, the end of youth. He was to be a father. He was to be locked for ever into this single embrace with this rather dowdy woman. And though in the ten preceding years Giuseppe had only rarely and very casually ended up in other women's arms, this new awareness of limitation suddenly seemed deeply disturbing and important. He would go through life hurrying home, trying to keep her happy (an apparently impossible task), missing dinners with friends, missing weekend conferences, losing out in short in every department. It had all been a terrible mistake. And just to show that he was not the kind of man to succumb to such servitude, he allowed himself to be seduced one evening by one of the girls in the lab; she was notorious. And it felt good, quite frankly, to be using contraceptives again.

Not that efforts weren't made to recapture that weekend ease and simplicity that had led Giuseppe and Hilda to believe they were so well suited to each other. For these two people were both well intentioned. They did not want things to go wrong. So perhaps in the evening he would begin to tell her about some curious case on the ward, a child with a kidney tumour, a pensioner whose prostate had returned to normal for no reason they could imagine. Hilda would give her opinion, but without the old sense of enthusiasm, the sense of participating as an equal. The truth being that hospital talk only heightened her feeling of regret, while for his part he was only half aware that she had lost some of her charisma for him when she had stopped working. She was less important now somehow. So that the conversations failed to engross as they once had.

Then the following day, ashamed that she was taking out on him what in the end had been the natural and obvious result of her own decision, Hilda would prepare a treat for his homecoming: a strudel, a plum cake with rum. After dinner she would present it, his eyes would light up and he would gobble it down on the sofa, watching television, looking up at her from time to time and smiling. It wasn't the kind of easy, light-hearted communion they had experienced in the past, there was something thin and rather pathetic about it, his quick smiles between concentrating on the inevitable game of something or other on the television. But it was better than nothing. And she vaguely wondered how it would be when she was cooking for a young child too, when there would be breathless demands for second helpings. Would she feel fulfilled then? Would it all have been worthwhile? Perhaps it was just a question of waiting, of not demanding satisfaction here and now. Perhaps, with time, she would find some useful part-time job in a private clinic or something, or doing research: one didn't need state authorisation to do research. Giuseppe was such a beautiful man, and basically kind. And perhaps anyone would be irritating once you started living with them. So probably it was just a case of hanging on and believing in it all. She stooped to kiss his neck, bent forward over her strudel, and smelt a strange perfume. Surprised, she sniffed again. There was also an unmistakable red mark just inside the collar, the kind of thing one wouldn't imagine girls did any more.

So two days later, when he said he was on night duty, substituting for a sick colleague, Hilda phoned the hospital, something she had never done before, since she knew how irritating it could be for everybody concerned if the doctor was constantly being dragged to the phone.

She asked for no explanations. She wasn't interested. It was extraordinary how suddenly, how firmly her mind was made up, how efficiently she packed, how quickly she penned her little note. With steady ruthlessness and immense clarity, she went towards a future she was still in time to turn into a copy of the past.

Some months later, seeing as he was scheduled to attend a renal disorder conference in Bonn, Giuseppe wrote to Hilda via her parents in Munich to try to arrange a meeting to discuss details of divorce. They eventually met in the foyer of a small provincial hospital some thirty kilometres outside Regensburg. It was raining heavily, and, being a Saturday afternoon in Germany, most of the shops and bars were closed. The hospital was scruffy and depressing, so they went back to her flat in his new Alfa 90. She made him tea and offered some of the heavy black fruitcake she always kept for herself for breakfast. He began to tell her about some of the new ways of treating renal failure that had been presented at the conference, and she asked if he could let her have a copy of the conference proceedings when they were available. Her own hospital, for she'd been unable to get back to her place in Frankfurt, was hopelessly provincial and out of it. She would be down in Apulia, she said, in September, with another woman, from radiology. They had booked two weeks in a Club Med, for lack of anything better to do. And of course she didn't want to forget all her Italian. Anyway, perhaps on returning she would stop by in Verona for a couple of days to sign the requisite papers and swear what in Italy inevitably had to be sworn. Giuseppe said yes, that was fine, but to phone him a couple of days beforehand just in case. Neither of them for one moment, not in the most allusive of asides, mentioned the abortion.

And then in September they made love again. She was so suntanned, so glowing, so horny to be quite frank, and he so relaxed, laid-back, self-satisfied with his various papers published and projects coming to fruition – with his clothes, his car, his expensive furnishings – that there was nothing easier than for them to make love with the same lightness, the same purely physical but tender pleasure of the years before. Even if, the following morning, they went just the same to sign the divorce papers on the grounds of complete incompatibility.

So, little by little, perhaps shamefacedly at first, but progressively less so, the weekend visits began again, the oases of holiday and eroticism in the midst of responsible, even commendable working lives. It was so much easier than taking local lovers with all their demands, their insistence on consequences. The distance, the travel, the hours in car or train (though Giuseppe travelled first-class now) seemed to purify them for each other and for the brief weekend that would follow. There were no friends involved, no distractions, they asked nothing more of each other than two days' medical conversation and as much sex as a married couple would manage in a month. Only when they parted, sometimes, did Hilda reflect what a sad comment it was that with all the advances in medical science it had proved impossible for two healthy young people to have a baby.

Something Odd

Friday after breakfast his wife noticed the perfume. He'd thought there was something odd. And immediately he was aware there had been a dream in the back of his mind for a couple of days now. Though quite what was in the dream...

Hazel said: 'Found a new aftershave, have you?' and although such a development would have been totally out of character for this busy man who usually took what Christmas and birthday brought his way and never thought twice about style or image, still his wife seemed perfectly cheerful and relaxed about it. 'Sign of age,' she said, 'when men start getting vain. And a bit sickly for my taste really, if you want to know. Not very masculine at all.'

Rod rubbed a hand across his stubble. Couldn't she see he hadn't shaved yet?

She was less relaxed when she found the hair, so very long and blond against the wine-dark of the sheets some sale had offered.

'What's this?'

It was Sunday morning now, and he was helping her with the bed.

'A hair,' he said.

She had plucked it off the pillow on his side and was holding it up against the light: 'A blond hair,' she said. It stretched out a good foot. 'A woman's hair.'

Hazel's own was jet-dark, though with strands of white now.

'How did it get there?' he asked.

'I thought you might be able to tell me that.'

He shook his head, but with the bewildered, vaguely guilty discomfort of one who suspects he knows, but doesn't know what.

'And the perfume, my love?'

His hand rose involuntarily to touch his cheek. The stubble seemed to come up thicker than ever these days. Perhaps he was ageing.

'Your new aftershave,' she reminded him.

'But I haven't shaved yet,' he protested.

'Precisely,' she said. 'It's called Fidji, and I never use it.'

They stared at each other across their marriage bed. Twenty happy if hardly exhilarating years. Two healthy teenage children, still asleep.

'I'm not angry Rod, but I would appreciate a confession.' And she burst into tears. When he moved instinctively to comfort her, she thrust him away and used the back of her hand to wipe her face. 'I suppose I knew this would happen someday,' she muttered. He sat down on the edge of the bed.

'But I've been sleeping here all night.'

'Perfume clings, dearest.'

'You would have noticed it yesterday evening.'

'I was already asleep when you came back.'

This was true. Saturday night was snooker night.

She said: 'Sometimes I wonder what you really get up to when you say you're going to play.'

'Oh, Christ, ask Neville.'

'How do I know he's not covering for you?' Then she laughed harshly: 'Rod, Rod, the funny thing is how you imagine you can hide it. You've been going round in a daze all this last week.'

'What? No, I haven't.'

'You most certainly have. Yesterday Anne asked you about twenty times if she could borrow the Metro, and you never even noticed. She and John were in stitches.'

He put his head in his hands and said: 'If I have, it's because of this dream.'

'I beg your pardon?'

'I've been having this dream for nights now. I keep waking up feeling really awful and I know I've had a dream, always the same one, but I don't know what it is, just that it's getting a grip on me. You know during the day, when you keep getting nudged by a dream...'

There was a short silence. They heard the sound of pop music coming on in John's room, then the tedious enthusiasm of the disc jockey.

'I think it's more likely because your new receptionist has long blond hair and a tight little arse.'

His wife had never spoken like this before. As he stood up and turned to protest, she tore back the sheets they had only a minute before so carefully arranged and tucked in. For a moment he didn't understand, then realised she must be looking for stains. Suddenly alarmed, feeling caught out, he looked himself. There were none. But then his wife bent down and with eagle eye plucked once, twice from the sheets. He couldn't even see what. 'Pubes,' she announced in her new harsh voice. 'Bleached blond,' and she turned and ran out of the room.

Rod showered slowly, and by slapping on a liberal quantity of aftershave and rubbing deodorant in all the appropriate places finally managed to wipe out that curious and curiously familiar perfume. Staring in the mirror at the wrinkles which seemed to be spreading so rapidly now across a once babyish face, he shook his head vigorously, then put a finger in his mouth, popped a cheek and, leaving the bathroom, tried to whistle. Oddly, what came out was 'Penny Lane'. He hadn't whistled that in years. And he stopped on the landing: 'Penny Lane the barber shaves another customer.' He stood, puzzled, scratching thinning hair.

Inevitably it was a difficult day. Hazel wouldn't speak to him. At first the children didn't notice, then thought it hilarious and started poking fun. His own attempts to be relaxed and offhand were particularly appreciated. Anne started copying every gesture he made, facetiously taking him up whenever he tried some new and ever more banal conversational gambit: 'The council'll really have to do something about that subsidence at the corner of Ballards Lane and Drummond Avenue.'

'A considerable traffic hazard, I agree.'

John wriggled with laughter.

Hazel turned off the burner under the frying pan and walked out. Rod looked at his children as they smirked. He found their confident young adulthood, the coltish uncontrolled movements of their now grown-up bodies disconcerting. Of course children inevitably reminded you how far over the hill you were yourself. Going after Hazel, he found she had locked herself in the bedroom.

The day dragged on in a series of false starts and unpleasant skirmishes, so that early in the afternoon Rod did something he had not so long ago promised he would never do again on a Sunday: he went to the office to mull over his company's order book. He sat on the red couch in reception, drinking mugs of instant coffee, but for some reason couldn't muster any of his usual entrepreneurial enthusiasm. His company was going on as it always did, splendidly. It was his life that needed attention.

Finally, when Rod and Hazel were alone together going to bed that night, he offered the explanation he had been casting about for all day.

'It must have been John.'

'You what?'

'John must have brought a girlfriend here, while you were out. One of the mornings you go to teach the Asian women, or to the institute. Haven't you noticed how sly he's been looking lately?'

His wife was still an attractive woman in her clothes, but undressed and without her make-up, both body and face tended to take on a slack and tired look that was at once poignant and uninviting. Now she twisted her features into her most sarcastic, do-me-a-favour smile: 'John is only fourteen, he has not been looking sly lately, and when I'm out teaching he's at school. We'd have heard if he was playing truant.'

Rod felt the considerable weight of this argument.

'Whereas someone else we know is perfectly free to leave his office for an hour or so any time he wants. Not to mention claiming to go there on a Sunday afternoon.'

'But I did go there.'

'Well I rang and nobody answered.'

'I suppose the switchboard was turned off. I had no reason to suppose anybody would phone.'

She didn't answer, but her face suggested what she knew. He felt desperate: 'Look, Hazel, I haven't done anything, OK, I swear. Why are you being so harsh? You've never been like this before.'

'Because I've never had cause to. And the moment you confess I'll go back to being my old self and we can talk it over. I do understand. Women age faster and men get randy. That's common knowledge.'

She turned out the light and very quickly climbed into bed, her back towards him.

Rod lay still. It seemed there was nothing he could do or say. Hopefully when he woke tomorrow the problem would have gone away and he would return to work with all his old interest. Then, as his mind drifted towards the pleasant confusion of thought and image that precedes sleep, he was suddenly aware, or imagined he was, of hair brushing across his forehead, followed, for just a second, by the most delicate downy touch of a woman's cheek against his own. 'Hazel?' he jerked awake, imagining she had decided to make up. Instead the same smell of that perfume was thick on the sheets.

'Yes. Ready to confess now, are we?' She didn't turn round.

'Hazel. Hazel, that perfume. And I felt someone touch me.'

'Well, you can rest assured it wasn't me.'

'But I did! Look, for God's sake, Hazel, I don't know, it must be some kind of, what do they say, visitation or something.'

There was a brief silence. Then she said crisply: 'You know, Rod Harper, I'm pretty impressed. I always thought you were such a prosaic kind of bloke. Obviously necessity has jump-started the imagination at last. Unfortunately it'll only make you feel sillier when you finally tell me the truth.'

'But can't you smell that perfume? I mean, one minute there was nothing and then the place is full of it.'

'Right, presumably because you just sprayed about half a bottle of it over the bed.'

'But...'

'You buy a bottle, planning to give it to we both know who. Then you use it to pull this ruse. Pretty smart.'

'Find the bottle then.'

'It's 11.30 Rodney Harper, and Mrs Harper is tired. Anyway, I don't doubt your ability to hide a bottle of perfume.'

He got up, found slippers and dressing gown and opened a bottle of beer. Drinking, he stared at the well-appointed kitchen around him, its fitted cupboards and polished granite work surface so recently installed. 'Padding the cell,' he liked to joke when friends commented on the Harpers' appetite for home improvement. But now he really did feel oppressed by it all. He closed his eyes and pressed his thumbs into them. The question was, should he tell Hazel that an ex-girlfriend had used that perfume? For that was why it was so familiar of course. The problem being that to do so would mean destroying the myth his marriage was based on. Rod and Hazel had been childhood sweethearts, though they hadn't married till their mid-twenties. In the years between, when he was away at university and later in Saudi earning the money to set up his company, he had had – what? – perhaps a dozen women, one or two semi-serious. But in the end he had always known he would marry Hazel, it just seemed to be his destiny, already decided, and so very sensibly he had never told her anything. Now, if he were to tell her about those girls, it might alter her whole vision of their life together. Or alternatively she would think he was spinning a crazy story with the most callous disregard for her feelings. Because the fact that somebody in the past had worn that stuff hardly explained its presence now.

What was worse, he couldn't remember which of the girls it might have been. After all, it was more than twenty years ago now. All he knew was that

that perfume reminded him of sex, and exciting sex at that.

As he drank his beer and mused, Rod heard a rustling in the lounge, then a little slap as of a book dropping on the floor. Hazel must have got up. And he decided he would talk to her. Yes, come what may. That was what wives were for, to offer companionship, intimacy. He would insist on his good faith and tell her everything.

But there was nobody in the lounge. The clock said eleven-thirty. Puzzled, he looked around for the source of the sound he'd heard, and saw that the middle one of the three wedding photos on the mantelpiece had fallen over. Yet, if it had fallen, surely it would have crashed to the floor; it must have been deliberately turned on its face. Rod shivered, whether from cold or fear he wasn't sure. He stared about him for a moment in a gesture of defiance, then hurried back up the stairs to their bedroom, threw himself into bed, heaved the sheets over his head and closed his eyes tight.

When he woke again, it was – as every night this week – to sweat and rigidity. Struggling to consciousness, he was aware that somebody was moving round the edge of the bed towards the door. In a reflex action worthy of a well-paid sportsman, he twisted round and lunged out over the bedside table to snap on the light, sending an alarm clock clattering onto the carpet. A rather thick figure in a white nightdress was standing by the fitted wardrobe with its gold edgings, a pillow in her arms.

'I'm going to sleep in the spare room,' Hazel announced.

He groaned, 'But why?'

'Because I've had quite enough of someone tossing and turning in his bed and calling out names. Not to mention that perfume.'

'Names? What name?'

'You know perfectly well what name.'

'But I don't. Tell me.'

Hazel laughed harshly, as one determined to maintain a minimum of dignity and self-respect, and walked out. Rod lay under the pink bedroom light. Picking the fortunately unbroken clock from the floor, a liquid crystal display told him it was now 3.15. Instead of going back to sleep he sat up and arranged his pillow so he could lean back against the head of the bed. The only thing he really remembered about his dream was that it always finished with a terrifying sense of oppression and suffocation which had him fighting like mad to wake up. This was not something he was eager to repeat right now. He stared about him at the prosaic bedroom, so harmless under electric light: the two white chairs, the wall mirror innocently reflecting drawn curtains. And he decided to go over it all, recapitulate, a habit he had developed at the office for when things got really hectic.

So, (1) he was having bad dreams and (2) calling out a name in his sleep. A hair (3) had been found and (4) there was a recurrent smell of female perfume which he recognised as having belonged to someone he had once made love to. As if that wasn't enough, his wife (5) had taken all the above as an excuse for acting like a jilted schoolgirl and seemed about ready to file for divorce. Then (6)... but Rod stopped. Yes, when you thought about it, you almost felt Hazel damn well deserved an unfaithful husband, the way she was carrying on.

No sooner had Rod thought this rebellious thought than an extraordinary warmth glowed through his body, a thrill at once of promise and comfort. The recapitulation was lost in a sudden welling of fierce self-justification. Had Hazel made the slightest bloody effort to head off this affair he was supposed to be having? Had she done anything to win him back these last two or three days she had begun to suspect? No. For months and months now – or why not admit it, years – her affection for him had been more maternal than passionate. Or as if she were a paid housekeeper. She looked after him very well, she was amiable and efficient, a good hostess when he brought home business guests; nor could he say she had ever denied him lovemaking when he asked for it, and yet... there was no spark there, was there? She had lost her personality somehow, become no more than her social role. She did not seduce him any more. She didn't allure him – the way other women did.

Again, on thinking these thoughts, Rod felt an extraordinary warmth flood through his body, giving him

a very pleasant sense of fullness. Yes, he had been looking at other women rather a lot lately.

He lay on his back again, head on the pillow and
hands under his head. He tried to slow his mind
down, to return to the orderly objectivity of his recapitulation. Let's think. He was not usually critical
of his wife. On the contrary, he generally struggled to
present his marriage to himself as well as to others
as a great success. So why should these subversive
thoughts be coming now? Why should he be trying to
justify himself for an affair he hadn't actually had?
Why did he feel so resentful? Of course Hazel was
no longer the most exciting lover in the world, but
it was understandable and certainly forgivable. You
had the kids, there were other interests, other sources
of satisfaction.

Suddenly Rod sat up straight in his bed. There had
definitely been a woman's soft chuckle in the room.
And again the overpowering scent of perfume.

'Who are you?'

He was bolt upright in traditional pale blue pyjamas, addressing the ordinarily expensive bedroom:
'Tell me who you are!'

Then he thought: 'For God's sake, I'm going off
my nut,' and he got up, found his dressing gown and
went downstairs again, this time to make himself
cocoa. A few minutes later, stirring his drink at the
kitchen table in the suburban silence of a house at
dead of night, he began to doodle on the back of a
letter in which Sun Alliance had suggested that for a

man at his time of life his pension scheme was under-subscribed. First he just drew his normal doodle of interlocking circles. Then, without having actually meant to, he found he was writing names in the circles: 'Eileen, Janet, Jackie, Heather, Pauline, Annette, Gail…'

Odd, Gail was also the name of the receptionist. Not a very common name either.

Rod wrote down three more names. He pored over them. Perhaps they seemed a lot, but it had been an eight-year period. Certainly he had never actually thought of himself as promiscuous. He might have a girl during term-time, then return to Hazel working in her boutique in Crouch End during the holidays. Nothing special about that. No, if there was just one thing he had been rather ashamed of years ago, it was how close the last fling had been to his marriage. Just a week. And that of course was Gail. The conference in Liverpool. Yes, yelling 'Penny Lane' together in the shower. 'Penny Lane is in my ears and in my eyes.' What fun it had been!

Looking at the list of names, Rod dimly remembered warm embraces, intimacies, the unrivalled excitement of undressing a different woman. And he was alarmed, yet, beneath that surface fear, pleased at this sudden breach in his usually sober state of mind, this rent in the backcloth of routine. Yes, you undressed them and made love to them and it was so so so wonderful; though of course when Gail had then written, quite desperately, soon after his marriage, he had dutifully written back to tell her that it was off, that now he was a husband he was determined to be a good husband. He had warned her after all. Though for weeks Hazel complained about his endlessly whistling 'Penny Lane'.

Head on the table, Rod was jerked to wakefulness by the sound of his wife's uncharacteristically sarcastic voice: 'Had a nice night out, did we?'

His neck was fiercely stiff, his head thick.

'Can't you see I'm still in my pyjamas? God, what time is it? I'll have to fly.'

'Well, somebody must have walked the mud in. Frankly, for a man committed to a life of deception you're not being very clever about it.'

'But what mud?'

'In the hall. It certainly wasn't there last night. I suppose I did you a favour sleeping in the guest room. Except of course I heard you sneaking down as soon as I'd gone.'

Rod stood up and went out into their narrow hallway, where, yes, the light showed muddy footprints by the door. Thick mud, as if somebody had thrown down a handful of earth and stamped on it.

'She was feeding me earth,' he immediately said, trembling and deeply disturbed.

'I beg your pardon?'

'It's my dream, she was feeding me earth. My mother.' Yet no sooner had he told her this than he knew it had not been his mother, but Hazel. Or rather, in the way people in dreams blend into each other, or will take on roles not their own, it had been both his mother and Hazel, Hazel as his mother, while the baby thus being fed was both himself and his children and all children. 'She was saying, "Come on, eat up now if you want to grow big and strong," and she was pushing spoon after spoon into my mouth, only it was earth, slimy and gritty and full of worms, and I was choking and retching, and she didn't seem to understand. That's the dream I've been having.'

Hazel said wrily: 'Not to mention groaning rhythmically after your receptionist. Gail, uh?'

Usually Rod found that even the worst dreams would vanish with the light of day, yet at the office this Monday morning his mind was prey to such an extraordinary variety of images, memories and fears, based and baseless, that there seemed no hope of concentrating on his company's fortunes. Towards twelve, therefore, he picked up the phone, got through to reception and told the new girl that if she didn't mind having lunch with him he would like to tell her a little more about the company, who did what, and what impression they were trying to convey, so that she could deal with clients more efficiently. Saying this, he was vaguely aware that on Friday he had been planning to explain to her that she would have to develop a rather more serious phone manner if she wanted to stay with Printek Plus for very long.

He came down at twelve-thirty and invited the girl to step into his Sierra so they could go a little further than the restaurants most of the staff frequented, a normal ritual with new recruits. She was a cheerful, rabbity-toothed, flirty creature, not the kind he would have chosen himself: Harrington, his junior partner, had been responsible. Too cocksure of herself by half for Rod's liking, too ready to be intimate with everybody. Which he found in rather bad taste.

But why in that case had he mentioned this girl's rather obvious and unsubtle physical attractions to his wife? Or had it been his wife, who, when he had said, 'Got a new receptionist at last,' had responded by asking, 'Nice?' to which, without giving it a second's thought, he had replied, 'Blonde, neat figure, snappy dresser – yes, rather attractive actually.' 'Typical,' Hazel had said, 'that's all you men think of, isn't it, a woman's figure. What I meant was, is she a nice person?' But Rod knew she hadn't meant that at all. No, it was as if for some time she had been looking for ways of setting him up, was eager to catch him at a game he wasn't even dreaming of playing. Perhaps because, fearing it must happen sooner or later, she wanted to hear the worst at once. Or, even more perversely, because she sensed that an aggrieved resignation in the face of the antics of one's husband was somehow a necessary part of the role of middle-class, middle-aged wife she seemed so thoroughly determined to play. And of course such a development, with all the legitimate resentment it would nourish, would inevitably give her more moral clout around the house, more power. She would run the family. He could run off and play and of course feel guilty about it. What was it she had said? 'I'm not angry. All I want is a confession.' That is, the advantage accruing from his deceit.

So was it possible she had put the hair there herself?

And the perfume?

And the fallen photograph?

No. In any event, she would certainly never have put mud on the good Axminster in the hall, since this, as she so often remarked, was the first thing a guest saw when he came into the house.

Or unless, in some extraordinary way, they had both been responsible for willing the appearance of these signs of a life more exciting than the one they were leading? Was that possible? Perhaps he should pick up a book on the paranormal.

Then, over Tandoori chicken and in the middle of telling the new receptionist that clients were always to be referred to as sir and never as love, or even worse as Mr Whatsit, he – Rod Harper, MD – let out: 'I had a girlfriend called Gail once.'

He was disturbed by this departure from his prepared spiel, and at the same time immediately aware that of course this was why he had brought the girl here. To tell her about the other Gail.

'Oh, did you?' She brightened up at once, as if at the arrival at last of someone interesting to talk to. Previously she had been visibly stifling yawns. 'Not a very common name neither, is it? You know, I never actually met a single other person called Gail. Apparently me Dad wanted to call me that because I was born in one. Even if it isn't spelt the same.'

'In Liverpool…' he was saying. 'I mean, she lived in London, not far from me actually, but we met at a sales conference in Liverpool.'

'Oh, I had to go to a load of conferences in my last job,' the girl laughed knowingly. She was speaking with her mouth full. 'I was secretary to this bloke in research at the Royal Free, you know. And he always used to say: men invented conferences for that.' Her laugh became a giggle.

'Yes,' Rod said, a little taken aback. For this was precisely the over-easy intimacy he had meant to warn her about. Drinking quickly from his glass, he hurried on: 'Though of course that was many years ago. Then I got married.'

The girl smiled at what she obviously considered a non sequitur.

'Before you were born, actually,' he insisted.

Again she said nothing. There was, however, a peculiar knowingness about her small pixyish features, a cocky assurance as she polished off her food, that both unsettled and intrigued the older man. The way the make-up had been put on too, at once lush and precise, the lips full, deeply scarlet, but so deft at the corners – it was unnerving. Her loose clothes expertly suggested the slim pertness there must surely be beneath.

'It's odd, isn't it,' he pressed on under the influence of he knew not what compulsion. 'I mean, that just hearing your name when Harrington told me he'd taken you on the other day made me think of her, when I haven't thought of her for years. Even started me dreaming about her, this other Gail. I've dreamt about her every night since.'

'Lucky you,' she said with a sly laugh.

Rod was acutely aware of having thrown away any chance of asserting himself in the cool boss-underling relationship he usually chose to establish. On the contrary, it was almost as if he were appealing to her somehow. 'No, I don't mean that kind of dream. Just vaguely, about her. If you see what I mean. She keeps coming into my dreams and I thought how odd it was.'

'That usually means the other person is in trouble and needs you.'

'Sorry?'

'When you dream about them like. It means they're in trouble. Me mum's a medium,' the receptionist added with the simplicity of someone not at all embarrassed by such confidences. 'Maybe you should look her up.'

'Your mother?'

'No, silly, this other Gail. You know, find out why you've been dreaming about her.'

Rod found a don't-be-silly expression for what after all were strong executive features. He was a big man and knew how to make his face stern. 'Oh, for Heaven's sake, that was twenty years ago. Anyway,

I'd have no idea where to find her. I just thought it was odd the way things come back.'

'What was her surname?'

'Zdansky. Polish father I think.'

'Piece of cake. There can't be more than two in the whole phone book.'

'But she'll have got married. Probably doesn't even live in London any more.'

'Trip to Somerset House. You could sort that sort of thing out in half an hour. I was down there regular in the last job. Tracing relatives of people with syndromes and things. You know? Rather exciting really. Like being a detective.'

He looked at her with new respect, but then bluffed, 'Sounds like a lot of hard work for a couple of dreams.'

'But it's interesting, don't you see,' she exclaimed, throwing down knife and fork on an empty plate. 'It's one of those things that makes life more than just getting up and going out to work, like. I bet you she's in some kind of trouble. Bet you a week's wages. Are you on?'

Feeding himself a forkful of rice, Rod suddenly had a distinct sensory recollection of the spoon entering his mouth, full of earth. He stopped chewing for a moment, tongue probing the warm food. And there was the earth in the hall too. Yet he hadn't really been dreaming of Gail at all. Why had he told the girl that? No, it seemed if anyone was in trouble it wasn't Gail Zdansky but himself. And being tempted into more. So that as soon as he had swallowed he said: 'What would my wife think if I started looking up old girlfriends?'

'Who cares? She wouldn't know.'

'I tell her everything.'

'Oh, pull the other one. Anyway, it's not even as if you're doing anything wrong.'

'But she might think I was.'

'You men,' the young receptionist laughed in genuine merriment. 'It's so funny the way you let your wives run rings round you. Dr Stafford was the same for all his talk. My last boss I mean.'

Then perfectly ingenuous, she added: 'I'll find out meself if you like. Give me two hours off work. Say, till four, and I'll find out. Write down the name on a bit of paper for me. Bet a week's wages she's in trouble.'

A few minutes later, winding up the lunch with some strange Indian sweet he wasn't particularly enjoying, Rod politely enquired: 'And why exactly did you leave your last job seeing as you seem to have enjoyed it so much?'

'You really want to know?' She was amused. 'I mean *really*?'

He nodded dumbly, feeling a fool.

'Well, after a year of beating about the bush, if you see what I mean, we went to bed together, me and Dr Stafford, then of course he had to go and confess to his wife and she got him to fire me. Serves me right, I suppose.' But this girl looked at Rodney Harper from two great eyes that all that mascara had only made more tremblingly large and alive. The MD asked for the bill.

Mid-afternoon he was sitting listlessly at his huge desk when the phone rang.

'I'm in Somerset House,' the chirpy voice said. 'You ready with a pen or somethin'? OK? Gail Zdansky married Godfrey Rhodes Mapleton of all people in 1970. Bit of a mouthful I know. She was living in Willesden at the time – him in Dulwich. The London phone book gives five G. Mapletons, but only one G.R. The G.R. lives at 32 Ashhampton Road, Kensal Rise, pretty near 'er maiden address in Willesden.'

Rod had barely told the girl how impressed he was and put the phone down before his secretary was announcing a call from his wife.

'You came back here this morning, didn't you?' There was more than an edge of hysteria to Hazel's voice.

'I most certainly did not.'

'The signs are all too obvious,' she protested.

'I think you've gone paranoid,' he told her.

'I would have expected,' she said, 'that after all the warning shots fired this weekend, you could at least have cooled things down a bit.'

When he protested, she said, 'Well, next time it won't be me on the phone, it'll be my lawyer. Understand?' And she hung up.

Rod was left staring at the mute receiver. Had she ever hung up on him before? Surely not. Yet, along with the sense of alarm came a perverse feeling almost of satisfaction. Something was happening in his life. Grim-faced, he buckled on his coat to step out into what was now a wet and windy afternoon in Shepherd's Bush. He climbed into the Sierra, consulted his Nicholson's Guide and set off along the Uxbridge Road.

The light was grey. The rain sluiced his windscreen from a low sky over the motley slate and brick shambles of London rooftops. The traffic was heavy as ever, pumping exhaust through the pinkish red of brake lights; it was stop-start all along Holland Park, with cosmopolitan crowds under umbrellas waiting to cross at every light. And Rod was struck by the contrast between this ordinariness, this seething ordinariness all around him, and at the same time the extraordinary folly of his journey, going to look up a girlfriend of twenty years ago. He began whistling 'Penny Lane' again. 'Penny Lane the barber shaves another customer.' How did it go? Something something. 'Then the fireman rushes in, from the pouring rain, very strange.' Yes, strange indeed. For as if by some extraordinary act of association, his memory, as he turned into Ladbroke Grove, now offered up the exact words of that letter he had received so long ago: 'Rod, dear Rod' – he even remembered the slant of fierce scribble on an office comp slip – 'I know I shall never never find another lover who excites me so much, who I'm so completely wild about. Rod, how can you just go back and marry your childhood sweetheart after what has happened between us? You're only doing it out of a sense of duty. If you really loved her, you would never have been as you were with me. Please, oh please Rod, think, think while there's still time. Save yourself and me – and her!'

Quite suddenly the car was filled with the clogging scent of perfume. Which seemed to function as a stimulant. Rod accelerated, driving dangerously fast across changing traffic lights at the intersection with the Harrow Road, then simply attacking Kilburn Lane the way a professional might take on a chicane, as if with this last burst of speed he could somehow recoup a deadline that had passed twenty years before.

Finding a slow line of traffic inching up Chamberlayne Road, he madly and quite out of character overtook one car after another, dodging an oncoming van moving far too fast for comfort, just squeezing in before a bus. Then he had reached the cause of the hold-up: a hearse and two funeral cars were crawling up the hill with majestic slowness, and so close together that there was no hope of getting by. Fuming, Rod consulted the guide on his knee and found that Ashhampton Road was only another quarter of a mile or so. There was nothing for it but to wait.

'Rod,' a voice whispered.

'Yes?'

'Rod, Rod, Rod.'

He sat rigidly still, staring at the vehicles ahead of him, engine fretting in third. Between the backs of heads in the car directly in front of his, blurred through rain-soaked windows, he could just make out the flower-bedecked coffin in the hearse beyond.

Why didn't they hurry up! Get the dead buried and be done with it, for Heaven's sake!

'Almost there now,' he said aloud. 'Next turn on the right. What number was it, 32?'

'Rod,' the voice said, soft but terribly audible.

He didn't dare to turn and look, but his impression was quite definitely of somebody sitting there. And the situation had begun to seem less rather than more strange, as though some destiny were being fulfilled here, something so necessary as to be obvious.

Then he was furious to see that the vehicle in front of him was indicating right too. The little funeral procession turned into Ashhampton Road. For one moment he pulled out, thinking he might manage to overtake in the empty side street, but there were parked cars and bollards, and anyway he must keep an eye on the numbers.

He had counted to 28 on the left side of the road when the funeral cars drew to a halt ahead of him. Then at last he understood. Somebody in her family had died. This was the trouble the receptionist had intuited. Clever girl. Somebody had died, her husband perhaps, yes, her husband, and she was calling him back to her. That must be it. She was calling him back to her and his whole life was going to change. He would leave his wife and go to this woman whose love for him was so great it had somehow broken through across the years, broken through all the physical barriers of West London's endless masonry, broken into his sleep, his dreams, his heart.

'Oh, Rod,' the voice said, thick with emotion now.

Three young children stepped out of the car behind the hearse and were herded into a mock-Tudor semi-detached by an elderly woman with a black hat holding two umbrellas. In the hearse beyond, a woman with blond hair was sitting beside the driver. The procession moved off, taking two lefts to return to the main road. Rod followed and, as if under hypnosis, found himself saying: 'I will come, Gail, I will. What a mistake it all was. The love we made, Gail. Never. It was never like that again.'

All at once, together with the perfume and the low soft voice speaking his name, he felt a hand settle on his thigh.

Holding his breath, he followed the cars at a stately pace.

The hand caressed his leg very lightly, and now slithered across to cover his crotch. He bit his lip.

'Rod,' the voice was so so tender. And very very gently the hand squeezed him. Until, suddenly overwhelmed by such a surge of physical longing as he had not experienced in years, he turned, his own hand lifting from the gear stick to reach out for her – and found nothing but empty space. She was gone. Not only was there nobody in the seat, nobody to touch, but no presence either now, no perfume, no voice, nothing. His hand came to rest on a pile of dusty lapsed client files he had been planning to sort through before throwing out. Jerking his head up at the last second, he had to brake violently to avoid going into the back of the car in front.

Ten minutes later, this tall man in business dress was winding his way amongst tombstones in the newer part of a large cemetery. Ahead of him trooped a party of three men and the blonde woman from the hearse, following four lads in ill-fitting suits carrying the coffin. Leading the way were a clergyman and an undertaker under two black umbrellas. The woman, Rod was sure, must be Gail, just must be. Calling him to her. In a moment they would be face to face.

The little procession shuffled to a halt beside a freshly dug, muddy grave. Under heavy rain the coffin was lowered to the ground, where the gravedigger had already laid two dirty nylon cords. The four lads hurriedly arranged themselves at the four ends of the cords and lifted, then rather clumsily trotted round in a little dance to manoeuvre the coffin over the grave. They began feeding the rope, and immediately, before the thing had even hit bottom, the clergyman was gathering the little group together at the head of the grave; with the undertaker holding his umbrella, he started to read from a Prayer Book, mumbling the words far faster than would surely have been decent in nicer weather. At the same time, Rod caught up with the others and, mistaken perhaps for a mourner by the clergyman, perhaps for some cemetery official by the mourners, took his place at the side of the grave, where he was finally in a position to see the woman face to face.

The coffin hit bottom with a muffled thud and splash. Rod stared. There were three middle-aged men, the two on each side standing close to support the one in the middle, who had begun silently to weep; then, beside them, but standing a little way apart, tall, slim and still unbelievably young, was Gail. Unmistakably Gail. Blonde, bright-eyed, a splendid bloom on girlish rain-wet cheeks as she stood erect without an umbrella, arms folded over her breasts. She turned to him, as if to greet an eagerly expected guest who is arriving late. They gazed mutely at each other across a corner of the grave. She was smiling, lightly, sadly. Then, still looking at him, lips mouthing something now, eyes seductively narrowing, she began to unbelt and unbutton her coat. Alarmed at this crazy impropriety, for the others must surely notice, Rod wanted to shout to her, but as in a dream found himself physically unable, voiceless, strangely paralysed. He could only stare as with teasing slowness her wet fingers loosened button after button until the raincoat flapped open on the very same peach-coloured nightdress and cami-knickers she had worn in that Liverpool hotel so long ago.

Rod started forward, but his beloved slowly shook her head, the lips mouthing he knew not what.

The clergyman suddenly raised his voice: 'Earth to earth, ashes to ashes, dust to dust.' As he spoke, he bent down, snatched up a handful of wet earth and tossed it over the coffin.

Momentarily distracted, Rod saw the loamy grain of the damp soil in the man's hand and vividly remembered in his dream how the spoon had approached his mouth, how he had kept his lips shut tight and how Hazel had insisted, 'But it's good for you Roddy. Everybody eats earth.' Then suddenly she had grabbed his nose, forcing him to open his mouth to breathe, and immediately the worm-laden earth had shot in on its spoon right to the back of his throat, and through that appalling sensation of imprisonment and suffocation, he was shouting: 'Gail! Gail!'

The earth hit the coffin with a thin clatter.

'Rod!'

But she had gone. The three gloomy men stood alone. The clergyman was taking back his umbrella. The young coffin-bearers were already scampering away for the dry of the chapel.

'Rod!' the voice positively shrieked, and it came from the grave. 'Rod, oh Rod...'

A man had already begun to shovel on earth in quick spadefuls. The mourner in the centre of the group covered his face and the others began to pull him away.

'Rod!' The voice became even more lacerating and imperative. 'Oh, Rod, too late.'

Lips and jaws instinctively shut tight, Rodney Harper stumbled forward and, as the others turned to go, found himself right on the muddy edge staring down into the grave. She was kneeling in her open coffin, still in the coat and silken underwear, but aged, horribly aged, and transformed by some awful disease that had pitted her face and swollen her body. 'Rod!' Her head was on one side, dull eyes imploring. Her arms reached up to him, beckoning, wrists wide in hopeless welcome, earth-grey lips parted in ghastly invitation, and Rod blacked out.

'Actually bloody fell in too, would you believe,' he was explaining an hour later at the office. 'I must have gone crazy, you know. Really psychic.'

The rest of the staff were gone, but the new receptionist had waited, curious to hear what might have happened. When he arrived, covered in mud and still trembling from head to toe, she was immediately solicitous, removing his coat and jacket for him, finding some whisky in the medicine cabinet, taking away his muddy shoes to wipe them off in the bathroom.

When she came back, he was sitting on the red sofa in reception, bowed forward, face in hands, shaking. She sat beside him, put an arm across his shoulder, her provocative, over-made-up face next to his. At which, with an instinctiveness he had supposed must have been lost with his early twenties, he turned and began to kiss her. The girl hesitated, apparently knowing better, and drew away. For a moment two perplexed faces stared into each other, and Rod sensed – no, knew – that his face was assuming the same expression of imploring invitation he had seen earlier on that afternoon.

The girl smiled. Then, very gently, she came to him again, lips wide, so that in only a very short time this couple were making love on what proved an extremely accommodating couch. With all the excited whispering of 'Rod' and 'Gail', and then the curious familiarity of her smooth young body beneath his, Rod wondered for a moment if he mightn't be back in that Liverpool hotel of twenty years before. Fearful, he raised his head. No, it was definitely the reception of Printek Plus: the red couch on a grey, smoke-stale carpet; the black L of the desk with its elegant electronic switch-board: and beyond that, the last of grey twilight retreating through a window that dimly showed rain-wet rooftops and skeletal TV aerials stretching north to White City. Then, looking down to find the corn-yellow of his receptionist's hair, the warm brown of her eyes flickering open, Rod became so engrossed in their lovemaking he might have been nowhere at all, or simply anywhere, and in any event a thousand miles from eating earth and falling into graves.

Later, holding tea in cupped hands, for the building was suddenly cold now the heating had turned itself off, Gail said: 'Oh, me mum could tell you endless stories like that. Endless. Perhaps you should go to one of her seances and try to get in touch.'

In a mood that somehow combined euphoria with a sense of solemnity and ceremony, Rod said, 'I feel I already have.' The girl was sitting on the sofa arm pouting a kiss, and he put a hand out to touch her mussed hair. 'You know?'

Then the phone rang.

'Oh, Christ,' he said, 'what time is it?'

The girl told him: 'Eight o'clock, Mr Harper, sir.' She seemed amused and got up to answer.

'No, not you, please!'

Rod moved quickly across the room to grab the receiver. In a soft voice, his wife said: 'I'm sorry, Rod.' After a pause she went on very lightly. 'Have I scared my little boy from coming home?' And when he still couldn't think how to respond, she went on: 'It's all my fault. You were right. John's confessed.'

'What?' her husband croaked.

She was laughing, though nervously. 'It seems with this teachers' work-to-rule he's been getting all these free periods, and when I'm away he brings this girl home.'

This news was somehow infinitely more unsettling than the straightforward battle Rod had been expecting. 'But that's impossible,' he objected brusquely, as if she might have been concocting a story to annoy him. 'I don't believe it.'

'I know,' Hazel said, 'I was shocked myself, but I suppose stranger things have happened. He...'

'You're not trying to tell me they made love in our bed? That that's what the hairs were about?'

'It would seem so.'

'But he's only fourteen! It can't...'

'As you said, he's been looking very smug lately. And as I said, stranger things have happened.'

Rod was suddenly struck by this phrase of hers.

Why had she said it twice? He hesitated. Had stranger things happened or hadn't they? Surely they had. They must have. But now it was as if something precious were being threatened. Then, with quite unreasonable abruptness, he protested: 'Oh, come on. And the perfume? The mud in the hallway? You don't want me to believe it was all Johnny and his little scrubber?'

There was a brief silence at the other end of the line. 'No doubt the truth will come out in good time,' his wife finally said with quiet dignity. 'But, for the moment, forgive me, Rod – I mean for jumping to ignoble conclusions like that.'

Holding the phone, Rod Harper saw the young girl standing with statuesque ease by the black gloss of the window. Her face in silver profile took on an unexpected simplicity and beauty.

'It doesn't matter,' he said quite harshly. 'I had to stay anyway. Rowlands sent in this huge job at the last minute and I'm stuck here trying to get it all sorted out for production tomorrow. I'll be another couple of hours at least.'

'I'll have something nice to eat,' Hazel said dutifully.

When he had hung up, the girl turned and said: 'Are you always so unpleasant when you talk to your wife?'

'What? Was I?'

'Yes, and it doesn't suit you. You're far too sweet for that.' She crossed the room and kissed him gently on the lips. 'So, do I get fired?'

Rod stood still for a moment, looking at her. At last he said: 'No, no, on the contrary, I think I owe you a week's extra wages, don't I? Wasn't that the deal?' He tried to make his voice inviting. 'Do you mind if I begin by paying in kind, taking you out to a restaurant?'

Gail the receptionist smiled, apparently indicating her acceptance. However, when he came back from a trip to the lavatory, Rodney Harper found only the brief note: 'I'm sure it would be wiser if we left it at that. See you tomorrow.' He stared at it in puzzlement and disappointment.

A little later Rod stopped at the Indian chemist's on Ealing Broadway and bought a bottle of Fidji, but then spraying it into the passenger seat of the car he was immediately aware that it was not the same. Not at all. Didn't remind him of anything. How could Hazel have made such a mistake? He frowned at the yellow liquid. Then he realised that this was probably rather fortunate. It would be foolish to get attached to the old smells when there were so many new ones to be had. He would leave it in the receptionist's drawer tomorrow. He wasn't going to let the little hussy get away with just once. Oh no. Not unhappily, Rodney Harper drove home to his wife and children.

In Defiance of Club Rules

In defiance of club rules, Robert took to going out on the river alone. It had become difficult to fit in with other people's plans. Arthur's wife was about to give birth, and this hitherto loyal friend now had no time. To go on the group outings would mean hanging around for hours waiting for others to arrive and argue about what they were going to do and where. Instead, after work, Robert drove straight to the club, pulled his kayak down from the rack and changed into his wetsuit.

This was January. There was even a patch of ice in the slacker shallows. Immediately he noticed that going out alone changed his state of mind. He was doubly anxious sorting out his kit as he got into the boat. He checked and rechecked that his life jacket was properly buckled. Sitting on the muddy bank, he ran his fingers around the cockpit at least three or four times before feeling reassured that the spraydeck was secure. Did he have the paddle the right way round? He placed his hands on either side of the boat and pushed off.

Just upstream of the club, the boys who competed in slaloms were running the gates beneath the so-called New Bridge in their long fibreglass boats. Robert wasn't interested in competing with anyone. The only thing he wanted to measure himself against was the river. He had a short plastic white-water kayak. And the first thing he did was paddle it to the middle of the river and turn upside down. The icy water gripped his head. It was dark and muddy. This, as far as Robert was concerned, was the defining experience of kayaking. You were alone, unseeing, unhearing. You couldn't breathe. You had a handful of seconds to return yourself to the normal world. Robert counted to at least three before coming up. It was important not to concede to the darkness that you were afraid. 'I am not in a panic or a hurry,' he told himself. He set up his paddle carefully and rolled up. The water streamed off him. There was the shock of the breeze on his face, then a rapid warming. He was master of the river.

He set off downstream towards the railway bridge. Often, to loosen up, he paddled backward, which gave him a view of the centre of town. The high red-brick embankment curved away to the left. There were pretty stone towers from centuries before, steep hills rising to walls and battlements, and, on a clear day, the mountains were just visible in sharp relief behind. The almost daily experience of this view reconciled Robert to his home town and induced a mood of acceptance and calm. For some years now, since even before his father's death, he had been increasingly disaffected with the place. He had been passed over for promotion at work. The area he lived in had been invaded by immigrants. Drug addicts left their needles in the gutters. He had seen his mother grow fearful and bitter. 'You mustn't go out in the boat on your own,' she told him. 'You are all I have in the world now.'

'The river is safer than the streets,' Robert replied.

After the bridge where the ring road passed, marking the end of the town proper, he was obliged to turn and paddle forwards. The river flowed a little faster now. The bank was untended, snagged with broken branches, bits of rubble, rusted iron. Occasionally the paddle scraped a block of cement. Sometimes there were fishermen, usually old. The man who haunted the right bank just downstream of the bridge must have been a thalidomide case. He gestured with a shrunken arm to show Robert where his line was. Robert steered clear. He couldn't imagine eating the fish from this river. On the left bank, truck drivers in the slow traffic were high enough in their cabs to watch him over the parapet. He imagined them envying his freedom. Some waved. Sometimes the lovers sitting on the steps halfway along would break off their kisses. If he was in a good mood, he would capsize and roll up for them. 'Exhibitionist!' his fiancée teased. He and Stella had been together for almost ten years now. 'Robert needs the river,' she confided to their friends. 'He has so much frustrated energy. Show your biceps, Rob,' she said. Neither of them was in a hurry to marry. An uneasy inertia had overtaken Robert's life. He was angry without even being aware of it.

Under the railway bridge, the club's rule about not going out alone made sense. But this was the only place Robert wanted to be. Carrying four tracks, the bridge was built as a viaduct, its five tall arches channelling the wide river into five narrow streams, with thick walls of masonry in between. At the same time, the water level fell almost three feet, so that with the sudden narrowing, plus the dive, the placid surface was transformed, for the twenty yards or so that it took to get through the tunnels of the arches, into a wild rush. This was most pronounced beneath the second arch from the right, where the drop coincided exactly with the beginning of the tunnel. Here, a strong V-shaped wave formed beneath the nineteenth-century masonry, powerful and irregular. At either side of the wave, great blocks of stone, placed just above water level to protect the bridge's stanchions, allowed for the formation of narrow lateral eddies of escape and refuge. After the frothing crest of the big wave, the stream swirled through the long arch in a tumultuous chain of lesser waves before tumbling out into a broad boiling expanse beyond, where sudden whirlpools could suck the boat under, front or back, before you had time to think.

There were all kinds of games to play here. When the water was high, the stream throbbed beneath the kayak. Pointing downward into the wave, face up-stream, you had a fantastic impression of speed. The river was pouring onto you, and you had to fight like mad to hold your position, curving to left and right, braking with a low brace when the nose sank in the trough, paddling hard on the crest when the water threatened to toss you out. Riding this wave, forced into a fury of concentration after his dull hours at the office, Robert had the exhilarating sensation of being right at the heart of life, in the secret pulse of the river, yet at the same time wonderfully static, in control. Sometimes a train thundered above as he surfed, packing his brain with noise and excitement.

But it was hard to stay on the wave for more than thirty or forty seconds at a time. Perhaps you exposed a little too much edge on one side or the other, or you let the bow sink too deep into the trough, or the wave itself suddenly changed with a hiccup in the current. Then all of a sudden you were blown off and careering down the wild water behind it. Often the fight to stay on the crest led to a capsize. Then you had to roll up in earnest. The swift current grabbed your paddle beneath the water. It was hard to drag it forward to the set-up position. Towards the end of the bridge on the left, there was a rock that might catch your helmet. Altogether, there were seven bouncy waves to get through before the stream spread out and steadied. Sometimes the best thing to do was just wait till you were past the roller-coaster, then come up in the muddled water beyond. It irritated Robert when it took him two or even three tries to roll up. He knew that one day he would fail and have to take a swim. He would have to save himself, his boat and his paddle all on his own.

Upright, he fought his way back up the narrow eddy along the inside of the arch and tackled the wave again. After half an hour, he might take a break. He got out of the boat below the bridge and sat on the blocks of stone that protected its masonry. There was a strong river smell here. Occasionally he saw a rat hurrying through the sodden vegetation. Men loading trucks behind a factory on the right bank might turn to watch. Robert nodded to them.

He began to like going out on his own so much that he felt vaguely annoyed, in March and April, when he arrived at the bridge to find some of his old companions already there, riding the wave, shouting: 'Whoa!' and 'Alrighty!' They shook their heads at the idea of his being there alone. Sometimes, they said, a piece of debris could form a strainer under the water. Upside down, you might get tangled in a branch that had jammed in the rocks.

The other canoe-club members who played at the bridge drove down in their cars, unloaded their kayaks, had a good time, keeping careful watch on one another, loaded up again, and drove back. They didn't like the long, dull paddle from the clubhouse or, above all, the fact that to get home you had to carry your boat upstream of the bridge and then fight the current for almost a mile. On the other hand, there was a risk in driving down; on two or three occasions, club members' cars had been broken into while they were paddling. The bank beyond the factory was quite isolated, and there was a gypsy camp on the wasteland a few hundred yards further on. Robert preferred to paddle back to the club. It kept him fit.

So, once he decided he'd had enough, he pulled his boat out, dragged it up the high bank and walked it upstream beyond the drop. It wasn't unusual, on this walk, for him to find a couple of unshaven young men sitting around smoking on the bank beneath the first arch of the bridge, with a fire lit perhaps, their women cross-legged in shawls and shabby dresses, the inevitable baby at their breasts. Sometimes Robert came across a pair of teenagers in sleeping bags, surrounded by sachets and needles. He was careful where he trod in his thin rubber kayak shoes.

When spring turned to summer and the weather grew warmer, a group of Moroccans would often come down to the bank and sit and smoke under the bridge, and sometimes bathe in exactly the place where Robert pulled his boat up on the bank. It was really the only place where you could get out of the water easily. Robert never spoke to them. He looked away. Out of the water, his legs stiff from being jammed against the footrests, carrying the heavy kayak on his shoulder, he felt vulnerable. This was a lawless place. There were all kinds of foul smells now that the weather had turned. Without wanting to be racist, Robert intensely disliked gypsies. 'They carry knives,' he thought. 'They don't clear up their litter.' But further upstream, where he relaunched, there were a couple of small gardens that backed onto the river, and often he saw a pretty mother playing with her young daughter there. Then Robert said hello, and explained to the little girl over the garden wall how the spraydeck worked. 'Goddam druggies,' the woman said, nodding towards the bridge. 'The police never bother them.' Robert shrugged. He got into the boat on the bank and let it slide the ten feet down the steep slope into the water. The bow plunged deep, then reared up. The girl cheered and clapped.

Paddling back, he had to keep tight to the embankment, out of the current. Sometimes there were strange blue-and-yellow birds nesting in the bushes that had burst out of the old brickwork, and on a mud bank just after the bridge that carried the ring road there were always geese and ducks. Once, Robert surprised a troupe of ducklings. They broke right and left in panic. Tiny flies swarmed over the mud and around his face. He reached forward with the paddle, torso swaying in a strong rhythmical stroke. The mother duck squawked and flapped.

It wasn't clear to Robert why he hadn't married Stella yet, why he wasn't having a family, like his friend Arthur. Sometimes he and Stella used his member's key to get into the canoe club at night and made love on the floor in the changing room. Lying in the damp dark, with the river flowing by outside, they told themselves they liked this better than finding each other in a soft double bed every night.

Mid-June, the river rose dramatically as the snow melted in the mountains, and rushed down to the plain. This was the time to ride the wave. But now there were more and more riff-raff enjoying the deep cool beneath the bridge. It was infuriating that the one place in the city Robert loved should be infested like this. One scorching day, three Slavic-looking men were standing on the rocks by the masonry of the second stanchion, right near the wave. They must have waded over from the bank under the first arch, where the stream was shallow, then worked their way around the rocks to the second. The men smoked and shouted, and one, wearing only soaking underpants, with a mobile phone in his hand, wanted to speak to Robert. He was laughing, gesturing, stout and moustached. From the signs he made, it seemed that he wanted Robert to lend him his boat, or at least his life jacket for a swim. Robert shook his head. He didn't understand their language. The men were passing around a bottle of something transparent. The current was dangerous. They waved the bottle. Did he want to try? Looking up from the water, Robert shook his head. The man seemed to want to take a photo of him with his mobile phone. He was a fat, heavy fellow, doubtless drunk. He kept leaning forward, grinning behind his moustache, pointing the phone. Robert decided to move to a different arch.

The central passage of the viaduct was just a quick cluttered rapid with no eddies at the side. All you could do here was push the kayak under a certain rock near the middle, where the stream poured over so hard that the boat would be suddenly sucked in and turned up more or less vertically on its nose.

It was while Robert was approaching this place that he saw something curious. It was trapped on a rock a little way up the rapid. At first he didn't understand.

It was greyish and almost round. It was a bone. Presumably an animal's bone. He got closer, forcing the boat upstream from one small eddy to the next. The thing was jammed between two rocks, and water was trickling through it. Now he realised that it was a human skull.

Robert held his kayak steady in the small churn of disturbance behind a half-submerged stone. The skull lay on one side. The jaw was missing. But it clearly was a skull. The water was passing through an eye socket. Though he couldn't have said why, it seemed important to Robert to retrieve it. The position was difficult. The skull was in front of him and to his right, just beyond reach. The water was powerful and cluttered with debris. Leaning the boat onto the rock beside him, unsteady in the line between eddy and stream, Robert raised his paddle in his right hand and swung it at the skull. On the third attempt, he dislodged it. It bounced on the rock below and into the water a good yard away. Switching his paddle to the other hand, he lunged out and grabbed at it. His fingers found it just as the boat capsized.

Here was a situation unprovided for in all the books he had read on kayaking. He was upside down in a swirl of water, helmet scraping on the rocks, with a skull in one hand and his paddle only loosely held in the other. If he took hold of the paddle to roll the kayak upright, he would have to let go of the skull.

And he wanted to keep it. He wanted to take it to the authorities. There was some mystery behind it, some missing person.

Underwater, Robert waited a second, until he felt that the boat had been flushed clear of the rocks and the arch. You always have more air than you think. That is a commonplace. He wasn't afraid. Encumbered by skull and paddle, he tried to force his body into the position from which, theoretically, with a wave of the arms, a toss of the head and a snap of the hips, he could roll upright even without the paddle. Sure enough, his head came up, but only enough for him to get a gasp of air. He had never been good at doing it this way. He tried again and just caught a glimpse of the Slavs by the first stanchion leaning out and shouting, as they watched the capsized kayak float out into the current downstream of the bridge.

'One more try,' he thought. He sat still, upside down in the churn of water; he leant forward; he stretched his arms – still holding skull and paddle – towards the gloomy light of the surface to his left. Then he threw his arms wide, in the proper rotary motion. This time he didn't even get his head up. He was tired. Very rapidly, he let go of the paddle, pulled the release tab on the spraydeck and popped out. Immediately, his face was in bright sunshine in the whirlpools after the bridge. With his free hand, he flipped the boat upright again, tossed the skull into the cockpit, and looked around for his paddle. It was only a couple of yards off. One hand on the back of the boat, he launched into a determined sidestroke. All was well. But now there was a shout right beside him. The kayak tipped as a big hand grasped the cockpit. One of the Slavs, it seemed, had jumped in.

Robert knew the river here well enough. Although to the unpractised eye it might seem one broad, uniform meander, there were in fact two fast channels, one on each side, and right across the middle, fifty yards down from the bridge, a great shale bank that would be exposed when the river was low.

If you steered carefully as you came through the central arch, it was only a short while before you were in water little more than knee-deep. 'It's OK,' he shouted to the wild foreign face now propped on the deck. Clearly the idiot had had no idea how cold full immersion would be. His teeth were chattering. This was snow water. He didn't have a wetsuit or life jacket. 'OK, OK. Take it easy. Wait. Just wait. OK, now!' Already Robert could touch. He waited till the water was just a little shallower and stood up, grabbing boat and paddle as the current tried to tug them on. Stumbling on the stones, the Slav yelled and pointed. He retched, then started yelling again. Both his friends were in the water, too, but they were flailing in the main stream, swirling rapidly away along the right bank.

Getting the man beside him to steady the boat, Robert managed to climb back in – something he always found difficult in moving water – and, leaving the Slav safe in the shallows, headed for the others. He always kept a sling around his waist and a throw rope in the boat beside his seat. He caught up with one man about a hundred yards down. He was panicking. Robert clipped the sling to the kayak's stern and told him to hold it. The man thrashed about, almost pulling the boat over. He couldn't understand the simplest of instructions. He was shrieking. There were gaps in his teeth. His face was white, ugly, and terrified. With a furious effort, Robert paddled him to the side, but the bank was high here and the water was rushing deep against the smooth wall. It was another hundred yards or so before there was anything safe to climb onto.

Then he went to look for the third man. Where had he gone? Only now did it dawn on Robert what had happened. They had thought that he was in serious difficulty. Drunk, and quite probably stupid, certainly inexperienced, they hadn't hesitated to leap to his aid, diving into the stream by the second arch, right where the current was strongest. It was madness. Robert paddled fast with the stream. The man he was looking for was the fat fellow with the mobile. Presumably, he had left his phone on the rocks. But Robert wasn't familiar with the river down here. All he knew was that the faint roar he could hear in the distance was the dam – none of the kayakers came this far – and that it was crucial to get out before it, otherwise the current would pull him down into the sluice and the filter.

He did paddle fast. He was determined to find the man. Only a hundred yards above the dam, he turned upstream and ferry-glided from side to side across the current in case the swimmer had fallen behind him. He had a clear image of the fat fellow with the black moustache leaning over the rocks beneath the viaduct, pointing his mobile phone, shouting, beckoning, offering him the liquor. It was just the sort of unruly vitality that had always bothered Robert. What a fool! He cruised back and forth for a good half-hour, at what he judged was the last safe position, but the whole business had tired him, and he needed to be sure that he could get out well above the dam. Eventually, he found a place on the left bank, climbed the high rocks and hauled the boat up after him with his sling. The skull banged about in the bottom. He had already forgotten it. At once he went to the police.

Stella thought him heroic. After some days, the police came to the conclusion that the skull was that of a prostitute who had been missing for more than a year. They were unable to trace the two Slavs whom Robert had saved, but the corpse of the third was picked up in the filter across the sluice of the dam. His mobile had disappeared from the rocks beneath the bridge.

'Why on earth did they jump in?' Robert kept repeating on the two occasions he was questioned.

'You were alone,' the policeman said. 'They thought you were in trouble.'

'But I didn't even know them or anything. I didn't ask to be rescued.'

The policeman shrugged. 'People imagine they can help,' he said.

Robert's mother seized on the drama to beg him not to go down to the viaduct again. 'Promise me,' she said. She hugged him tight to her thin shoulders. 'Promise me you'll stop now. I've got nobody else in the world.' She was a determined old woman. Robert solemnly promised.

But Stella was angry. 'What will you do, then?' she demanded. Her eyes burnt. 'How will you keep fit? You're so goddam moody when you can't get out.'

Robert stared at her. 'I'll go anyway,' he said. 'Mother will never know.' So most evenings, in defiance of club rules, Robert still pulls his kayak off the rack and paddles downriver to play the wave beneath the viaduct on his own.

Lebensraum

They announced their arrival – bridges long burnt – from Newport Pagnell service station. 'Of course you're welcome,' Kate said. An hour later they turned into the close just as freezing twilight was stiffening into fog. The evening was suddenly a huge milky whiteness, though fouled here and there by the sour yellow of street lamps.

'What a furry hat, Mum!' Kate greeted Mrs Taylor as the woman had to use her shoulder to force open the passenger door.

'Old age. Your hat gets furrier as your own hair falls out.' Hook-nosed, imperious, yet oddly raffish in her jumble-sale-salvaged coat and hat, Vi Taylor laughed with a sort of raucous cynicism. Climbing out of the opposite door, visibly exhausted by his long drive, a small squat man sent his daughter a look of pained resignation over the damp roof of the Fiesta. The women were embracing. Then the children came running through the surreal light of the fog. 'Have you got anything for me, Granny, Grandad? Come and see my new garage. Come on, come with me. No, me!' Their small fingers clutched and tugged at coats. A fat red smile on his face, Grandad Taylor had already opened the back of the car and was pulling out packages.

'Are you mad, Rupert? For Heaven's sake, they'll freeze to death if they start fiddling with their presents out here. Put them in my bag.' The group walked up the path to the small block where the Langleys had their flat. Halfway up the stairs, Mark Langley appeared. 'Got a lot of work to do, I'm afraid,' were his first words, not out of character. Nevertheless he seemed pleased to see his in-laws, and embraced them both warmly, though winking at his wife over the old woman's shoulder. 'To what do we owe the pleasure?' he enquired.

'The ants in his bloody pants,' Vi Taylor said with grim mirth. 'If he doesn't do a thousand miles a week he gets fretful. Because at home of course there are only a million and one things need doing he'll never lift a finger to sort out.'

'Single-handedly supporting the whole Middle-Eastern economy,' Kate suggested, but now grand-mother had been kidnapped by children determined to be spoilt.

Walking back to the car to help with the luggage, Mark facetiously suggested that Rupert Taylor could write to Ford and offer his vehicle with its almost 200,000 miles on the clock for some advertisement on the reliability of their products.

Stout Rupert said nothing. Apparently impervious to the freezing fog wreathed about the salmon pink of his bald scalp, he leant on the car and found cigarettes and matches in his jacket. It seemed he was in no hurry to get back to the warm company of the flat. Then he said, 'I was thinking: I'm seventy-one next month, I could buy a new Escort on the never-never, minimum down payment, and I'll be dead before I've repaid the half of it. They can come and repossess the thing for all I care. Vi won't want it.'

In the back Mark found the usual orange box full of home-made jams. There was also a narrow roll of old carpet, a child's bicycle covered in rust and a small bathroom cabinet, perhaps produced in the late 1950s. Together with the Taylors' huge old tin suitcase.

'I couldn't stop her,' the old man remarked. 'As far as I'm concerned you're perfectly welcome to bung everything in the bin the moment we're gone.'

Mark began to carry things back to the flat, leaving his father-in-law to smoke in peace. But he was then overtaken on the path by a now urgently scurrying Mr Taylor. The old man tossed his cigarette into the white gloom of a winter garden. 'You want to bet,' he panted, 'you just want to bet she'll be giving the kids their presents while I'm not there.' He staggered on up the stairs, presumably putting considerable strain on his heart.

The following morning, Saturday, towards seven, or perhaps it was nearer six-thirty, Kate and Mark, who had a child wheezing and sniffling between them, heard Grandfather Taylor cross the living room, where he and Mrs Taylor were sleeping on the sofa bed, and pad to the phone in the hall.

'Larry? Good. Sorry, I just wanted to be sure of catching you before you went out.'

Kate had to quickly stuff two knuckles in her mouth to stop herself from giggling. On a Saturday morning her brother was unlikely to be awake if he could help it before nine and gone.

'Yes, we're at Kate and Mark's. They'd like you to come over for lunch.'

'Oh, thanks for the info,' Mark muttered.

'No, today. We've got to get down to Salisbury tomorrow. It doesn't matter why. Well, bring Sabine with you if she's there.'

'Oh, not fucking Sabine,' Kate muttered, apparently in no danger of laughing now.

There was a fairly long silence, after which Mr Taylor said, 'Of course I understand. Just that I would have imagined that when it was a question of your father and mother you might have seen your way to changing your arrangements a bit.'

'Hang on in there, Larry boy,' Mark encouraged in the dark of their bedroom.

'Yes, I know, but we only decided to come at the last minute. Well, because that's how your mother is. It's hopeless asking her to plan anything.'

'He'll give in,' Kate announced gloomily. 'He's worried about his inheritance. And I'll have to spend the whole morning shopping and cooking.'

'Anyway,' Rupert Taylor was saying, 'Sabine may as well get used to the family if she's going to become a part of it.'

This brought low groans from the married couple. So much so that their child, alarmed, began to cry and had to be hushed. Otherwise they would have lost what the old man was saying.

'And then it's little Sylvia's birthday. Yes, Kate was saying you'd have forgotten. Just tell them you can't. It's not work after all, is it? I could understand if it was work. Speaking of which, I've got to talk to you about a little problem I've got. I was wondering if maybe you could arrange for a few tests. I've been going to the toilet a lot at night.'

Mark and Kate had hardly got over the surprise of hearing it was their daughter's birthday before they were offered this juicy titbit. Again the whining child was hushed.

'You think so? It's not fatal is it?'

'Every time he had a stomach ache he was convinced he was going to die,' Kate whispered.

'You see! Tell Sabine she probably won't have to put up with us for much longer, so she may as well get the benefit of our wisdom now.'

'Oh, Christ,' Mark said.

'See you around one then. Don't forget to bring a couple of bottles of wine.'

There was the sound of an old man scratching at flesh under pyjamas, then padding back to the sitting room.

'Dad?'

He retreated a couple of paces to appear at their door, paunchy in pale pyjamas. 'I got Larry to come for lunch,' he announced brightly. 'He's bringing Sabine.'

'But you know it's not Sylvia's birthday for another couple of weeks.'

'I don't see why that should stop us having a little party today.' The fat old man was clearly cheerful and proud of having managed to twist his son's arm. He moved away whistling softly.

However, a moment later there came the sound of raised voices from the living room.

'Mother doesn't want to see our Austrian friend,' Kate commented.

'Who does?'

Mrs Taylor was shouting: 'The girl is bad for him. He shouldn't be encouraged to think we think he's doing the right thing!'

'Nobody,' her husband was impassive, 'ever thought you thought they were doing the right thing. And least of all did they care.' At eight o'clock he went out into a bleak morning, ostensibly to pick up a news-paper, though Vi Taylor said it would be pointless expecting him back before ten at the earliest.

The other adults were now eating breakfast.

'But where does he actually go?' Mark enquired of his mother-in-law. For this was the kind of enter-tainment that compensated for the hassle of their visits.

'God knows.' The old woman had a habit of laugh-ing over things she obviously didn't find at all funny. 'He says he needs his *Lebensraum*. You know how he likes to use words like that, thinking I won't know what they mean. I said, what I want to know is when *I'm* ever going to have any, thank you very much.'

'Take some,' Kate suggested.

'I have. I've stopped cooking for him.'

'Really?'

'We go and eat in a transport place every day.'

'You're joking.'

'No. I said if, now that you've finally retired, you're still too lazy to mend the roof that's been...'

But the children arrived and this conversation had to be interrupted while slippers were found and milk warmed.

'I better get weaving then,' Mark said, and stood up. He was referring to an article he had told his wife had to be ready for four o'clock that afternoon. He would have to take it in personally. And if there was to be a big family lunch...

'Oh, go. Do please go.' Kate raised her voice in sudden exasperation, though without turning to look at him. 'Off to your room, go on. Work. Kiddies, say bye-bye to Daddy now. He's going to lock himself up in his room and work on a Saturday morning.'

His two small children, four and two, turned to look at him from wide, surprised eyes.

'Kate, look, I can't quite see what I've done to deserve this. Somebody has to produce the...'

'While I look after two kids and shop and cook for eight.'

'But we've been over this before. Anyway, you've got your mum. Come on, let's not argue in front of...'

'Just don't be surprised,' Kate was almost shouting, 'don't be bloody surprised if I start taking myself a bit of *Lebensraum* in future. OK?'

'And what's that supposed to mean?'

Mrs Taylor, however, was making all kinds of mute gestures for Mark not to worry but go off and work. 'You should be lucky,' she interrupted to tell her daughter, 'that you've got a husband who wants to work at all. I wish Rupert would. Maybe we wouldn't still be driving that filthy old car and visiting jumble sales.'

'You love jumble sales,' Kate snapped.

Mark stood uncertainly for a moment, but then, unable to get any further change from his wife, re-treated down the passage where the Taylors' thread-bare carpet had now been laid. In his tiny study, sitting at his desk, he pressed his thumbs into his eyes. He listened through the thin modern walls to his wife telling Philip not to do his Nazi salute when Auntie Sabine came. He heard his mother-in-law objecting strongly to his wife's use of the word 'auntie'; heard his wife reply that she couldn't see why her mother expected her son to marry any more intelligently than either she or her daughter had; heard the mother saying that at least she had been a good wife to Rupert, kept house and brought up children for him, whereas sulky Sabine only thought about her own career; heard his son Philip announcing he needed a poo, his wife telling her mother Sabine was right, his daughter Sylvia saying she wanted a glass of choc-olate milk, his mother-in-law saying that hundreds of young English girls would be happy to marry a doctor and wait on him hand and foot, his wife urging his son to hurry up and get to the loo before he dirtied his pants, and telling her mother what stupidly old-fashioned ideas she had, nobody wanted to wait hand and foot on anyone these days, least of all on their husbands. Then while mother and son were in the loo, grandmother began to teach granddaughter 'Little Tommy Tucker'. Her rich old voice moved up and down in warbly nursery-rhyme cadences until she finished: 'How shall he cut it without a knife, how shall he marry without a wife.'

Odd rhyme, Mark thought, and carefully inserted fresh earplugs. Immediately the room, although still oppressively small and with only a lavatory-size square of window, was nevertheless freed of the oppression of sound – might even, since the window was frosted and let in only a dim glow, have been floating in some silent outer space. He looked at his watch: seven hours till paradise.

Towards mid-morning this struggling freelance journalist turned off the processor, removed earplugs and listened attentively. Given that his wife and mother-in-law, not to mention the dear children, were notoriously incapable of making anything less than an unholy racket about a hundred per cent of the time, it was reasonable to suppose the coast was clear. He walked confidently down the passage, planning to treat himself to a phone call, but then had the good sense to glance in the kitchen first, where unfortunately he found Mr Taylor poring over copies of *The Sun, The Independent, The Economist*.

'Just grabbing a lightning coffee,' he explained.

The old man nodded. 'Have you seen about this character wants it to be illegal for you to hit your children?' Short fat legs wide apart, elbows propped on the paper on the table, double chin in hands, Mr Taylor communicated an impression of quiet, adult enjoyment.

'Must live in a bigger bloody house than we do.'

'Claims it teaches them to be violent.'

'I can think of no more useful education.'

The two men laughed together very cosily and with what both recognised these days as an antique male solidarity. Indeed Mark was aware that this might be one reason why his father-in-law liked to visit. The kettle whined for attention.

'Carpet in the passage blocks the living-room door,' the younger man remarked.

'Talk to Vi about it.'

'Of course it's nice of her to bring things. I mean, the thought.'

The old man laughed: 'Lack of it rather.'

Hazarding, with what was on his mind, rather more than he had in the past, Mark said: 'You know, given that you and Vi are always, well, often arguing, I was wondering, didn't it ever occur to you that maybe it might have been wiser, er, I don't know, to separate or even divorce years ago?'

Mr Taylor was reading an editorial in *The Independent* and at the same time licking his fingers clean of something he had presumably just finished eating.

'Divorce?' he said mildly, without looking up. 'I should have bloody well killed her.'

Yet all was sweetness and light a couple of hours later when Mark again emerged from his room, having picked up, in his muffled, earplugged world, the booming voice of brother-in-law Larry. And sure enough the big boy – for it was hard to think of him as a man and even less as a doctor – stood in the passage by the front door, beaming greetings and holding high a cake box to keep it above the greedy assaults of the children. Handsome, tall, with full mouth and laughing eyes, Larry radiated vitality and ingenuous good will, kissing and calling to everybody. Beside him, small and rather plain, glum Sabine unbuckled her raincoat.

Mark called hello, then went through to the kitchen, where Kate was preparing an elaborate lunch. 'Oh, who are you?' she demanded of her husband, who stood dazed by the winter sunlight that found its way into this part of the flat. 'Pulitzer-Prize-winning article on refuse collection in Haringey?'

'And Hornsey,' he corrected. 'Can I help?'

'I imagine,' Kate said, 'that when they've cleaned the last corpse away from Armageddon, you'll arrive offering your valuable assistance.'

'I imagine,' Mark mimicked, 'that having claimed you hate cooking, you are now slaving to produce the unnecessarily elaborate cordon-bleu fare, *n'est-ce-pas?*'

'I don't see why I should be taken for granted just because I take pride in what I do.'

He was opening his mouth to snap back the usual reasoned male objections to unreasoned female resentment (why was his wife like this?) when Grandmother Taylor, in high spirits with having had the children all morning, pushed into the room and told him not to think badly of her daughter. She had always been like that. 'Haven't you, Kate?' It was just her character. She meant no harm and loved him very much really, otherwise she would never have stuck with him so long. 'No need to argue,' she said. And wasn't it good the children could play in the passage now there was a carpet? She went to the cupboard to pull out some of the home-made jams for her best boy Lawrence. Finding a smile, Mark took steaming dishes from his wife and began trying to get the children to the table. In the sitting room, Larry could be heard telling his father that his problem might be anything from a banal urinary infection to cancer of the prostate and imminent death. Rupert Taylor seemed gratified by both possibilities.

'But the most normal diagnostic profile would be a slight hardening of prostate tissue accompanied, if not exacerbated, by weakening of the bladder and sensitivity of the lower urethral tract.'

The speaker, in a monotone, was Sabine. 'Chronic and incurable,' she added in an English as impeccable as it was forced and painful. 'Perhaps mitigable to a certain extent by mild tranquillisers.'

'Private consultation. Cost you thirty quid,' Larry said, stooping to squeeze the girl affectionately and help her off with her coat. 'She'll examine you later if you like. Did we bring any gloves, darling?'

Vi Taylor in the kitchen pulled a face that meant to say, 'Listen to her! Is that any talk for a woman?' The children laughed and spluttered food. And now their grandmother was saying: 'Yes, Mark, you know, just the way Rupert and I have always loved each other despite the fact that he's a presumptuous fool. Haven't we, Rupert?' As the mild, balding man came into the kitchen, she went over and embraced him warmly. Although the look on Mr Taylor's face was one of weary condescension, he nevertheless returned the hug with obvious pleasure at this animal contact and promising lunchtime atmosphere of détente. The two swayed a moment together as if they might fall over. Sabine of serious face took the opportunity to stand on tiptoe and whisper something in her boyfriend's ear. He told her reassuringly not to worry.

'Aren't you going to kiss Grandad, who bought you your new Transformer?' Mr Taylor broke off one embrace and was sentimentally looking for another. What was family for after all?

Little Philip said: 'But Granny gave it to me.'

There was general laughter. From where he was spooning food into daughter Sylvia, Mark shouted to his brother-in-law to open the Frascati in the fridge, and very soon six adults and two children seemed to be rather enjoying themselves. The little folks were fed and chased off to their room with threats and promises, and the small kitchen table was extended, covered with a red tablecloth and extravagantly laid with porcelain white plates and side plates, paper serviettes, water tumblers and crystal wine glasses. The guests, though none had been invited by the hosts and two had come only in response to third-degree coercion, sat down in excellent spirits, while Mark served what the inexplicably aggrieved Kate was so expertly preparing.

An opening course of vol-au-vent was thus suitably oohed and ahed over. Fat Mr Taylor was particularly appreciative of his daughter's cooking. It was one reason why he had liked to come, he said. Sabine likewise ate with a gusto one wouldn't have expected from her diffident air and Teutonically clipped speech. Only Mrs Taylor seemed less than engrossed in her food, while Kate didn't eat at all, but went on working at the oven.

'Not going to sit down with us?' Larry shouted to her.

She shook her head. 'I'd be fat in a second if I touched that stuff. I just make it and watch you lot eat it.'

The trim young woman made no attempt to hide bitterness and even a certain note of criticism here, as if dissociating herself from the delicious food she had made and those carefree enough to be eating it.

'Oh, come on. When all the family are together. Just this once.'

Mark made a face to his brother-in-law which meant, 'Don't bother, it's not worth it, she's always like this.'

But the good-hearted Larry insisted, 'It just feels wrong, us eating while you're working.'

'Oh, if it makes you feel guilty I'm sure you must have your reasons for being so. Anyway, I thought guilt was supposed to spice things up.' Mark concentrated very seriously on his food. Then his wife added, 'I take after father, that's my lot. Hereditary. I'd be a barrel if I ate that stuff.'

From another room came the sound of the older child bossing the younger. The little girl was playing something 'the wrong way'.

'Whereas your father here has never missed a single meal in his life, nor ever forgotten to ask for seconds,' Mrs Taylor said, voicing her own mixture of contempt and merriness. 'Not a place we go but he doesn't tell whoever it is they're the best cook in the world and yes, he'll treat himself to a little bit more just this once.'

'Actually, it's called politeness,' her husband remarked.

'And you know why he gets up in the middle of the night? You know why? Not to go to the loo at all. He thinks it's to go to the loo, he likes to think he's ill so he can curry some sympathy, but really he gets up to go and look in the fridge. A glass of milk at one o'clock, a ham sandwich at two o'clock, a boiled egg at four o'clock.' She mimicked the gesture of someone peering into a fridge, frowning and pulling things out to eat. 'A yoghurt at five o'clock. A piece of apple pie at six o'clock. By the time I arrive in the morning there's nothing left. So you know what the first thing I say to him in the morning is? I say, "Rupert dear, Rupert my darling, have you said good morning to the fridge yet, Rupert? Have you asked Fridgie if he's feeling well today?" Because every time I turn round he has his big nose in there, doesn't he?'

A plump little darling in short pigtails appeared at the kitchen door weeping. 'Philip won't let me play with his train,' she wailed. 'He pushed me.' An older but shriller voice shrieked, 'There's not enough room for both of us.' A door could be heard slamming.

Swallowing vol-au-vent, Mark told her kindly: 'Well, you go back and tell him he's a very naughty boy, and if he doesn't open the door and let you play I'll give him the worst spanking he's ever had.'

Apparently reassured, the girl toddled off. The group sat in silence a moment to hear the baby voice in another room comically relaying her father's threat. Sabine, who had discussed this at length with Mark on previous occasions, said abruptly that in her experience if someone actually went and talked to the children there would be no need to keep threatening violence. Mark seemed pleased she had brought up the issue: 'At least I didn't say I'd beat the living daylights out of him,' he smiled.

Mr Taylor explained: 'The fact is that eating is really the only pleasure that remains to me. Presumably Kate has other sources of satisfaction, otherwise she'd be guzzling here with the rest of us.'

'The only pleasure!' his wife protested. 'Oh, that's good! And the other?'

'Oh, come on, Mum,' Larry was laughing with a full mouth. 'Give us a break.'

'Just three hundred and sixty-five times a year,' she insisted. 'No, honestly, I'm not joking. There's nothing wrong with his prostate, I'm telling you. He nudges my leg and it's...'

A pained look crossed fat Mr Taylor's face: 'Do we have to? Isn't there some rugby on telly this afternoon?'

'I can't think of any other satisfactions at all,' Kate said. 'Mark and I gave up sex when Sylvia arrived.' She walked to the table for a moment to pour out the last of the first bottle of wine and, diet or no, drank it at a gulp.

'Don't exaggerate,' Mark said defensively.

'Oh, don't worry,' Kate said. 'Nobody's questioning your libido. I blame it all on my frigidity.' But then she bent and kissed him with mock passion on an ear.

In her tone of somebody used to killing conversations quite dead, Sabine announced: 'Surveys showing mean frequencies of intercourse are known to give misleadingly inflated results. People tend to...'

'Mean?' Mrs Taylor interrupted. 'There's nothing mean about his frequencies!' She laughed immoderately and was obviously drunk on a single glass of wine.

Again there came the sound of squabbling from the other room.

'I'd better go and spank the both of them,' Mark said, and pushed back his chair, smiling deliberately at Sabine.

'It's always fun when you actually get here,' Larry confided to his girlfriend. Sitting tall and square beside his fat and shrunken father, the athletic young doctor stretched an arm around him: 'Listen Dad, when I'm on casualty, you know how many old blokes I get coming in who've had heart attacks trying to get it on? You wouldn't believe it. And almost all of them overweight. So if you want to stay on the job you'll have to cut down on your eating. They're mutually exclusive pleasures.'

'Oh, if you believe the half of what your mother says, you're more of a fool than I took you for.'

Poor Sabine said: 'He is not a fool. He got one of the best degrees they've ever given at the London School.'

Kate explained wrily: 'Freedom of calumny is one of the tenets of the Taylor household. You'll have to get used to it.'

'In the absence of *Lebensraum*,' Mrs Taylor giggled with thoughtless wisdom, draining a second glass of wine.

'I beg your pardon?' enquired Larry.

But Sabine felt this could be nothing less than a below-the-belt jab at her origins. 'I can't see,' she said with sudden acrimony, 'what concepts like that have got to do with it at all. I don't...'

'It means,' Kate placated, 'that not being able to get away from one another, they take delight in making hell for each other.'

The Austrian girl glared. 'It seems to me *Lebensraum* is a culturally specific term and I think it would be better if it wasn't mentioned.'

Larry hadn't understood, as indeed he understood little that wasn't strictly to do with urogenital functions. 'The truth is, though,' he said, 'that Mum and Dad really love each other, don't you Mum? The arguing's all a show to keep themselves on their toes. Right?'

'I love him very much,' Mrs Taylor said with sudden alcohol-aided solemnity.

'Pass,' Mr Taylor said wearily. 'And can somebody please get another bottle out.'

'For example, I was perfectly happy to give up my career to wash and cook for Rupert. When we first moved into the place in Drummond Road and there wasn't enough...'

There was a danger that the party would now have to hear a long account of the older woman's sacrifices, which were indeed many. But Sabine abruptly interrupted to offer the kind of hard information she was never short of: 'Statistically, married people live longer than single people. So there must be some advantages.'

'Determination to outlive the other and have a few years' peace,' Rupert Taylor had no difficulty explaining.

Returning from the children's room, Mark stopped off briefly in the bedroom, opened a drawer and slipped something into his wallet. Arriving in the kitchen just as Kate was serving a dish of veal escalopes with *champignons* sautéd in red wine, he found the room steamily cosy and a fresh glass of wine by his place. Suddenly elated by these luxuries and the spirited company, he decided to go to his father-in-law's aid at once, as if the man had somehow been stuck there with his back to the wall all the time his son-in-law was out of the room. Rubbing his hands over his food, he said brightly, 'It seems to me perfectly reasonable and healthy that Dad should want a little action every day. To make up for all those lost years in Saudi. I'd take it as a compliment if I were you, Mother.'

Mrs Taylor snorted: 'If it wasn't me it'd be someone else. And when he was away in Saudi, no doubt it was someone else. Or some others rather.'

Mr Taylor wanted to know, 'Can't we have a quiet lunch for once?' though he didn't appear to be suffering greatly.

'He just never wants the truth to come out,' Mrs Taylor told Sabine, briefly forgetting that the girl was an enemy. 'Not that there's much danger of him recognising it if it did: he's got such a high opinion of himself.'

Rupert Taylor may indeed have wanted a quiet lunch, but was nevertheless incapable of remaining passive in the face of such naked aggression. He broke off chewing his veal to remark acidly: 'The truth about my going to Saudi, for those who have eyes to see it, is that finding myself condemned to spend my life with an argumentative, ignorant woman who just would not understand where my or her own responsibilities lay, I chose, what? To leave her in the lurch as any normal man would? – no, simply to work overseas for a few years so as to avoid insanity or suicide or worse, sending ninety per cent – and I repeat – nine-zero per cent of my salary back to her. Any objections?'

Larry clapped as if applauding two combatants. 'Attaboy,' he remarked. But Sabine, who was new to all this, seemed appalled. She said: 'If you'd kept your job, Mrs Taylor, you wouldn't have needed the money, and you could have split up if you wanted to.'

'He wouldn't let me keep my job,' Mrs Taylor muttered grimly. 'You obviously don't know Mr All Important I Can Manage Everything, My Wife's Not Going To Work, Leave It All To Me.'

'Rubbish,' Rupert Taylor said, helping himself to more wine. 'She couldn't wait to stop working and have kids. And quite right too.'

'You did say, Mum,' Kate remarked, eating a spartan piece of meat with no sauce and only a few leaves of plain salad, 'that you willingly gave up your job to be a good wife.'

Mrs Vi Taylor suddenly changed tone, became jolly, almost coquettish. 'Well, I had my illusions then, didn't I, Rupert dear. I was in love. I thought he was right. I respected him.'

Pressing her point, and with a wink at her father, Kate said: 'So given that you admit yourself that it was an illusion, why complain about the fact that Sabine wants to work?'

'I never complained about Sabine,' Mrs Taylor lied with enviable fluency. 'I only said life might be difficult if they were both working.'

'When has life not been difficult?' Mr Taylor enquired rhetorically, sensing a consensus in his favour.

It was a characteristic of these conversations, however, that the youngsters would mercilessly keep the ball in motion at the expense of their elders, who anyway appeared to take pleasure in a gladiatorial performance that had begun almost forty years before. So after a moment's pause now, Mark said archly: 'You are just concerned for their welfare, right, Mother?'

Mrs Taylor pouted. Although her body still seemed solid and trim, her face had a sort of savage, haggard dignity about it which only age could confer, hook-nosed and bluishly gaunt to her husband's rosy mellow chubbiness: 'No,' she said, 'the point is, it's *right* for a woman to have illusions when she marries. I didn't know I'd married a fraud. In Larry's case it's different, and I just think with all respect to Sabine that as a doctor he would be better off married to somebody who would stay at home and cook for him.'

Sabine rather surprisingly said: 'So do I.' With what she had been drinking, her accent was creeping out, so that 'so' became a rather ominous 'zo'. 'Naturally it would be better for him. But I am not like that. I want to work and I don't want children.'

Mr Taylor was signalling to his daughter to bring him another helping of veal. 'You insist on holding contradictory positions,' Kate needled her mother, standing up. 'You can't say your life has been a disaster and then expect everybody else to repeat it.'

Mark promptly came to the old woman's aid. 'It's just that your mother has a sense of the ideal, a vision of how things might be in the best of best possible worlds. That's why you never wanted to split up even when things were bad, right Mum?'

Mrs Taylor nodded vigorously. 'You're the only one who ever understands me,' she said to her pleasantly smirking son-in-law. 'A sense of the ideal is what it is.'

'And no sense of reality.' Mr Taylor's policy, having said his piece, now seemed to be to keep out of the spotlight and just toss in a grenade from time to time.

'You what?' Mrs Taylor shrilled, perhaps more theatrically than from real shock. 'Me got no sense of reality? Who washed and cooked and slaved for forty years? While somebody else we know hasn't even got the time and energy to fix a leaking roof, has to jump into the car and go gallivanting off to see friends and relatives every time he can't think of a better excuse.'

Larry said ingenuously, 'Well, I'd much rather have a wife with a career. So please don't anyone worry about us,' and he turned to Sabine and kissed the graceless young woman on the lips. 'I don't want my wife at home.'

'More fool you,' Mr Taylor came out at his driest.

'You see!' his wife shouted.

'In marriages where both partners work, the divorce rate is much higher.' Kate cheerfully took a leaf out of the Austrian girl's book. 'I saw it on telly.'

'So be it,' Sabine said. 'We divorce then. Why is everybody so scared of that?'

'Just do it before you have any children,' Kate said sincerely.

'But I told you: I don't want any children. No problem.'

'When I was thirteen' – Kate found it hard to keep a note of condescension out of her voice when talking to her brother's girlfriend – 'I wanted to be a film star. When I was twenty-four, I was quite a good radio producer. Now I'm a housewife.'

Sabine didn't seem to appreciate the point of this.

'She'd always sworn she'd keep working,' Mark explained to Larry, 'otherwise I'd have found a job that took me out of the house.'

At which somebody observed that the children had been screaming loudly for some minutes now, so once again Mark went off to sort them out. Returning, he stopped in the bathroom and examined himself in the mirror. Was his skin smooth enough, or did he need another shave?

When he returned Mr and Mrs Taylor were arguing, presumably after careful prompting from Kate and Larry, about some event of twenty and more years ago, when Mr Taylor had walked out of the house one Saturday, apparently to get cigarettes, and had not come back until two days later. Mr Taylor was vigorously denying this scenario. It merely indicated how little his wife had ever listened to what he said. Because in fact he had been going to a conference and had told her so. But then as an afterthought he remarked that if he had ever thus walked out in desperation, which of course he hadn't, then rather than just getting hysterical about it, his wife might have done worse than to ask herself why a man to all intents and purposes so sensible and responsible should have done such a thing.

Kate innocently enquired whether this had occurred before or after the introduction of decimal currency.

In response to a question from Larry, Sabine claimed that her parents never argued, though her mother had a fetish about bathrooms: she would only ever use her own bathroom in her own house, which meant that she refused to travel, so that once a year her father, who loved travelling, went on holiday on his own.

'Excellent arrangement,' Mr Taylor thought.

Mrs Taylor weighed in that having shared a bathroom for forty years with a man who didn't even know the seat could be lifted up, for her the toilet was one of the pleasanter aspects of travel.

'If it's any comfort, they'll be giving me a colostomy bag soon,' Mr Taylor came back.

The battle smouldered on. It was pushing three o'clock now. The windows were definitively steamed over, and anyway the winter light was already fading. The family gathering had eaten their apple crumble and were now enjoying whisky in their coffee, and out of it too, in the case of Mr Taylor. There was, on their six faces, the glow of people having a good time eating and drinking and merrily exorcising all the little irritations that made living together so heroic.

Inspired by the bathroom conversation of a moment before, Larry now launched into an enthusiastic account of a man brought into urology in the small hours a couple of nights back with a severe bite on his genitals, which he had ludicrously tried to pass off as the result of a toilet seat falling while he was urinating. Sabine abruptly interrupted to ask why Mr and Mrs Taylor were going off home in such a hurry. Wouldn't it be nice perhaps to go to a restaurant tomorrow, Sunday evening?

Whether the Austrian girl found what her fiancé was saying distasteful, or whether she was deliberately trying to win the favour of her in-laws, or merely thought that such invitations were the 'done thing', the suggestion came as a surprise, if not a shock. The atmosphere in the little suburban kitchen grew suddenly tense.

Mark said quite cheerfully that he was on for it, knowing as he spoke that his wife would immediately trot out the excellent excuse of the children.

She did.

'Just with Larry and me then,' Sabine said. 'You're not on call, are you?'

'I second the motion.' Mr Taylor raised his hand with a provocative light in his eyes. 'As long as it's a good restaurant and expensive. To my daughter-in-law, Sabine,' he added, raising his whisky glass.

Sabine beamed. 'Larry and I will offer, won't we, Larry?'

'No,' Mrs Taylor said. 'Rupert, we've got to get to Salisbury tomorrow.'

'Why?' Kate asked. 'Who's in Salisbury?' And she said: 'You did get that they're offering to pay, Mum?'

'Go on,' Mr Taylor said, 'tell them, Vi. Listen to this everybody. This is the real reason things don't get done around the house. Not my mythical laziness.' And he poured himself a second full glass of whisky, at which his son protested: 'Dad, it'll kill you.'

'We have to go and see a very dear friend of mine.' Mrs Taylor was dramatically tight-lipped and solemn.

'Who she has neither thought of, spoken about, nor in any way communicated with for twenty years.'

'Who is it though?' asked Kate.

'The woman who taught dressmaking with me after the war in Manchester. Valerie.'

'But can't it wait till Monday, so you could eat together tomorrow? Seeing as you've made all the effort to drive down here.'

'She's dying,' Rupert Taylor explained drily. 'Last week it was someone called Hannah in Glasgow who

I'd never heard of before, a month ago somebody else in Preston, not to mention the endless visits to the Leeds Infirmary to visit every declining pensioner within a five-mile catchment area.'

'Valerie's an old friend. We had good times together,' Mrs Taylor insisted. 'It was her birthday party we first met at.'

'We met at Talbot Road bus station,' Mr Taylor corrected. 'And you wouldn't even have known she was ill if you hadn't run into a friend of a friend who has kept in touch.'

'We had such laughs together,' old Vi Taylor repeated. For a moment it seemed as if she might cry. Her eyes watered. 'Anyway, I would have kept in touch with all sorts of people if somebody had given me the kind of life where I had time.'

Mr Taylor lit a cigarette.

Mark said nostalgia seemed a perfectly legitimate reason for visiting people.

'Maybe one day you'll feel that way about me,' Kate said.

For some reason Larry laughed quite immoderately at this.

Mark said, 'Hardly.'

Becoming unusually aggressive, Mr Taylor said that it wasn't nostalgia. It wasn't nostalgia at all. It was just a morbid bloody desire to bury one's contemporaries and savour one's own imminent end into the bargain, an occasion to be at once smug and self-pitying. Because Vi never went to see somebody unless they were condemned. It was like the kiss of death when old Vi came to see you. You knew you'd be in your box before the week was out. She was a stupid, insensitive woman.

Scathing and loud, Rupert Taylor appeared to be losing control.

Mrs Taylor said quietly: 'Rupert's just scared.' Then she said: 'More often than not he naps in the car while I go in, because it upsets him to see people who are ill. He can't face death.'

'You could refuse to drive,' Mark suggested to his father-in-law. 'After all, it's dangerous in this weather. What with the fog we've been having.'

'I like driving,' Mr Taylor snapped. 'I hope to die in a car accident. That's how scared I am. At least I won't have to suffer her ministrations in some miserable hospital.'

The fat old man so obviously meant this that the jovial veneer of enthusiasm and banter at last went out of the conversation. There was silence. Unless it was just that the soporific and depressive effects of the alcohol were now replacing the initial sense of exhilaration. One or two people sighed. Larry yawned, smiled: 'God, I feel good. Haven't eaten so well in years.' But nobody responded. The verbal carnival was over. They were tired after eating and drinking; the grey twilight through misted kitchen windows contributed to a general Lenten feeling.

Then Mark said: 'Oh, shit, I've got to get that article in. I'll be late.' He jumped up from his seat.

'Here we go again. The busy man only has time to sit and eat,' Kate said. Then she shouted far too loudly: 'Come and say goodbye to Daddy, kiddies. Off he goes out to work on Saturday afternoon!'

'I hate you,' Mark informed her in a tone that might have been suited to a purchase over a post-office counter.

Larry was the only one who could still laugh at this charade. Sabine said a polite goodbye. Mark took a last look at himself in the mirror in the bathroom and escaped.

When he returned, it was almost midnight. Unusually, his wife was up waiting for him.

'Sorry, they dragged me in for editing,' he said. The flat was quiet, so that a faint swish of traffic on the high road could be heard. 'Garry was off sick.'

'Oh really?'

'Yes, what a bore. Except they'll have to pay of course. Which is nice.'

'Just that I've been phoning all evening,' she said quietly. 'And you weren't there.'

There was no interruption in the flow of Mark's movements as he slipped off his coat. Nor did his expression betray even a flicker of concern. He had already decided long ago, and in this he was taking a leaf out of his father-in-law's book, that whatever came to light, whenever, and however damning, he would brazen it out to the end.

Offhand, unwinding a scarf, he complained: 'Give

me a break. If you'd phoned, which I can't remember you ever doing before, they would have called me, wouldn't they? And then why on earth should you phone all evening?'

'Oh, only that mother killed father,' she said.

This thin woman, his wife, was sitting cross-legged and stony-faced on the sofa.

Mark, holding his wet overcoat, didn't believe her.

'They had an argument. I don't know. About who had wanted to sell the place in Kirby and move to Broughton Street. It would have been funny. Until suddenly he lost his head: why would she never never let be, etc. etc., why wouldn't she let him breathe, and he hit her.' Kate paused. She spoke quietly, almost crisply. 'They started hitting each other. I tried to stop them. The kids were terrified. Then she gave him a big push. He fell backwards over the coffee table and banged his head on the corner of the cabinet. The next thing we knew, he was dead. The doctor said it was a heart attack.'

Mark sat down in a green upholstered armchair.

'Jesus,' he said. 'And your mother?'

'They took her to hospital with him. Naturally she was desperate, saying how much she loved him and never wished him any harm. I phoned for Larry to go and be with her.'

As so often before, Mark couldn't help feeling his wife had flint in her heart. So unlike the woman he should have married. And all the time, while trying to take in his in-laws' tragedy, for he had always felt a very deep affection for the old couple, his mind was nevertheless racing against time to find answers to the questions she would be asking any moment now.

'So I phoned you up,' she said, 'only about ten or fifteen times, so that you could come and look after the kids and I could go and be with my mother. And you weren't there.' She paused. 'And now you come back and you say you *were* there.'

Boyish Mark looked at the woman he had married. He remembered that ten years ago they had been very much in love, very much, so that a confrontation like this would have been unimaginable.

Kate had aged more markedly than he. Above all, her features had dried and hardened around their handsomeness.

'Well?' she demanded.

Fortunately, at this very moment a little boy came scuffling into the room. 'I had a bad dream,' he wailed, and went straight to his mother.

'What about?'

'I don't know,' the boy said, trembling. 'But it was horrible.' Then he said: 'Sylvia was a horrible monster.'

He clung to his mother. She kissed him softly, and her hard features smoothed a little. The father watched. For a moment there was the satisfying intimacy of a family dealing capably with the classic traumas, bringing the children through.

Mark said: 'Listen Kate.'

She didn't look up.

'Kate, listen, we're going to have enough on our plates the next few days, sorting everything out, aren't we?'

'And so?'

'Well, so I was thinking: can't we, maybe, I don't know, let this argument wait?' Raising his eyebrows, he managed to half-laugh in an attractive, winsome way. 'I mean, wait thirty years or so. How about it when the kids invite us to lunch some time.'

'I can't imagine we'll make it thirty years,' she said.

'It seems people do, though,' he said. 'You know, Kate? We could bring it up over twenty-first-century vol-au-vent. We wouldn't even be sure we'd remembered it right. It'd feel like it didn't matter at all.' After a moment's silence he added, 'The way your father goes out to a café every morning, for his *Lebensraum*.'

She lifted her dark eyes to look at him now, the child wriggling on her lap. Very coldly, she sized him up.

'Used to go,' she said tonelessly. Then began to cry, rocking back and forth with her child, shivering silently. 'Now he's got all the room he needs,' she sobbed.

'Kate,' he said, but was afraid to go and comfort her. The little boy burrowed into her breasts and clutched her.

Annette and Frank

Shortly after his wife's untimely death, David Markham vacated the small flat by the river that he had used for many years as a studio. There was no longer any reason not to work from the bigger house in the suburbs. All the same he was reluctant to sell an asset that might come in useful for the children some time. There was also a sentimental attachment: it was here that he and Monica had first lived together in a time now utterly remote. So he put the flat in the hands of a real estate agency, and only a few days later found himself being invited to meet the prospective tenants.

In their early twenties, Annette and Frank were about to get married. Immediately, David was aware that he had seen the girl before. She had straight blond hair, a strong chin, blue eyes and, most unavoidably, two beautifully full breasts held in evident tension in a tightly buttoned white blouse. Seeing the older man's eyes raised inquisitively, Annette smiled and said, 'The new café in Roland Street.' Of course, not two hundred yards from the flat. He had grabbed a coffee there three or four times. The girl made a good cappuccino. The agent, a plain, lanky man in his thirties, invited them to sit down around his desk, and with monotone punctiliousness proceeded to give details of the couple's income and their ability to pay. Frank, it seemed, of Italian parents, worked in the back of the café making the pastries and sandwiches. They ran the place together. There was thus the problem, the agent explained solemnly, that the tenants' earnings were liable to fluctuation depending on the fortunes of their business. In such circumstances, it was normal practice... But David waved the complications aside. He liked the couple.

There was now the question of furnishing. David wanted to rent the flat furnished, so that it would be easier to evict if he needed to get it back for one of the children. The girl was eager to know what he would be buying in the way of a bed, a sofa and an oven. Endearingly businesslike, she put on a pair of red-rimmed glasses and made careful notes on a little pad. As she did so, her young man slipped an arm round her waist. Frank was medium height, wiry, with closely cropped hair and soft brown eyes. His body was strong, his manner modest. They discussed the deposit, the method of payment, the way complaints might be made on either side, the question of whose name the utility bills would be in. As they spoke, David's eye moved back and forth from the young woman to the young man, she taking notes, he listening carefully, occasionally asking a question, squeezing his arm around her, teasing. Very obviously they were a couple, David thought. There was an attractive dynamic to their relationship. 'My only condition,' he said, 'and I think this was clear on the ad, is that you are non-smokers.' Frank and Annette assured him that they had seen the condition, there was no problem, and the agent then fixed the rent at the going rate, not a penny more, not a penny less.

David now had two weeks to get the furniture together. He found himself spending more than he expected. On removing all his work and tools from the place, he had had to have the walls replastered. They were clean and white. Now he walked round a furniture warehouse rejecting the cheaper items suggested by the salesman. He didn't want to be thought mean, especially if he was asking the youngsters not to smoke. Good furniture will last longer, he told the salesman, and the tenants will be more inclined to respect it. In particular, he chose a good bed with a rather attractive satin oak headboard that sloped up and away from the pillow in a soft curve. While he was studying the quality of the carpentry in this bed, trying to make up his mind about spending the extra money, he suddenly imagined the young couple making love there. He saw the girl release her bra, perhaps coming in from the narrow passage to the bathroom. Frank would be waiting on the bed, in boxer shorts no doubt. He saw the breasts released into their natural shape, more innocent naked than pressed into that cleavage. In just her pants she would step the two or three paces to this handsome bed, the simple white cotton of her underwear betraying the shadow of her sex. 'I'll take this one,' he announced to the salesman's pleased surprise. David left the warehouse in something of a daze.

When the furniture was in place, David arranged to meet the couple at the flat to go over the inventory and give them the keys. 'It's hard for us to get away together,' Annette told him on the phone. David said it seemed important that all three signatories be present. Perhaps Frank's sister, Annette eventually decided, could look after the café for an hour or so. They couldn't afford paid help as yet. In the event, to David's surprise, since he imagined everything had already been agreed, they brought along the estate agent as well. Tall Mr Halliday was dressed in a chalk-stripe suit and plain tie.

The flat was on the ground floor, and Frank was worried that there were no bars to protect the windows exposed to the street. David had never had any unwelcome guests, he said, but he was willing to consider the possibility of bars. 'Doesn't it get damp, being so near the river?' Annette asked dubiously. With a dry cough, the agent remarked that the rent had been adjusted downward in line with the well-known disadvantages of a ground-floor location. The proprietor was under no obligation to affix bars. Damp, in a rental contract, could only be an issue when it actually occurred. There was no recent history of flooding in the town. A good six inches taller than any of the others, there was something at once incongruous and reassuring about Mr Halliday. He had the discreet authority of the funeral director. With linked arms, Frank and Annette proceeded into the building.

All their conditioning, David noticed, as the two youngsters now examined cupboards and kitchen fittings, warns them to be cautious. They are expecting to be ripped off. Were there enough electricity sockets? the boy wondered. There were sprinkles of white flour on his jeans, David noticed, just above the knees, where his apron ended, presumably. Annette was looking suspiciously at the neatly fitted kitchen. Storage space was a bit on the short side, she thought.

Eventually it was the agent who remarked: 'Well, Mr Markham does seem to have been extremely generous with the furnishings. No wonder he doesn't want smokers.' After this, the couple began to relax.

'Try it out,' David suggested, gesturing to the small plush red sofa. As they sat down together – she in a tightish skirt, her breasts as ever pressed high – the wiry boy turned to his future wife and kissed her quickly and spontaneously on the red lips. As he did so, Annette's eye caught David's for a moment over her man's shoulder. David thus had a vision of the strong nape of Frank's shaven neck and the girl's clear blue eye betraying at once pleasure and modest restraint. The older man was instantly and intensely aware that something had changed. He had fallen in love with the young couple.

'No idea how lucky they are,' commented the agent, as he and David left the new tenants to take measurements and make plans. 'Actually,' Mr Halliday confided, 'perhaps I should say that I know Annette's family quite well. I'm sure that even if the café were to go through a bad patch, they would always guarantee that the rent was paid punctually.' Still struck by the vision of the lovers on the sofa, David thanked the man profusely for this reassurance.

Nothing like this had ever happened to David before. He did have three children – all grown-up and away now – but their girlfriends and boyfriends had only irritated him, or made him anxious for them. He had never wanted to picture what their sex life might be. Trained at the city's finest art college, he had failed in his ambition to become a serious sculptor, but for more than twenty years, as a result of a completely fortuitous early contact, he had specialised in the creation and repair of metal artefacts used in the Christian liturgy. Churches of every denomination for more than a hundred miles around sent him damaged communion chalices, font covers, bishop's staffs, reliquaries, aspersoriums and censers. David was not himself a believer as his wife had been, but this had never prevented him from respecting and enjoying the rituals of the cult and all the beautiful objects they had produced. He had become an authority. When a fashionable young priest asked for a modern communion set, something that would inspire the appropriate sense of occasion without looking old-fashioned, David knew just the mix of hexagonal silver plate and semi-precious stones they were after. For the traditionalist, he could reconstruct from art books almost any chalice, candlestick or casket that had ever been. Now though, as he worked in the large semi-basement of the family home repairing a small bas-relief Nativity scene damaged in a fire, he found his mind constantly wandering. He imagined his tenants sitting on the sofa in the old studio, perhaps with their dinners on their laps, watching television, absorbed. After the plates were put away, their fingers would intertwine. Now she swings a leg over his knees. Soon they are making love, strenuously but tenderly. David couldn't stop thinking about it.

Over the next month or so David visited Frank and Annette's café on four or five occasions, though there was now no reason for him to be in this part of town. 'Paradise' they had called the place.

'One expects a waitress clad in fig leaves,' he said brightly. 'Or with wings.'

Annette didn't understand. The girl seemed friend-ly, but cautious. 'We're having problems getting the vent on the cooker to work,' she told him.

'Tell Frank his almond croissant is a masterpiece,' David said. He was disappointed when he didn't see the young cook. It was the vision of the two of them together that so aroused him. For all her physical beauty, Annette was only interesting with Frank.

When spring came round and the days grew longer and the river rushed more eagerly through the town with the melting snows, David contrived to be in the vicinity of St Mary Magdalene the afternoon of the couple's wedding. He sat in a pub across the street, watched the small crowd gather, saw Frank in a black suit laughing and joking with some other young men his age. They began to fool around, pushing and shoving each other on the damp patch of grass in front of the church. More and more, David liked the boy. He was reminded of the morning of his own wedding. 'The kid's nervous,' he thought, 'he senses life's seriousness creeping up on him. After all, these two must have been having sex for some time now. What marriage ushers in are babies, responsibilities.' If ever David had had a chance of becoming an artist, he thought, the arrival of the first-born had certainly put the dampers on it.

When everybody had gone into the church, David slipped in after them and took a seat towards the back beside a pillar. Before hiding behind it for the closing procession, he was just able to glimpse how the light from the rose window in the chancel made the bride's white dress faintly see-through. Tinged with pink, you could catch the shadows of her young legs striding slowly in the soft material. The estate agent Mr Halliday stood out among the family friends walking behind her.

Throughout the following week, using photos of similar artefacts, David set about recasting the donkey in the damaged Nativity scene. At the same time he was constantly disturbed by the idea that Annette and Frank would soon be having a child.

'They are making love to have a child now,' he told himself. 'It isn't just eroticism. And this of course makes it so much more erotic.' Again and again he laid down his tools and played out the scene of their lovemaking in the old flat he knew so well. 'Monica and I only had a mattress on the floor when we started,' he remembered. The girl's belly would swell up, he thought. Her sex would disappear beneath. Now she would sit on top of him. 'You are sick,' he told himself.

Eventually it became necessary to look for some kind of help, or at least to talk to someone. Martin Ingram was both an old acquaintance and an analyst with a successful practice in the town centre. They had a hurried lunch together at a wine bar opposite the man's studio.

'The fact is,' David told Martin, 'I'm thinking about it really all the time. It's scary.'

'Do you masturbate over these images?' Martin asked.

'I might start to,' David admitted, 'then something blocks me. I never come.'

'So what blocks you?'

David tried to think. He recalled the times he had stretched out on the old sofa in the semi-basement among the sour smells of cleaning fluid and plaster of Paris. 'I think,' he said eventually, 'it's because I can't see any role for myself in the scene. I mean, I don't want to have sex with them. I just want to contemplate them, even encourage them. As though it were somehow important for me to tell them I approve.'

'Have you been to any peep shows?' Martin asked. 'See if that does something for you?'

David was irritated. He began to feel the man didn't understand. Martin, who had put on a lot of weight since they last met, was watching him, dabbing at the corners of his mouth with his napkin. Eventually he said: 'Perhaps the best way to understand this, David, is as part of your bereavement.'

David couldn't see it. The analyst sighed: 'Idealising this young couple, you seek to recover the early years of your own marriage.'

'Sorry, but no,' David said. 'Those years were hell for us, I'd never want to recover them. We weren't like these two at all. We weren't in love. We were always arguing. It was a miracle we stayed together. Or rather, a disaster.'

Martin didn't reply. He was evidently in a hurry to leave.

'Then, even if it were true,' David insisted, 'I mean that I was trying to recapture, etc. – even if it was true, how would that help?'

'Actually, not at all,' Martin agreed. He stood up. 'Perhaps you should tell them how you feel, though, this young couple. Say what you want from them.'

'They'd never speak to me again!' David protested. 'They'd go to the police.'

Martin raised an eyebrow. 'Why do you say that? It's hardly a crime, is it, to want to watch two people making love?'

David reflected on this while they sorted out the bill. Out in the street, he said: 'I don't think they would understand how benevolent my feelings are. They would find me gross.'

'You bet they would!' Again Martin laughed. 'In the end, even if it was God watching us, we'd still think he was a dirty old man and draw the curtains.'

Back in his studio, David was annoyed by the lightness with which his old friend had treated his problem. For some weeks he made a determined effort to repress any thought of the couple. In particular, he renewed his relationship with the woman who had been his lover at the time of his wife's illness and death. But despite the fact that Carol was an attractive and affectionate lady, her caresses brought only the most fleeting pleasure. His mind raced on. She sensed this at once.

'You are still mourning for Monica,' she said. 'You feel guilty because you were cheating on her when she was ill.'

David said nothing. He really didn't feel this was the problem. If anything, he felt guilty because he hardly thought of his wife at all. He didn't seem able to. She had died. She was gone. 'You don't know how much it bothered me,' he suddenly told this other woman, 'that Monica smoked. You know? It seemed so out of character with her being such a good mother and always going to church and so on. Drove me mad.'

'Hardly an excuse for screwing around,' Carol said. He did not contact her again.

David had now finished the restoration of the Nativity scene. The oxen, ass and shepherds once again gazed on the Holy Child in the arms of the Blessed Virgin. The ambiguous Joseph loomed behind. 'Here is a rebus,' David thought. 'I am attracted to something pure, but in a morbid way.' It had been a mistake, he decided, then, to move his work into his own home, to be surrounded, even where he lived, by these sombre religious images. It had been better when life was compartmentalised. Yet he could hardly just go and tell Frank and Annette that he wanted his old studio back. They had only been in it for three months. Again, he began to imagine their lovemaking. He couldn't resist. 'They are blissfully happy,' he thought. Soon Annette would be pregnant. His and Monica's first child had arrived quite unplanned, and some months before their marriage. It had been an unhappy time. Perhaps the angst of those days showed even now, David thought, in his daughter's troubled face. Sarah was doing some secretarial job in a town three hundred miles away. When she called each weekend to ask how her father was, he would say, 'Oh, bearing up.' There were long gaps in the conversation. His daughter, David felt, unlike the two sons who had followed, was finding it hard to get a start in life, to feel she was a real woman. He knew he couldn't help.

Then David started to think that he would, in fact, talk to the couple about his fantasy. Perhaps, if they would let him into their intimacy in some small way, he would get over this obsession. 'You are too much on your own,' he told himself. First the children leaving, then Monica's death. Perhaps Annette and Frank would be more open than he imagined. He went to their café again. He sat at one of the small tables outside and drew Annette into a discussion about service charges. They talked for quite a few minutes. Apparently he had chosen a good time of day. Then Frank came out of the kitchen to say hello. He grinned. Standing at the door, the two youngsters leant their bodies against each other. How beautiful they were! David despaired.

'Not expecting, are we?' he suddenly asked.

'You what?' The girl's voice was abrupt. Her hands moved down to smooth her apron.

'Just something in your faces,' David blundered. 'You looked so happy.'

'Well, I certainly wouldn't be if I was pregnant!' Annette declared.

Frank turned quickly to go back to the kitchen. David was appalled with himself. But thinking back on it at home, he was disappointed with them too. Didn't she want a child? 'I am lost,' he thought.

Some days later, with a growing sense of fatality, he put the matter to Father Dickinson. Dickinson was one of the few priests he knew who might have something sensible to say about a problem like this. In charge of the diocese's artistic heritage, he had brought David a very old chalice that had lost two precious stones some very long time ago.

'Can it be wrong,' David asked him, examining the settings, 'to be constantly fantasizing about something that is essentially good?'

'These thoughts are sent by the Devil,' Father Dickinson said with surprising conviction.

David protested that he didn't believe in the Devil.

'Then your question, "Can it be wrong, etc." is meaningless,' Dickinson told him.

'The stones would be a ruby,' David said, 'to represent Christ's passion, and a sapphire to represent eternal life. It'll be pretty expensive to replace them.'

When the priest left, pulling up the skirts of his cassock as he climbed the stairs from the semi-basement, David felt more strongly than ever the now definitive loneliness of his existence in this large house that he and his wife had bought just before her cancer was diagnosed. 'Did Monica and I really love each other?' he wondered. This strange obsession was no doubt a morbid form of self-pity.

Then one evening in late autumn an opportunity at last presented itself. Returning late from a delivery in a different town, David stopped at a riverside pub that had once been a regular haunt. Perhaps there would be an old friend to talk to. Irritatingly, the main bar had been transformed into a place to watch football, with three or four screens in various corners. Turning from the counter, pint in hand, David saw his tenant Frank sitting alone, intent on the dying moments of the game.

'What'll you have?' the older man offered. They sat together watching.

'Bloody bore,' Frank pronounced when the final whistle blew. 'No one really going for it. Just cancelling each other out.' Then he lit a cigarette.

David was taken aback. 'But...' he began. The boy had obviously forgotten he wasn't supposed to be a smoker.

'Yes?' Frank asked.

'Er...' David couldn't bring himself to say it. 'Is everything OK?' he asked. 'The flat? Annette?' One couldn't stop liking the boy, he realised, just because he'd lit a cigarette.

Frank opened his mouth, let the smoke coil there, inhaled. 'Yes and no,' he sighed. 'Trouble is, running a café doesn't give you much time to live, you know. There are days you feel a bit trapped, stuck in the kitchen, like.'

It was closing time. Having come on foot, the boy accepted a lift back to the flat. David's mind fizzed with possible gambits. 'If you really want something enough,' he remembered being told, 'sooner or later you will get it.' Or: 'When God wants to punish a man, He gives him what he most desires.' 'Oh, punish me,' David prayed. He pulled the car over to the kerb.

'One for the road, Mr Markham?' Frank offered. 'I've got a decent whisky if you're up for it.'

It was a quarter to midnight. 'I am so near,' David thought. His old front door opened into the couple's sitting room. It was a stale clutter of unemptied ashtrays. A laundry basket crammed with dirty clothes occupied the red sofa. There were dirty plates on the table. David stood and stared. In the kitchen corner of the room, Frank was banging open a cupboard. He moved a few things, looking behind them, then went to another. 'It's not where you bloody well think it is!' shouted a voice from the bedroom. 'So there's no point in looking, is there, stupid!'

Turning to David, Frank exchanged a glance of weary male complicity. 'Guest, Annie!' he called. 'We have company.'

Almost at once the girl appeared in the doorway. Her long hair was uncombed. She wore a crumpled blue cotton nightdress. Her face lacked the composure make-up gives. 'Mr Markham!' she said. She held a freshly lit cigarette in her right hand, and was immediately embarrassed.

'He bought me a pint in "The Castle",' Frank was saying, and he added in a lower voice: 'Actually, I didn't think you'd be back.'

'I hope this isn't inconvenient,' David began. His mind was racing.

'Oh, not at all.' Annette stubbed out her cigarette. 'I'll just fetch the bottle.' She disappeared into the bedroom section and came back a moment later with a dark cardigan over her shoulders. 'Thursday I go out with the girls,' she explained. 'It's our only night off.'

Though he didn't need it, David asked if could use the loo. Walking down the narrow passage, he paused to get a glimpse into the bedroom. Clothes were strewn everywhere. There was a beer can on the bedside table. The sheets were lemon-coloured and seriously tangled. A black bra hung from the door handle. How many memories it brought back! Inside the small bathroom cupboard, among the standard array of creams and conditioners, was a large, un-opened box of condoms.

'Frank was telling me,' David began on his return to the sitting room, 'how difficult it is to get away from "Paradise".'

'Dead right,' Annette agreed. 'It's more like Purgatory at the moment.' In just a few moments she had contrived to empty all the ashtrays and open the windows. David found himself facing a generous glass of Ballantine's and, to his surprise, a full dish of vanilla ice cream. Frank insisted on clinking glasses. The boy now seemed determined to be cheerful.

'How come at "The Castle" then, Mr Markham?' Annette enquired.

'Call me David,' he insisted. He explained about the delivery he had made, a silver crucifix, about two hundred years old. ' "The Castle" was an old haunt of mine.'

'That's such an interesting job you have,' Frank said, shaking his head. 'I mean, your work really lasts, instead of just getting gobbled up.'

'Some of the best things in life are gobbled up,' David risked.

'Dead right,' Annette said again. She exploded in a coarse, nervous giggle. 'Have you seen our crucifix by the way? I'm Catholic, you know.' There was an ugly wooden image over the door. 'Though that's another thing about running a café: you can never get away to church.'

'You wouldn't go if you could,' Frank objected.

'I would so.'

'You would not. When did you ever go to church?'

'Only all my life,' the girl insisted.

'My wife never missed,' David put in. This was not something he had planned to say, but it seemed to create a certain effect.

'Separated are you now?' Frank enquired.

'She died,' David said. 'We lived here once you know. We had our first child here.'

'Oh, God, I'm so sorry.' There was a short silence. 'That's awful,' Annette said.

To check a welling emotion, David hurried on: 'Seriously though, kids, if the café ties you down too much, why not employ someone else?' Both young people replied at once that they couldn't possibly afford it. 'Well, if the rent for the flat here is a significant part of the equation,' David said quietly, 'don't think that we couldn't renegotiate.'

The youngsters were suddenly alert, one each side of their landlord around the table. 'What do you mean?' Annette asked. He felt their heightened attention. He swallowed. 'Well, perhaps we could find... I don't know... some other way of satisfying our requirements.' As he said this, sweating, he noticed the down of blond hair on the girl's forearms. The two had argued together of course. Hadn't he and Monica fought almost daily in the early years? They had imagined each insult was of monumental importance; then, when their bodies met again in bed, they would make up, they would make love. 'The same will be true of these two tonight,' David suddenly realised. He knew it. What a pleasure it would be to savour those moments of reconciliation. The naked young bodies under the rumpled sheets, the initial resistance, some last recriminations, then a forearm meeting a soft flank, quite casually at first, then with quiet purposefulness. Passivity turns to welcome. A sigh of surrender. 'I love you, I love you,' as they approach climax.

'But what way?' Annette repeated.

Rather unsteadily, David got to his feet. 'I'll have to go,' he said. At the door he found himself looking straight into the young woman's eyes. There was a knowingness there. 'Thanks again, mate,' Frank shouted. He seemed relieved that the evening hadn't ended worse. 'The woman is my only chance,' David told himself, descending the stairs. He knew women. He could go through the routine seduction – something in her eye had told him that was possible – then say what he really wanted. Sitting in the car, looking at the chinks of light round their curtains, it occurred to him he might wait ten minutes, then go back to the flat and say the car wouldn't start. 'At my age,' he wondered, 'how can I be so ridiculous.'

The following week, David began designing a portable communion set for a priest who took mass to the dying. The pieces must be simple and practical and stack into a small case, the kind of thing you could take to the scene of an accident. On the other hand they must convey the solemnity of the occasion, the most solemn occasion of all. David pondered over his previous efforts in this field. His wife had been so concerned about receiving last rites that she had taken them four or five times. It took her quite a while to die. How can such a ceremony make any difference? David wondered. Was there something Monica had felt particularly guilty about? 'Thursday evening is my night with the girls,' Annette had said. David forced himself to wait two weeks.

He was a completely free agent these days. There was no one to nag him when he returned home late. He had plenty of time to sit in the car and watch the couple close up the café, see them walk back to the flat, wait till Annette slipped briskly out of the main door of the block of flats towards ten. She was smartly dressed in a tight white skirt, heels. He must contrive an encounter. She had turned along the embankment, heading towards town via Victory Bridge no doubt. David started the car, crossed to a parallel street, drove two hundred yards, took the third left, parked, got out, made for the corner.

He would meet her as she came the other way. He didn't. The embankment road was empty. The river slid coldly by in the winter dark. David hurried to the first, he thought insignificant, cross street. Not a place for a night on the town. Just as he turned into it, a door was closing, on the left, among darkened shop fronts. David waited a moment, crossed the street, walked quickly by. It was the estate agency. Two hours later, from the windscreen of his car, he saw Annette reappear at the door with the chalk-striped Mr Halliday. At the corner with the embankment, she stood on tiptoe to give him a quick kiss.

In a state of some confusion, David drove quickly back home. He poured himself a whisky, turned out the light, sat on the sofa. Then noticed the answering machine was flashing. There was a rare message from his youngest son, Ian, asking for an increase in his allowance. University was proving hellishly expensive. He drained the whisky. Then, lying on the sofa in the dark, David tried to imagine Annette making love to the estate agent. It was repulsive. 'I must tell poor Frank,' he thought. 'Except...' It occurred to him now that he was in an excellent position to blackmail the girl: 'Let me watch you two make love,' he could say, 'or I'll tell Frank.' But what kind of lovemaking would this be? A charade of intimacy! Not the wholesome, beautiful thing that had enchanted him. And what if she said: 'Oh, Frank knows.' Or even: 'Don't you think Frankie sees someone else himself from time to time?' 'Perhaps our own marriage wasn't so bad after all,' David suddenly thought.

He took a double dose of tranquillisers to sleep, then woke in the middle of the night with a start. How much money was it his son had asked for? He stumbled downstairs and listened to the message again. 'Christ! I must try and earn more,' he thought. His head was groggy. 'I should take on some different work.' He stood in the dusty sitting room in his boxer shorts. How long was it since he had actually noticed the photos on the mantelpiece? He picked one up. She didn't smoke in photographs. 'How could I imagine giving up the rent?' he wondered then. 'If anything, I should increase it.' The following morning he phoned Mr Halliday and complained that despite the contract they had signed, his tenants were smoking in the flat. He had actually seen them doing so, they had invited him in, but he felt too embarrassed to speak openly to them.

'They'll have to leave,' he said abruptly.

'I will explain,' the agent promised, 'that either they stop smoking, or you'll be obliged to quantify the additional deterioration vis-à-vis the furnishings.'

'No, they'll have to leave,' David insisted. 'They lied to me.'

There was a pause on the line. 'Mr Markham,' the agent said, 'I understand your anger, but don't you think you should give them a second chance? After all, they've always paid the rent promptly.'

David couldn't respond. He hung up. 'Monica,' he said, as he banged the receiver down. 'Monica, Monica, Monica!' He burst into tears.

Globetrotters

Being temporary, the plan was to muddle through with what they'd got, what furnished flats provided. No need to buy anything. Or perhaps it was just that they were both tight with money, both appreciated wealth in terms of figures on bank statements rather than its translation into the more concrete luxuries of consumer goods. They had no television; the washing machine was ancient and frequently flooded the bathroom. It was difficult really to see how they might have come by this characteristic tightness, since neither had any history of poverty or insecurity. Nor did they have a particular goal to scrape and save for. They weren't interested in buying a house, for example. Perhaps it was just that, their money being paid as it was by the hour, when it came to spending it they had such a strong sense of the seconds and minutes being traded away they would think twice before lashing out. 'Every four hundred lire,' they would often remark, 'is a minute spent doing something you don't really want to do, being with people you don't really want to be with.'

And, of course, they were only temporary. What was the point of buying a new cooker or getting an Italian plate for the car? Next year they might be back in France, or on to Hungary. Why not? No point in fixing the dripping loo or painting the sitting room.

It became a way of life.

They met in Chartres, where she was running the Speak Out Language School. She was rather bossy. As a new teacher, he met her bossiness with a witty, robust gallantry that was never quite facetious. She found him fun.

Neither was particularly good-looking. She wore comfortable clothes: slacks, loose home-knitted sweaters, flat shoes. Her figure was boyish, her face thin and wry under pageboy hennaed hair. What did she have in the way of charms? A ready generous laugh, in the course of which she would often take a knuckle into her mouth; an unmistakable motherliness which went hand in glove with that bossiness and likewise with a certain pride in being outspoken on any and every subject. After a few weeks, it was clear that she had begun to mother Jack, and she found him a better room, in the same building as her own.

Jack wore his wiry hair rather long. In the early 1980s he was under the illusion that this was still in fashion. Or it may just have been that he found it difficult to imagine himself any different than he was. He couldn't quite bring himself to get it cut short. The same was true of his beard: despite its prickly unpleasantness on summer nights, he was afraid he would look foolish without it. Soon it was discovered that Mary was a dab hand at trimming hair and beards, and this, quite apart from removing the anxiety of what a foreign barber might do, was a not inconsiderable saving.

Jack had been to Cambridge and taken a first

in modern languages; Mary had been to teacher-training college and taught for three years in a comprehensive in Balham. Both were comfortable with this state of affairs: without 'real' experience Jack obviously needed mothering, and mothering him Mary raised her status; he found his verbal wit and mental superiority without a challenge; the repartee was all his; she looked after the practical side of things and counted the pennies.

Or rather the centimes. And later the pesos. And later the lire. For they were never going back to England. At first they thought of this as a courageous, adventurous decision which had made their lives so much more exciting than those of many other people. And Mary would always speak of it this way. But Jack was too intelligent not to appreciate over the years that there were other, less flattering motives: the easy status she found in her expatriate position; his own slight sense of shame at underachieving, which was more easily kept hidden abroad.

Without being particularly highly sexed, this mild, genuinely well-meaning young couple eventually found themselves in bed together.

It took some years to get married. There was no reason to hurry. And if Jack played something of a waiting game, not wishing to say goodbye so soon to a young man's dream of more and more beautiful women (there were his students after all), it must be said that he was always faithful. Perhaps for the same reason that he could never quite see his way to shaving off his beard. Things were OK as they were. He didn't want to make a fool of himself.

In the meantime they moved on: Marseilles first, then Barcelona, Cannes, Mantua. They took up photography and bought a slide projector, second-hand. The other lavish expense was classical records, of which they regularly bought one a week. For news and entertainment they relied heavily on the BBC World Service, yet could never quite see their way to buying a decent short-wave radio – the things were so unreasonably overpriced; so that dinner was often eaten against a background of fierce static through which Jack listened intently for cricket scores, Mary for signs that the British economy had finally gone to pieces. It was nice to think one had left a sinking ship.

In Marseilles Mary had become a vegetarian, half from conscience, half from thrift – and then it suited her conversational style, which involved fielding strong opinions. Not being a cook himself, Jack was obliged to settle for the odd supermarket cold cut on the rare occasions he ate on his own. In Barcelona they became attached to a cat, which was henceforth to make holidays rather tricky. In Cannes they lashed out on a second-hand Dyane van into which they often boasted they could fit all their worldly possessions – and frequently did, including the cat. But not the money, of course, which was transmitted safely and electronically from one bank to another. The next year they were in Mantua.

What was it they were living for exactly, or didn't they suffer from existential problems? Despite all their moves, life had a surprisingly smooth routine. They got up late and taught in the afternoon and evening. Conscientious teachers, they took satisfaction in their work and were popular with their students, predominantly middle-class people in their twenties and thirties, paying privately. But despite being so friendly, they seemed to lack the facility – or perhaps really it was the desire – to make permanent friends. Occasionally another English couple came over to dinner. Occasionally they accepted invitations out to French homes, Spanish, Italian; but they resented being shown off as oddities or interesting acquisitions to friends of friends, and then each was painfully aware, in each new country they visited, of the other's imperfect command of the language: Jack's quips, to Mary's embarrassment, would not quite be understood by these continentals; Mary's outspoken opinions grated all the more on Jack's ear as she struggled to separate Spanish from French, Italian from both. For the most part they drove about in the Dyane taking photographs sparingly, or stayed at home with the cat and the growing collection of classical records.

In Cannes, making their first tax declaration, they married. Immediately the question of children was in the air. And there it remained – in the brisk sea air of the Côte d'Azur, in the minty air of a North Italian spring. Jack and Mary had no mechanism for making momentous decisions of this kind. When they decided on a move, it was because they had heard of a job offer through the grapevine, or because an old acquaintance got in touch; when they took on the cat, it was because it was already living in the garden of a flat they had rented. Both came from large families and both, in principle, were very much in favour of having children. They retained an unspoken, to some extent even unconscious respect for the family ideal. If they had a vision of themselves in the distant future, it was that at forty or fifty they would be there with a family around them. Yet this future didn't seem to grow out of their present. The moment was never quite right for a pregnancy. They were temporary. The Italian health service was questionable. It would be expensive. There were other moves to be made, countries to go to. And if only they could have made suitable arrangements for the cat, there were holidays too. Jack very much wanted to photograph Prague, assuming they could get there in the Dyane. Mary did skip her pills for a couple of weeks once, teasing fate, but fate didn't bite; nothing came of it. So she kept her lean boyish figure; it was Jack who filled out and had to start watching his starches.

Still, for Mary's motherliness there were always the outlets of Jack, of the cat, and of what Jack chose to refer to as her 'lame ducks'. For if this expatriate couple were in general sufficient unto themselves and felt no need to cultivate friendships, there were nevertheless those who occasionally felt the need to cultivate them. Or rather, there was the occasional lost young Englishman, far from home, far from knowing quite what he was about, who needed Mary, who felt immensely attracted to her staunch and sexless English woman's common sense, her knowing, caring smile, her housework-red hands.

Such was Nigel Winslow-Adams.

Jack met him through an expat cricket team he'd joined to keep his weight down. He told him there was work going at the Balmoral school where Mary was teaching. And within a few weeks Nigel was pouring out his sorrows to her in the breaks between lessons.

How did it come about that what began as such a big joke could bring them so near to disaster? Nigel's manner was so hilarious, such a marvellous combination of caricature physical features, Ned Seagoon accent and downright neurotic gestures. His skin, drawn tight and ruddy across prominent nose and cheekbones, had a peculiarly polished woodenish quality to it, on which he chose to sport the most carefully trimmed, almost carved moustache, geometric above girlish red lips. The expression he most frequently assumed with this odd, slightly elongated face, was one of arrogance mixed with knowing sarcasm, a sort of fragile smugness constantly belied by the nervous tic he had of twisting and twisting at the corner of that wooden moustache. His hair was worn Twenties style, ruthlessly slicked back from a tall forehead. His eyes were glassily green.

But it was Nigel's voice that transformed all the rest into comedy. He spoke with a painfully slow, aristocratic, adenoidal drawl which he contrived to combine with the most drastic of stress patterns in such remarks as: 'How *very, very super*', or, 'Mary, my d*ea*r, you have my most *heart*felt, my *warm*est thanks', or even, 'Jolly good *show*, Jack my man, jolly jolly good *show*'.

'Like listening to Kenneth Williams dragging out the last fifteen seconds of *Just a Minute*,' Mary observed. 'Only without the humour.'

Jack soon became expert at mimicking this voice and the things it would say, to the point where he and Mary would spend entire mealtimes in stitches, missing *News about Britain* entirely. Not that they were in any way mean to Nigel. On the contrary, the entertainment value he provided made them more generous with their time and attention than they might otherwise have been. And in any case, they were both quite sensitive to others and their problems, perhaps because they were not without a certain underlying fragility themselves. Nigel became a regular dinner guest. He brought boxes of slides he had taken on his kayaking expeditions, for he a*dor*ed kayaking. He showed them his new Sony ICF 7600 digital short-wave radio, and insisted on having them listen to English broadcasts from Tirana and the Arab Emirates. He described a computer programme he was writing for teaching English. Occasionally he said: 'Of course, *you* fellows can't really understand what it's *like* for a poor chap like yours truly to be *liv*ing on his *own*. Entirely on his own.' Sometimes he might even add: 'Without a *glim*mer of hope.'

Nigel was thirty-two and had spent a year some while back in a psychiatric home in Surrey. His problem, he explained to Mary on only the second occasion they spoke, was a dominant mother figure, a successful musician who had given him an acute inferiority complex. His father had died when he was still a child. The inferiority complex had made it very difficult for him to work or to have relationships with girls. And if he was in Italy now doing a job that was considerably below his capacities, it was because he felt so much better when he was a long way from his mother and his mother's criticism, and because he found Italian girls, with their more formal manners and expectations, easier to approach.

Mary remarked to her husband that sometimes Nigel's ears were the colour of tomatoes, and that his Italian, when he spoke to the rather pretty secretary at the school, was simply a riot. 'Eton Mantovano,' she said. 'Has to be heard to be believed.' But in her motherly way she did feel genuinely concerned for Nigel – his sadness at living alone and yearning for romance – and she always listened, however boring or pompous he was, and was always ready with small gifts of home-made cake or jam, or suggestions or invitations that might cheer him up. Not believing it for a moment, but nevertheless out of real kindness, she would regularly assure him that he was bound to find a girl sometime with the looks he had. In bed she and Jack debated whether he might be a virgin or not. Jack said: 'I really would be *most grate*ful for a teensy bit of *han*ky panky,' and they both went into convulsions of laughter.

Nigel repaid their meals and attention with gifts so large and lavish it became rather embarrassing: a new oven was delivered, a state-of-the-art, auto-focus carousel slide projector, and for Christmas there was an Amstrad computer. 'Not to worry you *chaps*,' he said. 'I've got nothing *else* to spend the *lol*ly on, and you're the ones who need it, *you're* the ones who'll probably have a family, *not* little old Nigel.' Soon after the Amstrad, he began to arrive for every evening meal uninvited.

Jack and Mary found themselves defenceless in the face of this invasion. It was perplexing. Nigel would settle before their computer screen, which only seemed to get turned on when he came, and proceed to enthuse over some new piece of software that had just arrived from England. He was '*fasc*inated', he said, by the possibility of combining, for example, a regular spreadsheet programme with a commercial language course. 'Just *fasc*inated.' Rapidly he keyed in some figures. 'Just a*maz*ing the tricks these little *jig*gers can play.' His voice was awesomely slow, so adenoidal, it seemed it must be a parody of itself. And when Jack showed some scepticism, Nigel said: 'I sup*pose* you don't i*mag*ine this old boy is really *up* to that kind of thing. But I'll sur*prise* you all one day, you mark my words, *surprise* you all.' And there was that smile of fragile smugness, thumb and index finger fidgeting at the corner of his moustache.

He began to arrive at weekends too now: 'Chaps, listen, I've bought a duck for Sunday lunch. What do you think about that? Haven't had duck for ages. No one to cook it for me.'

They had been planning to go out, but were somehow unable to resist Nigel's flair for the fait accompli. So Mary cooked the duck, but wouldn't waive her vegetarian principles to eat the thing – leaving all the more for Jack and Nigel. And over the bird their benefactor talked incessantly, as he would when warmed with wine, about the beauty of which- ever of his students he happened to be infatuated with at the time: 'The pastel *drama* of her face; the *pride*ful arch of those *eye*brows, the soft, the ins*tinct*- ive lightness of her arms.' But for the absence of static, Jack thought, they might have been listening to some idiot on *Meridian*.

'You *fell*ows just can't *imag*ine what it's *like* for a chap like me to be *so* in love and *so* hopeless.'

He turned to Mary for her look of motherly sympathy, but for once, from over her cold beans and salad, she said rather brusquely: 'Why don't you just bloody well ask the girl out then. She's only human.'

'Yes,' Jack came in with false innocence, sipping the Cabernet Nigel had also supplied, 'why don't you just, er, ask the young filly out. Maybe she's ripe for a bit of the old one-two.'

Nigel laid down his fork. 'I'm afraid *you* chaps just don't under*stand* the kind of respect a fellow like *me* has for a young, er, *lass*y like that. And she is definitely *not* human. I*lar*ia is di*vine*.'

He pronounced her name with a wildly exaggerated travesty of an Italian accent.

'She doesn't shit?' Jack enquired.

'Oh, Jack,' Mary snapped, and to Nigel: 'I just meant you should be a bit more practical, love. If you want to have any hope at all.' She cocked her head rather sweetly to one side, remembering motherliness.

'I sometimes *do wond*er,' Nigel reflected in his slow smug drawl, 'whether *hope* isn't more *cru*el than des*pair*.'

The previous week he had talked in a not dissimilar way about a girl called Silvia. The following month it was Luisa, and later Mariangela. 'The fact is,' said Mary, who enjoyed indulging in a sort of Sunday-newspaper psychoanalysis, 'he seems permanently trapped in an early-adolescent-crush phase.'

'And we with him,' Jack remarked. 'He's here every bloody evening, not to mention Saturdays and Sundays.'

They took to getting up much earlier than they normally would have at the weekends, even skipping their ritual breakfast, to be out before he came. Still bleary-eyed, they climbed into the Dyane and drove off with the camera to photograph the snow up in the mountains, the cherry blossom in the hills, the fields scarlet with poppies, or simply some village their guidebook had told them was interesting, a carnival parade or snail fair. But the day was marred by the certainty that at the end of it they would find Nigel waiting patiently on their doorstep.

'This is worse than having a kid,' Jack said. 'Let's tell him to fuck off. Could you *please* fuck off,' he added in Nigel's drawl.

'Oh, you have to feel sorry for him though.' Mary said.

'I feel sorry for God knows how many million blacks dying in Ethiopia, but I don't have them over to dinner every night, do I?'

'He's so generous,' Mary said, 'and he does mean well.'

But what she meant, Jack knew, was that they had taken too much in the way of loot just to tell him to get lost now. They should never have accepted those first gifts of course, that was the truth. They should have nipped the whole thing in the bud. But it had been so tempting to come across such major acquisitions while still keeping all the cash in the bank. And because of that double-barrelled name they had somehow imagined Nigel was quite rich and it meant nothing to him to lash out on a washing machine, a slide projector. Whereas now it transpired, from a letter Mary had seen in his locker at the school, that he had nothing more than his salary from the Balmoral. His famous mother was always in debt.

So they would get home from the mountains, from the lake, from Vicenza, Bologna, Venice, and there, sitting on the low wall outside their block, reading his computer manual, swinging his legs, was Nigel; with a present of six crystal wine glasses, perhaps, under the arm of an incongruous tweed jacket. Only now it was too late did they appreciate how completely they had been bought.

'So the obvious thing to do,' says Jack, 'is to move, flit, do a bunk.'

They had never seriously argued before. Mary had sometimes got on to Jack about his laziness in the kitchen; he had occasionally objected that she was obsessive about house-cleaning and the role she thought he should play in it. Sometimes they had shouted at each other. But they were cautious rather than passionate people, and each had a strong sense of the contract they had entered into and the reciprocal benefits that it brought. They had no intention of messing up their lives. Except that now there seemed no hope of compromise: Jack wanted to go, at all costs, and Mary was equally determined not to.

'Move? With a washing machine?' she protested. 'And an oven, and a colour TV? How are we supposed to get those in the Dyane? We're so well set up here now. We can wait at least a couple of years before moving.'

'By which time we'll need a fleet of removal trucks. Not to mention an extra space in the car for Father Christmas.'

Then Jack might say: 'We managed well enough before without all this stuff, didn't we?'

'*I* managed,' Mary came back. 'Anyway, a vegetarian needs good cooking facilities. Otherwise you end up with a rotten diet.'

'So buy another oven when we get there.'

The proposed destination was Athens.

'What's the big deal? They don't cost the earth,' Jack insisted.

'And what are we supposed to do with this one? And the washing machine? And...'

'Sell them,' Jack said. 'Or leave them with Mr Bountiful, seeing as he...'

'Don't be silly.'

But Jack couldn't see why he was being. 'You don't want to be stuck in stupid provincial Mantua for the rest of your life, do you? With that great adenoidal albatross round your neck.'

'What does he need a washing machine for?' Mary asked. 'He only has his own underwear to do. And when he doesn't eat here he goes to the pizzeria. You can't go giving people things back. They'd be offended.'

Man and wife looked at each other.

'I'm happy here,' she said. 'The rent's low. We've got everything we need.'

'We are living with constant harassment,' Jack said, slowly and carefully, almost menacingly now. 'We are sharing every spare moment, our entire social lives, with a goof, one of the walking wounded, and an arrogant stupid bastard into the bargain. And the way you talk one can't help suspecting that you don't really mind. That you feel flattered. Next thing we know, he'll be elbowing for room in our bed.'

'I don't know what you mean to insinuate by that.'

'Or buying us a bigger one to make sure he can fit. 'Just a little *thought* of mine, you *fel*lows, since we've all become such *sup*er pals.'

'Stop mimicking him. It isn't funny any more.'

'Precisely. It isn't funny any more, it's got to stop.'

'Look, Jack' – Mary was terse and earnest – 'you like to play so tough, but the fact is he would quite probably commit suicide if we just walked out on him. He's always saying we saved his life. You know he's had problems.'

Jack's groan was interrupted by the sound of the doorbell, and before anyone went to answer, this childless expatriate couple stared daggers at each other.

Their friend had bought bubbly and a packet of cream cakes. The threesome sat down to dinner.

'By the way, Nigel old chap,' Jack brought out with cavalier facetiousness over a vegetarian quiche. 'We've decided to move on, split the scene. Athens, you know.'

Nigel hardly blinked; he might perfectly well have been expecting it.

'Marvellous,' he drawled. 'Jolly marvellous. I've always wanted to see the Parthenon. Some of the finest sculpture in the world, you know.' After a few minutes he added, 'Coastal area too, excellent sea-kayaking. Not to mention the photos you chaps can take.'

In bed later Mary laughed. It was hardly worth

going, if little doggy followed. Was it? So he could forget that idea. But Jack said on the contrary, they could pack the car and flee at night – go to Yugoslavia or somewhere. Or South America. That should be far enough.

'Oh, come on, why don't you just be sensible and forget it. It'll blow over soon enough. Anyway, he's not such bad company.'

Jack experienced a sharp and growing sense of impotence; or perhaps, to be more precise, it was a sense of Mary's awareness of his impotence: to which he reacted over the following days and weeks with an increasing internal fury that found no outlet. He had lost command of the situation, of his life, and couldn't seem to regain it. He was doomed to having this unpleasant saphead at his table for the rest of his days. Normally quintessentially pleasant, Jack became gruff and aggressive. And raised the stakes. If she wouldn't go, he would go on his own.

'Oh, that'll be the day.'

An atmosphere of armed truce had crept up on them. 'But surely you can't be happy with things the way they are.'

Oblivious to removal costs, Nigel had bought a crystal-topped coffee table in a taste they didn't quite share, but knew was expensive.

'Everybody should be willing to look after at least one other person in life. You can't just go on living entirely for yourself, pushing everyone else away. No man is an island,' she said.

And when they were getting up one morning she remarked: 'Anyway, what about the money in the bank?'

'What about it?'

'When you go off on your own.'

'Oh, so you want me to go off now?'

'I didn't say that. I said what about the money?'

'Split it fifty-fifty.'

'No way,' she said, drawing her lips thin.

'Why not?'

'No way,' she repeated, as if somehow this might be a trick of his. 'And what about our marriage?'

'We wouldn't be the first,' he said.

Not having really argued before, it all sounded very dramatic, and made Jack at least feel rather ill. Without actually having made any practical plans, he continued to refer to his departure as something which became more imminent every day. 'Mary Rogers,' he needled, 'trapped by the arrival of a washing machine and an oven. Her mind was too small for electrical appliances not to loom large in.'

'Fuck off, Mr Witty,' she said.

The result was that now they couldn't even enjoy themselves when Nigel wasn't there. They stopped going off on their photography expeditions, stopped buying their classical records, stopped discussing students and lessons, prices and rates with each other. Increasingly hostile, they became strangers. Indeed, it began to seem as if they simply didn't like each other any more.

So that Jack now announced that he would definitely be going at the end of the summer term, some six weeks away, with her or without her. It was a firm decision. However, having set this deadline, he immediately became feverish about it. Because even if he felt he couldn't put up with the situation as it was a moment longer, still it was hard to revise one's vision of one's life so radically.

'Don't imagine,' she said grimly, 'you can scare me into changing my mind,' and she rolled away from him across the bed. Love hadn't been made for upwards of a month now. Jack had had to trim his beard on his own.

But Nigel appeared to notice none of this. Regularly there at dinner, he took advantage of their having given up their weekend trips to spend all Saturday and Sunday with them. His gratitude was as effusive and mannered as ever, his supply of slides, 'poor-me' stories and gifts quite endless. And as the weeks slipped by and the end of term drew near, Jack despaired of Mary's motherly tone, of the complacent way she took and stashed away the contraband, the way she said: 'Oh, don't always be so pessimistic, Nigel love, I'm sure things will look up in the end.'

He was slumped on the sofa, playing with the corner of his moustache. 'You are *super*, Mary dear, but I'm *afraid* I'm al*ready* a confirmed *ba*chelor really. Just have to thank one's pro*ver*bial stars that two such' – he paused – 'such m*arvel*lous people are willing to make a *home* for me.'

Jack groaned. He could perfectly well see them moving in together the moment he was gone. But he could never have guessed that just a week, a mere week away from having his bluff called, things did, as Mary had unwittingly prophesied, look up for Winslow-Adams. And the tide turned.

'*Some*one,' Nigel announced completely out of the blue and with quite boundless smugness from over a plate of artichoke pasta, '*some*one, I'd have you chaps *know*, gave me a *jam tart* last night. Now *what about that?*'

This startling non sequitur was such a splendid example of Winslow-Adams-speak that Jack and Mary immediately exchanged the kind of glance they hadn't indulged in for many weeks. Jack had to clench his teeth together.

'I beg your pardon?' Mary asked.

'Yes, *some*one here's been *rat*her a lucky *boy*, I'd say. My *word* I would.' With finger and thumb he carefully smoothed out that moustache. His wooden face beamed.

They waited, not realising how fateful the moment was.

'Aren't you going to tell us?' Mary enquired.

'Yes, do spill the beans, m'dear.' Jack screwed his face into a parody of camp public-school eagerness.

Nigel continued to smooth his moustache under the polished nose. It was infuriating, after his months of moping, how much he appeared to enjoy the sudden superiority a secret gave.

'Yes, I'd say *some*body was *rath*er su*perb*ly enter-*tain*ed last night.'

'You what?' Mary was getting angry.

Jack laid a hand patronisingly on his wife's arm. 'I believe the somebody must be himself, while the entertainment may refer to the fact that he was here for dinner last night.'

'Oh, *gett*ing warm,' Nigel clapped his hands, immensely amused. 'But *not* very.'

Mary obviously had half an idea they were both taking her for a ride in some way. 'And the jam tart?' she demanded. 'Did you go out somewhere?'

'Yes, now I come to think of it, you did leave rather early last night,' Jack mused, remembering his surprise and relief. 'Off to the discothèque, I imagine.'

Nigel beamed: '*Some*body had a rather super time,' he repeated. But would say no more.

In bed the intensity of Mary's speculation far outweighed the animosity of recent weeks. They were talking again. 'If he's got himself a girlfriend,' she protested, 'why can't he just damn well tell us? He's always told us everything before.'

'Nothing worse than a loser with the whip hand,' Jack observed, keeping a told-you-so tone just hovering beyond the edge of his voice. What he personally found fascinating was the extent to which 'jam tart' was, yes, a sexual innuendo – inevitably so – but then at once so explicit and so left-field it seemed impossible Nigel could really have intended it as such.

Eventually, after a considerable amount of more teasing on Nigel's part, and after his skipping dinner for two evenings in a row – unheard-of – it emerged that he had been taken over by the teenage girl who worked in the *pasticceria* a couple of blocks down from his bedsit, and who now regularly brought him any remaining cakes or fruit pies at the end of the day. Monica and her jam tarts.

'A slut,' Mary pronounced grimly, for she had immediately gone over there to have a cappuccino and spy out the land. 'Overdressed – short skirts, tights with seams at the back, Madonna lookalike hair – flirts with all the men who come in. Kisses all round.'

'My kind,' Jack said.

'But don't you see? He's convinced she's in love with him while she probably imagines he's got money because he's so generous. When she finds out and lets him down, he's going to be destroyed.'

For in fact Nigel was referring to her now as his 'angel' and his 'dove'.

'That's his lookout.'

'You may not care, but I for one don't want to see him going to pieces after all we've done to get him on an even keel.'

Jack had nothing to say to this.

Over the following weeks, while Nigel's visits became less and less regular, his smugness when he did turn up grew all but intolerable. 'My *God*,' he chuckled, twisting the end of his moustache, '*there* you are just going about your ordinary everyday business when something like this *pops* up and *bonks* you over the head.' He laughed out loud. ' "Bonks" perhaps not the very *best* choice of *word* in this context. *Ha ha*.' He beamed complacently. 'I *imag*ine you chaps must *env*y me, eh? But then *ev*ery dog must have his *day*, as they say, don't you think?' And he said: 'I sup*pose* you could say I'm com*mit*ted to Italy heart and *soul* now. Have to let *you* fellows jolly off to Athens on your own, you know.'

'Oh yes?' Mary said. She seemed intent on taking the whole thing as a personal affront. Not a single gift had arrived since the evening of the jam tart, not a single confidence had been confided, just ambiguous allusions in rather dubious taste. Jack, on the other hand, was immensely relieved to have been let off the hook. There was no more talk of his going off on his own now. And while he and Mary hadn't exactly 'made it up', he was so much enjoying her disorientation it was very much as if they had. Life was pleasant again. He felt in control.

'He hasn't actually said they've been to bed yet,' Mary observed, clutching at straws. Nigel had left this evening almost as soon as his minestrone was swallowed. 'Where *bet*ter than a *pasticceria* for *dessert?*' He smiled knowingly, arching a thin eyebrow.

'Yes,' Jack said, teasing, 'you wish he'd just come out with it and say she was a damn good lay, instead of all this sibylline "*Some*one was a rather lucky *fel*low again last night." '

'I meant,' she insisted, 'that there was still hope of him not being completely hooked. After all, he's had his crushes before.'

Jack said nothing.

'Shows what kind of bloke he is, though,' she said, opening a cheap pack of biscuits to eat with their imported instant coffee. 'Over here for dinner every night for yonks and then he drops you just like that for the first silly scrubber who thinks his money's worth the effort. And never even bothers to invite us to meet her.'

'Perhaps they're really in love. They don't have time for anybody else.'

'Don't make me laugh, he just buys her gold earrings and dirty underwear and she thinks he's good for a giggle.'

Jack shook his head: 'Too exciting for me,' he said. It never crossed his mind that Mary might perhaps have appreciated the occasional diamond and lacy undies.

When the true extent of their friend's infatuation finally came out some days later, it was with an expression Jack could never have imagined hearing in Nigel's mouth. Sprawled in their one comfortable armchair, polished face radiantly smug, nose shining, apropos of nothing, he began: 'No *doubt* you will think it *ra*ther pre*cipi*tous of the old chap, but Nigel and his little *lady* have decided to, er, *shack up* together.' He smiled very knowingly at their amazed struggle for something to say. '*Found* ourselves a little *pad* by the lagoon.'

'Very nice,' Jack smiled weakly.

Mary began: 'But don't you think…'

Nigel, however, was in triumphant mood and didn't even appear to notice she was speaking. 'Yes, it *does* rather *seem* as though the miracle has *finally* taken place. I can't see *any* other way to *look* at it really. This little *angel* has *saved* old Nigel's life.'

Mary's open mouth snapped shut.

'And not before *time* either, I'm *sure* you would agree.'

Jack was thoroughly enjoying himself. He crossed his legs and twined his fingers round the uppermost knee. Smiling innocently, he rocked a little from side to side. 'So we can, er, look forward to some jolly old dinner parties together, eh? All four of us. Goody-oh. More the merrier.' And then when Nigel said nothing, he added, '*N'est-ce-pas?*'

They were all surprised by the short but rather awkward silence that followed. Wasn't it an exciting prospect? Nigel fidgeted.

'Well, a good*bye* party certainly. I *thought* you brave *globe*trotters were off to Athens. Er, *rather soon*.'

Mary and Jack exchanged brief glances. Uncrossing and recrossing his legs, Jack said: 'The move isn't exactly a hundred per cent wrapped up as yet.'

'Ah.' Nigel seemed to make no attempt to hide his disappointment.

'Wouldn't you rather we stayed?' Mary resorted to her maternal tone, though it wasn't without a slightly peeved edge to it. 'I mean, you've only known the girl a few weeks, and if things go wrong...'

'Yes, of *course*, of course.' Nigel paused, not so much hesitating as calculating it seemed: 'Just that *if* you chaps *do*, er, feel it's *time* for you to *toddle* along, young *Ni*gel here was rather *count*ing on your, er, leaving behind the cooker and fridge, and *may*be the coffee table too. You see, the new, er, es*tab*lishment is somewhat *spar*tan to say the least, and I always *feel* it's the *man* about the house should lay on the a*me*nities.'

Later on in an evening whose atmosphere always seemed brittle under the weight of things left unsaid, Mary proposed with fake brightness and apparent practicality that Nigel might just have Monica sleep over at his place and forget the new flat for the moment. 'At least until you're sure it's the right thing. No point in rushing everything and then finding yourself in a mess.'

'Oh *real*ly, Mary,' this ex-psychiatric patient chuckled over a Glenfiddich that had been one of his last gifts, 'that *is* really rather un*worth*y of you, you know. I mean, *caut*ion and *love* can *hard*ly make good, er *bed*fellows, if you'll excuse me my little innuendo, *can* they Jack? In for a *pen*ny, in for a p-o-u-n-d. And then, of course, I *dear*ly want to make the little lady a *prop*er home, such as she most *roy*ally deserves.'

'Spot on,' Jack agreed. 'Champion. My sentiments entirely. Marry her as soon as you can, I'd say.' He smiled at his wife, wondering if her famous outspokenness was about to prompt her to tell Winslow-Adams his beloved was a whore and had frequently been observed embracing men who came into her shop and even leaving it with them, etc. etc.

But Nigel was imperturbable. 'Well, now you mention it, I *have* popped the *ques*tion of course, but the di*vine* creature says she's worried about *rush*ing me into things, you know. Very con*sid*erate of her, when you think about it.'

'Oh, God,' Mary couldn't help saying, and went into the kitchen to heat coffee and milk on the two next-to-new, stainless-steel burners she loved so much. And as soon as he had gone she announced: 'I'll phone the landlady tomorrow morning first thing. I don't suppose she'll need more than a week's notice.' Then later she said: 'He can have his bloody appliances for all I care. If that's all he cares about friends, giving people things and then taking them back. And after all the meals we've cooked for him!'

She had already begun to pull things out of drawers, dust off the suitcases.

'Otherwise how are we supposed to get everything in the Dyane?' she said, as one demanding the obvious. 'Or no?'

'Yes, that would be a problem,' Jack smiled, and before going to sleep they made love quite passionately, though without the rhythm and proficiency of the routine past. Lying on their backs not quite satisfied afterwards, she said: 'Maybe it's time we had a baby, Jack.'

'Maybe it is.' He was looking through the dark at the bulky shapes of the furniture, furniture they would never have chosen if the place had been their own. 'Bit difficult just when we're planning to move again, though.'

News of Nigel and Monica's first-born arrived a year or so later, when they were packing up their fifth-floor Athens flat and moving off to the cooler climes of Stockholm. Jack had been suffering a lot from the heat, though he still kept his beard and spreading paunch.

'Us lucky chaps have had a little boy,' Nigel's card said. 'Eight pounds, the little blighter. Called him Arthur, after Dad. Nothing like exorcising the old ghosts, eh? Hope to get together with you fellows again before too long. NWA.'

'You wonder why he doesn't sketch in the stress pattern when he writes,' Jack remarked. 'It would add so much.'

They were in Copenhagen when they heard of the second, a little girl; and if the angelic Monica frequently and blatantly cheated on him, as a mutual acquaintance they came across on a Channel ferry hilariously explained, dear Nigel didn't appear to know anything about it. His brief letter oozed the joys of parenthood. He'd be so delighted, he said, if they came to see his children.

'Well I'd bloody well tell him,' Mary observed grimly to Jack, but then apparently forgot about it. Her face had shrunk dramatically under high cheekbones.

Lisbon brought news of twins, this was '89, and two years later, finding themselves in Munich, nothing would be easier for this well-oiled couple than to sort out a good selection of slides and drive down to Mantua for the weekend in their Datsun jeep to pay the man the visit his letters always asked for. For curiosity's sake, if nothing else. After much map consulting and stopping strangers, they found the place way out in the suburbs towards the industrial south-west of the city, a fourth-floor flat in a six-storey run-down condominium.

'*Welcome, wel*come to our humble abode, oh, how *jolly* sp*len*did to see you fellows again. Monica! Oh, Monica!' Older but unchanged, enthusiastic but smugly so, as if this uninviting apartment were telling an unqualified success story, Nigel turned woodenly to his wife, and in a parody of the local dialect announced: 'Monica angel, these are the two dear people I told you about who saved my life when I was so down, otherwise we might never have met.'

A plump bright young woman with two toddlers clinging to her jeans burst out of a door and all but rushed to embrace them, arms wide open, chubby red cheeks beaming, lips parted in a huge welcoming smile, though one tooth was grey. And as her generous mouth gaily found his cheeks, brushed just lightly across his beard, poor Jack was overwhelmed by the sudden communication of an immense wave of emotional warmth. It was almost as if an oven had been opened full blast in his frosty face. The little woman kissed him, briefly hugged him and, in that instant of innocent ritual contact, this now middle-aged man found himself intensely aware of the gift of her body, her vitality, of a sudden charge of life thrilling through his own flesh. She stepped back. Sparkling dark eyes looked up warm and plainly naked into his cold green. Jack tingled. There had been a definite whiff of sweat and cheap perfume, extraordinarily intimate. Then the whine of a little girl called Monica away. Jack sat down on a shabby armchair. He hadn't felt like this since he was sixteen.

'How insufferably complacent,' was Mary's comment, no sooner than the jeep was on the road the following afternoon, for they had a cat back in Munich who couldn't be left on her own too long. 'I don't know how we ever put up with him. And with that ridiculous voice he has.'

'You'd promised not to criticise,' Jack said, 'if I remember.'

'Well, anyway, I told him what Alec told us. I felt it was my duty really as an old friend. I mean, you can't leave somebody in total ignorance, can you? It's quite clear she plays around, just look at the way she couldn't leave you alone all weekend, all that squeezing your arm every time she spoke to you. Oh, don't pretend you didn't notice.'

Jack had no comment to make.

'And you know what he said?' Mary demanded.

'Hit me with it.'

'He just gave me one of his snortiest laughs and

said Alec was jealous because his own wife had left him. Alec jealous! I mean, it's incredible. He's obviously never dreamt of what she's up to. After all these years, it's still "my angel, my little darling"; you know how he was.'

Jack said nothing. He felt depressed and somehow couldn't bring himself to imitate Nigel just at the moment. After a while he offered vaguely: 'Nice kids.'

'The girl is a bit boss-eyed,' Mary said. 'They should get her seen by a specialist.' And she said: 'Good job we didn't have kids, though. Look what it's done to her figure. And then being forced so far out into the suburbs like that to find space. Those Italian estates are the pits. Plus they're short of money, obviously. The furniture was the end.'

'At least they chose it themselves.'

'What's the point when you can't afford what you want? Not to mention her teeth. She should really get something done about that.'

That evening, since they had arrived home in good time, Jack and Mary had Trevor Godwin over to dinner, a nice young Oxford graduate, rather lost in Germany, perhaps homosexual – it was a frequent subject for speculation in bed. They ate a mushroom risotto with a bottle of Custoza which had been Nigel's parting gift, and showed slides of Copenhagen. Trevor was moody as always, Mary at her kindest and most motherly. Jack cheered up and became hilariously witty as he told their guest the story of Nigel. '*Some*one,' he announced, 'gave *this* lucky fellow a *jam tart* last night.' It brought the house down. Except that with the shocked flush brought by Monica's embrace still vivid in his memory, the woman's sparkling eyes, her smell, Jack now had a sudden inkling of what Nigel might really have felt that night of the first jam tart. And he experienced immense regret.

Playing with an Ariel free-gift solar-battery calculator in their bedroom that evening, however, it was discovered that this forty-four-year-old globetrotting couple did have the equivalent of £120,000 sterling in a German bank. 'Which very approximately,' Jack remarked, 'amounts to spending twelve thousand hours being with people you don't really want to be with, doing things you don't really want to do.'

'But not to be sniffed at all the same,' said Mary.

Dives

At the 1964 Olympics, Steve 'the lightning bolt' Lozinsky invented the triple somersault with a tuck and roll between the first and second and the second and third turns. Even before he hit the pool in perfect perpendicular, all the judges but the Russian were preparing to show ten. A naturalised American, Steve was born in the U.S.S.R. Celebrating his gold, he spent several drunken nights with the Polish women's 400-metre relay team, causing teenage wife Sophie to return to her parents with baby Boris.

Lozinsky missed the '68 Olympics having damaged his back practising a sequence his trainer described as 'sheer folly'. But the long hospitalisation brought about a reconciliation with Sophie, and their daughter Natasha was born in 1970. The little girl was thus present at the pool in Munich in 1972, when Lozinsky took gold again with the simply astonishing corkscrewed backward somersault and double sideways roll. Everybody remarked on the apparent impossibility of the diver's body straightening up before hitting the water. Nine-year-old Boris plunged his head in his mother's breasts and refused to watch. An excellent violinist, the boy had never learnt to swim. 'Diving is about getting the most out of that very short space of time we all have before gravity catches up with us,' Lozinsky told the press, before himself setting off to catch up with Bavaria's bars and brothels. With her parents in a rest home,

Sophie turned a blind eye. Boris' schooling did not come cheap.

After the motorbike accident and ankle amputation that put an end to his career in the pool, Lozinsky took up white-water kayaking. His one regret was that he could never get Boris to join him on his descents of the Rockies' most challenging creeks. Daughter Natasha's bronze at the cross-country skiing championships in 1992 left him unimpressed, perhaps because it coincided with the divorce that saw Lozinsky leave Sophie for a pretty Japanese would-be model.

Fortunately, there was Boris at home to keep his mother company. In his thirties now, he was struggling to get his music performed. 'It's rather more difficult,' he would point out, 'to get people to understand a musical score than a triple forward somersault.' Sophie said she thanked God every day that her boy had found a steady job at the bank. When father and son met, Lozinsky demanded to know why on earth his son wasn't playing the stock market. In 1999 the ex-athlete made a fortune on the NASDAQ, only to lose everything two years later. He declared bankruptcy, sold his house and moved into a bedsit in the Bronx. To everybody's surprise, the Japanese girl stayed.

In late January 2004, Boris left the bank half an hour early, took the subway up to the Washington Bridge, set out to walk across it, but, before even reaching the river, jumped over the parapet onto the rocks sixty metres below. Heartbroken, Lozinsky could never understand why his son hadn't walked just that little bit further, 'so at least he could have dived into water'.

Mary Knew about Marilyn

Mary knew, or had known, of course, about Marilyn, but not about any of the others, until one day Richard felt moved to give Norseha the key to his apartment. Why had he taken this extraordinary step? To date, only two people had keys apart from himself: Mrs Liang, the cleaning lady – a tiny Chinese woman, as discreet as she was industrious – and, naturally, his wife, or ex-wife, Mary. In Richard's defence, it must be said that he had no idea how often Mary visited the apartment when he was away. His routine absences she kept clearly marked on the calendar in her kitchen. When they dined together each Wednesday, assuming he was in town, Richard freely told her of any special missions. There was a presentation he must give in Berlin, a conference in Sarajevo. Then, knowing that he was away, Mary would climb the shabby stairs two floors to the gloomy little apartment Richard had found himself in such haste nine (or was it even ten?) years ago, when she threw him out.

In the early days, the overriding purpose of these visits had been to reassure herself that the bitch Marilyn had really gone. But very quickly Mary had grown to like just spending a quiet hour or two in her husband's living space, stretched out on the sofa perhaps, or wandering back and forth between shadowy sitting room and spartan bedroom. Though Richard had not, as it turned out, been true to her, he was unvaryingly true to himself. The place was scrupulously tidy. All his old cassettes, CDs and videos were carefully shelved in alphabetical order (apparently he had chosen not to bother with DVDs). The books and files likewise. There were no ornaments, just one carefully circumscribed space, in the bathroom, for a collage of photos, none less than fifteen years old. Though he was rich now, the furniture was all simple and second-hand, as if the better life of bourgeois middle age were yet to begin. Mary sighed. In the end it was very like being back in their old apartment before the breakup. Her husband was the sort of meticulously tidy man who left little for a mother, wife or cleaning lady to do: just vacuum and wipe the dusty surfaces. Nothing was ever out of place. On occasion, Mary had found herself weeping here. But more often than not she took a melancholy pleasure in the material expression of her man's personality. Sometimes she would take off her clothes and lie down on his dark sheets. She was careful to leave no trace.

Of all his girlfriends, Norseha had lasted so long, she explained to Richard, because she was the exact blend of Mary and Marilyn. She gave him spice in bed but was never bitchy out of it. Or unfaithful. If there was one thing this young woman loved to talk about with chirpy confidence and shining eyes, it was how they had become lovers, how she had understood that she was the girl for him. 'I'm a whore and a Madonna,' she announced complacently. 'All your other women were one or the other.'

Richard, it has to be said, was rather fat these days, and hardly in good shape with all he smoked and drank. His skin had an unhealthy pallor, his head was settling into his shoulders, his long hair, tied back in the ponytail of twenty years before, was thinning. All the other women, he reflected, had been at least ten, if not twenty years older than Norseha. He couldn't get over the willingness of this pretty young student to share his bed, her apparent contentment with a body that could hardly compete with the physique of her contemporaries. But Richard did have a ready wit and a great ability to tell stories, talents he used to best effect when offering anecdotes and character studies of the long line of Norseha's predecessors. This was a strategy he had developed over the years both to make himself more interesting and to lower a new lover's expectations. Like any incumbent looking at a list of those who have held the post before, the girl was bound to understand the inevitability of closure. One day she too would be history. And though Richard would never do anything so crass as to begin at the beginning and end at the end, it was impossible, considering them together, for a new girlfriend not to notice a definite and disquieting trajectory to these stories: first the wholesome project of monogamous marriage; then the tremendous flood of passion and betrayal that had swept it away; then the tawdry chronicle of a dozen and more doomed attempts to recover that passion. There must have been few of Richard's girlfriends who had not at some point felt their hearts sink when once again he described how the mythical Marilyn had tightened a silk stocking round his throat and dared him to enjoy life to the full. It was a hard act to follow. The haunting presence of the supposedly *ex*-wife was also disquieting. When Richard first took Norseha away for the weekend – he was giving a conference in some upmarket seaside town – she had been surprised on checking into their hotel room, when Richard broke off the first impetuous embrace to telephone Mary. The older woman was having a wart removed from her hand. She would not understand, he said, if he did not call to ask how the little operation had gone.

But little Norseha was unperturbed by these idiosyncrasies and surprisingly optimistic about their future. 'It's because I'm Malaysian,' she said. 'You never had an Asian girl before.' It was hard not to be endeared by such bright, youthful confidence. Added to this was her apparently insatiable desire to explore every pleasure that sex can offer. When had a sweet girl actually asked Richard for anal sex before, actually insisted he watch her masturbate? For a man who could no longer rely on achieving full erection, never mind orgasm, this was heartening.

With his men friends, Richard had been in the habit of joking that he measured the health of a relationship by the lapse of time between climax and the moment he wished the lady out of his bed, his apartment, his life. An hour, he would say, was the peak of health. When this length of time shrank to nothing, to the point where the intensity of physical pleasure coincided with the thought, 'I want to be alone,' then it was definitely game over. Hence the first time Richard spent an entire day in bed with Norseha was clearly a major development. He lay in the tangled sheets, making and taking the day's inevitable calls on the cordless while she rubbed his back or lit his cigarettes or held his ear in her mouth or pressed a finger into her sex and smeared its dampness on his beard. 'I don't think I've ever felt so relaxed about a relationship in my life,' he told her. The twenty-two-year-old was proud of herself. Even Mary, on their Wednesday dinner together, remarked on how well he was looking. 'I've had news that Dad's a little better,' he explained.

Every summer Richard and Mary would travel north together to visit Richard's decrepit parents. The old people hadn't been informed of the marriage breakup: it would break their hearts, their son had always thought. In the early years, Mary had been resentful. 'You only spend time with me to fool your parents,' she complained. Later, as the old people sank into torpor, she enjoyed the trips for themselves: the long day's drive, some modest country strolls, an evening or two in the pub. It was rather like old times, but without the sex, which perhaps they'd never been terribly good at anyway.

'And Mum?' Mary asked.

'How's the hip?' Richard cast about. He seemed to have forgotten what they were talking about.

'No, she's doing fine too,' he eventually said. 'It's such a weight off my mind. I find it hard to enjoy life when I know they're ill. Perhaps we won't even have to go and visit them this year.'

'Richard, sweetheart,' Norseha said, 'when you're late, I have to wait in the street, you know.' She said no more than that. She was careful never to give the impression she was complaining. Then at the end of what was now a fourth or fifth weekend together, she talked to him about the gap between morning rounds at the hospital and late afternoon lessons in the campus on the other side of town. She lived so far away from both. The university library was full of people eating and talking these days. It was hard to study. And despite the spring the weather had been rainy and cold. 'I must have a key made for you,' Richard said at once, as if this was the only natural response.

But in the hardware store, as the metal of that new key screamed in the jig, he realised that something had changed. 'I have never done this before,' he thought. 'I haven't spent consecutive weekends with a woman since the madness that was Marilyn.' Yet this was different. Why did he feel so relaxed with Norseha? Not passionate and tense, but easy, even happy. 'I never even imagined a person like her,' he realised. It was her foreignness perhaps. None of the regular defence mechanisms seemed to be in operation. 'Thanks,' she said. She took the key and kissed him. 'That's so sweet of you.'

At once it became clear that the pattern of his life would not be the same now. He returned from trips and conferences, or even just a day at the hospital, to find the girl in her white cotton underwear watching television, making herself a snack. It was certainly unusual, but not threatening. 'I like this,' he decided. Then just before he was about to give the inaugural speech at the year's biggest international convention in New York, Norseha phoned across all the miles and time zones to say she had just met his wife.

'You met Mary! Where?' Looking out across Manhattan from the twentieth floor, he was astonished. 'How did you know it was her?'

'In the apartment,' came the girl's voice. 'You didn't tell me she had the key. I was here in the apartment and she arrived.'

'Are you sure it wasn't Mrs Liang?'

But Norseha laughed. She had already met Mrs Liang various times. 'Your wife's not Chinese, is she? She has a limp, right?'

'Right,' Richard admitted. He was stunned. 'And she came up without ringing?' He couldn't take it in.

'No, she rang the bell, but I thought if I ignored it, whoever it was would go away. I didn't know anyone else had the key,' she repeated.

'But what did she say?' Richard demanded.

There was a short pause. 'Oh, she just seemed surprised,' Norseha said. 'She was very polite.'

'Yes, but what did she actually say?'

'Not much.' A more careful tone had crept into the girl's voice.

'And you?'

'Not much,' Norseha repeated.

For the first time Richard felt angry with her. He put the phone down. 'Here you are far from home,' he thought, 'and your entire world is being turned upside down.'

He had to hurry now to make the conference. Arriving at the podium, he felt breathless. It went badly. He couldn't concentrate on what he was meant to be saying, what people on the floor were asking him. The audience was disappointed. As soon as it was over, he rushed to his room to phone back, but Norseha was no longer in the apartment. At great expense, he called her mobile.

'But why did she go there?' he protested. He was smoking as he spoke. 'I mean, she only has the key for emergencies. In case I lose mine, you know, or some workman has to get in while I'm away.'

'There didn't seem to be any emergency,' the distant voice told him. 'She didn't leave anything or take anything or say anything needed doing. We just chatted for a moment or two, then she left.' Cautiously, Norseha added, 'I thought she was rather sweet.'

'Yes, of course,' Richard said testily. He felt he must know exactly what had been said, but was unable to demand that she tell him.

'What are you worried about?' she asked.

'I'm not worried,' he answered, 'just a bit irritated.'

Still, when he put the phone down, he found himself more anxious than he had been for years. He cancelled an interview and a dinner appointment. 'Mary will call any moment,' he thought. 'Mary will phone and demand an explanation.' The only thing comparable was the awful evening when his wife had found out about Marilyn. But everything had happened so quickly then, there hadn't been time to be nervous. She had given him his marching orders at once. He had accepted them without a fight. And of course the thought that his life would be with the other woman had even created a naive fizz of excitement. Now he expected Mary's call at any moment. She didn't have his hotel number, of course, but she was hardly the person to worry about the expense of calling thousands of miles to a mobile, or not at a moment like this. Any minute now she would be on the phone, weeping, accusing him of paedophilia, telling him she couldn't believe it possible. Probably it was only because he'd had the mobile turned off in the conference that she hadn't called already.

Unable to wait for the inevitable in his room, Richard went down into the street. He walked through the busy city traffic. He hadn't told his wife about any of the other women after Marilyn. What was the point of hurting her? On the other hand, she surely couldn't imagine that all these years had gone by without his having sex with anyone, whereas he felt fairly certain her life was sexless. There was between them that ambiguity that develops between some parents and their adolescent children. Everybody continues to behave as if they had no sexual life, even though it seems impossible that this can really be the case. 'Oh, why can't Mary make this a bit easier?' Richard moaned. He stumbled on the kerb. The sidewalk was packed and busy. It must be rush hour. He walked on blindly. He was jostled. Whatever direction he took, he seemed to be going against the flow. Now, of all the women to know about, Mary had met not the sensible Stacey, the decidedly mature Amanda, but this exotic little creature, Norseha. She would have been curled up on the sofa in her underwear. The dark hair of her sex was always in evidence. She didn't shave. The dark hardness of her nipples was something no bra could hide. Or not her bras. He could see Mary's face as she confronted this pornographic vision. Why does the red light district so often coincide with Chinatown?

It had begun to rain, some time ago perhaps. 'I'm wet,' he realised. People were moving faster. Then just as he was crossing 39th and Broadway, the phone began to vibrate in his pocket. This is it. In the mêlée as the light switched to WALK, one hand thrust in his pocket, Richard panicked and stumbled. He was down on the wet tarmac. Somebody tripped over him. 'I'll be trampled,' he thought. He seemed unable to move. A young Hispanic face appeared. The man was going to mug him. Richard felt strong hands under his shoulders. He was dragged to the sidewalk.

'Are you all right?'

'I guess I fainted,' he said. The man was gone. Richard was sitting with his back to a wall, the base of some tower block. The phone was still vibrating. She wasn't going to leave him be. Answer it, he decided in a daze. In the event it was a colleague wondering if he might still change his mind about the dinner appointment. 'I'm really not feeling well,' Richard said.

Why hadn't she called? He sat in his room smoking and watching television. He had found the erotic channel. Certainly she had reacted swiftly when she had found out about Marilyn. It was the obscenity of it, she wept. She had found his letters on the computer. Those were the days before people understood things like temporary internet files. 'I can't believe you'd want to be with someone with such a filthy mind.' After she had asked him to leave, Richard had never wanted to go back. On the other hand there had never really been any question of their not seeing each other on a regular basis. There was still the joint bank account. How would she have bought herself an apartment, opened a business without his spectacular professional success, his unfailing generosity? Richard watched two Asian girls licking each other. He had promised to call Norseha, but felt no desire to do so. Perhaps Mary was not calling because she had cut him off completely. The successful doctor took twenty drops of Bromazepam and eventually fell asleep.

The following day he flew home. He was concerned the Malaysian girl would be in his apartment. In the event he called Mary from a payphone in the railway station half a mile from home.

'Richard?'

He waited.

'Richard?'

'Just back,' he told her. 'Bugger of a trip.'

'What happened?'

He couldn't understand.

'Oh, I performed miserably. Let everyone down.'

'That's not like you.'

'Oh, I don't know. I was upset about something. Couldn't focus.'

'What is it?' she asked. She was concerned.

He flustered. 'Oh, just life,' he said.

'No, tell me,' she insisted. Her voice was quiet and caring and determined.

Inventing more fluently now, he mentioned some tests he would have to do. The bladder. You spend all your life lecturing on diagnostics and then you have to let someone else decide what's wrong with you.

'You can't see inside yourself,' she announced with characteristic primness. He felt immensely relieved and extremely perplexed. 'By the way,' she was saying, 'I know it's generous of you, but do you really think it's wise to let the cleaning lady's whole family take refuge in your apartment?'

'I beg your pardon?'

'You did say they could, didn't you?'

Standing outside the station in the square where the buses stopped, Richard said nothing.

'It's just that I had to pop round there while you were away and when I went in, Mrs Liang's daughter was there.'

'Really? Oh, I don't mind,' Richard said foolishly. Having braced himself for the conflict, the definitive exposure of self, he felt disorientated.

'She was making herself a coffee, if you please. Asked me who I was. I was going to drop off the shopping there while I did a little browsing you know, but then thought better of it. She seemed a rather sneaky thing.'

'She's a student, I think,' Richard got out. 'Or so Mrs Liang said. I said I wouldn't mind if she took refuge there when I was away. I think she has a complicated timetable or something.'

Mary repeated that he really was more generous than was good for him. Palms sweating, Richard ended the call. Settling into a cab, he realised his relief was soured by a growing awareness of humiliation. 'You could have told the truth,' he accused himself. But how painful that would have been for Mary.

'Hello, my love!' Pushing open the door there was Norseha's chirpy voice, her smiling presence, a distinctive perfume. She was wearing green, satiny shorts, a tiny white top which made the skin of her belly darker. Could Mary really have imagined she was Mrs Liang's daughter? He knew his wife had met the cleaning lady – they had all spoken together once – and the Chinese woman was in her mid-sixties, lighter-skinned, and with a local accent. Certainly Norseha would never have made up a story like that. The girl had too much self-confidence. She would have seen no cause.

'Oh, but we've got to fuck at once,' the girl was laughing. 'To fuck and fuck and fuck. Oh, we must.' She was bringing him a glass of bubbly, wiggling her arse. Her accent was comic: 'Do you like the music?' She had bought some new CDs. Jet-lagged, Richard sat on his bed and lit a cigarette. 'Sweetheart,' he smiled. She had begun to peel her top off, dancing to the beat. He watched. About forty-five minutes after making love, Richard began to feel that he would really like to have the apartment to himself now.

The Old House

Once the dramatic circumstances surrounding Albert's death had relaxed their grip on her mind, Charlotte found herself possessed by a new optimism. The time had come to put the family property in order: the old house on Grange Street, the 'chalet' behind, and the so-called 'prison block'.

It was a complex territory. The old house fronted directly onto the main road, and was divided into two apartments with the attorney's widow upstairs and the Serb couple beneath. The other two buildings faced each other across a couple of acres of grassland behind the old house, the only access being through a pedestrian gate. There were no parking spaces. The chalet, built in a hurry some fifty years ago, was a primitive single-storey construction in a state of abject disrepair. Albert had taken to sleeping there when the previous tenant died, so it was vacant again now. Opposite, on the other side of this piece of land that everyone referred to as 'the savannah', the prison block was a rectangular concrete structure without façade or roof. Albert had never really finished it, though the four apartments had been occupied forty years and more. The Johnson sisters were spinning out their old age in the top left, the Greek forestry student was underneath, the luckless Budgen family had the top right and Charlotte herself the bottom right.

All this domain was now in Charlotte's power. 'But remember, Mum,' the children told her, 'you don't actually own it. You only have the usufruct.' Actually the situation was a little more complicated than that. Charlotte owned the old house outright, since that had been her father's. But not the chalet and the prison block. If she should be so bold as to sell the old house, though no one imagined she ever would, the property as a whole would cease to be worth the astronomical sum the children were expecting from it when she died. The savannah backed onto the river at its loveliest. The suburbs of the nearby town were on the point of catching up with this ramshackle, once-remote settlement.

The first thing, Charlotte decided, was to get the savannah properly levelled, cleaned and seeded. Then the brickwork of the old house needed re-painting and the chalet must be replumbed. Most of all, the prison block must be given the dignity of a proper slanting, tiled roof, and brick, pebble-dash or stucco façade.

There were unforeseen difficulties. No sooner had work begun than it emerged that Albert had never had either the chalet or the prison block properly connected to the electricity mains. He had simply taken cables from the old house and strung them up with the telephone wires (though there had never been a phone in the chalet). A delay was inevitable while the utility companies came to sort out the mess and a fine was negotiated.

Having never held a bank account all her life, not even jointly with her husband, it took the eighty-year-old Charlotte a while to get a grip on things. Her daughter drove down from up north to help.

'Who's the old guy who hangs around the gate?' Elizabeth asked.

'How the hell should I know?' Charlotte wasn't interested. 'A gypo, obviously.' The workers were refusing to tile the chalet floor, she said, until they'd been paid for the new plumbing. And there were arrears.

'Can you lend me a couple of thousand?'

'Take it easy, Mother.' Elizabeth was concerned. 'Just do the essential. Keep things ticking over.' The old woman refused to see that as soon as she was gone all three properties would be demolished and redeveloped. Elizabeth and her brother Paul would be rich.

Elizabeth stayed a second week to sort out the piles of papers that her father had left in the drawers of the chalet. The more she looked, the more difficult it became to understand what the old man had been doing with his money. As an itinerant construction-site manager, he had had a good salary until fifteen years ago, then excellent pension arrangements. Yet he owed the bank ten thousand and Paul three. Or so Paul claimed. Nothing had been written down. Elizabeth herself had footed the bill for the funeral. Her mother hung around in the dingy living room while she tried to make sense of all the old bills and letters and receipts. The only thing that was clear was that her father had eaten out a lot.

'Where do you think we can have them bring the gas in?' Charlotte asked. The chalet had never had hot water or central heating. 'I thought we might break the wall below the kitchen window.'

'We're going to have to put our foot down,' Elizabeth warned Paul on the phone. 'Or we'll be up to our ears in debt long before we inherit.'

But the old lady was oblivious to all vetoes. At mealtimes she was cheerful.

'Look at this umbrella I found.' It had been in the bin at the bus stop. Only one of its spokes was broken. 'You can't say I cost a lot,' Charlotte laughed. It was quite a raucous laugh. Once again she described how she had pulled her shopping trolley out of the river. Her skirts and jackets were from charity shops. 'Even this ham we're eating,' she boasted, 'is from the reduced-items shelf.'

'There was that old bloke at the gate again this morning,' Elizabeth said. 'I can't work out whether he's begging or what.'

'It's because of the town coming closer,' Charlotte said. 'Tell him to go to hell.'

Soon after Elizabeth went back north, the tenants began to phone her. Charlotte had begun to demand that they contribute to the improvements being made to their apartments. Violet Johnson was in tears. Her voice quavered. 'We would love new bathroom tiles, but we have no money.' Mr Budgen pointed out that the plastic components he and his wheelchair-bound wife assembled in the apartment brought in only the most modest of incomes. The attorney's widow warned of a letter from the lawyer. Fyodor Samsich said he would willingly do some gardening in return for, say, fifty square yards of the savannah to grow his own greens. It seems he and the Greek student had recently cleared a little patch of the river-bank and often sat there fishing in the early evenings. 'They should pay,' Charlotte complained. 'They leave their cigarette butts everywhere.'

After taking advice from the Small Landlords' Association, Elizabeth explained to her mother that the only thing she could legally do was to increase the rents, which were very low. 'The fact is the tenants aren't responsible for major improvements.'

'The bastards are so tight!' Charlotte complained. 'What would it cost them? Your father treated them too well! "Oh, I'll take you to hospital, Joan!" "Oh, let me run you to the supermarket, Sandra." He was always flirting with the Budgen bitch. I practically had to kick her out. They've had a free ride for years.' The problem, Elizabeth explained carefully, was that rent increases could only be made when present contracts expired: the first would be the Johnson sisters in a few months, the last the Greek student in a couple of years.

Charlotte seethed. She walked back and forth across the savannah, tugging at thistles. Fyodor had cut the grass with a billhook, but it could hardly be called a lawn. Albert had always refused to buy a mower. It should stay wild, he said. If the prison block were given a proper roof, Charlotte thought, it would cease to be a prison block. With the proper improvements the chalet would become a bungalow. Already two or three people had come asking to rent it, though Paul and Elizabeth insisted it be kept free. They might spend weekends there, perhaps moor a boat on the bank. 'All my life that man prevented me from living decently,' Charlotte raged. She slammed the gate. When the place could have been a paradise. And now he had deliberately left her with no money to put things in order. 'I have no money,' she had to tell her two workers, 'until the rents are paid.' Since the men were unemployed, they came regularly to ask for what was owed them. 'At least I always pay cash,' Charlotte said. But if she couldn't even buy the building materials, they complained, how could they start work on the tiles, even if they were willing?

Paul told Elizabeth to tell Charlotte that a mortgage on the properties was out of the question. The elder of the two children by four years, Paul was firm, but found it difficult to take on his mother directly. In general he let his wife deal with life's unpleasantnesses; with mother it seemed more appropriate to leave Elizabeth to grasp the nettle. Intuitively, the tenants sought out the daughter rather than the son. 'She's been having people come in to look at the house,' Fyodor complained to Elizabeth.

He always phoned in the evening as soon as long-distance calls became cheaper. There had been arguments, he said, because the widow upstairs wouldn't let anyone in. She had even emptied a bucket of water from a bedroom window onto the car of the visitors beneath.

'Mum is trying to sell the old house,' Elizabeth told Paul. It was an emergency. Only the day after that phone call, Charlotte's daughter received the following letter:

Dear Ms Marshall,

There is something you should know. You have a baby brother. My granddaughter would never admit it. We are bringing him up in our religion. But it is your brother. We cannot live without some help. God is great.

Otilla Rakhevitch

In her mid-forties, Elizabeth was childless. She had married a man much older than herself, who had promptly developed a prostate cancer that kept her occupied a dozen years and more. Alone again now, she made a modest living running a flower shop. Paul was a painter who had renounced fatherhood for his unremunerative art. His wife, some five years older, was a ward sister in a busy hospital and did not appear unhappy with the sacrifices she had made. Everybody knew they would be well off when the old folks went.

'Are you really planning to sell the old house?' Elizabeth demanded. It was getting quite hard to find her mother on the phone, perhaps because it only rang in the front room, where the increasingly deaf Charlotte had no call to go.

'How else can I get the money to do up the property?' the old lady complained.

'But that's the family house,' the daughter insisted. 'You can't sell it.'

'It's not where I live,' Charlotte told her. 'I want the building I live in to look respectable. I want this property to look respectable. I'm not going to die in a place people call the prison block.' Suddenly Charlotte began to shout: 'Your father did it deliberately. Why didn't he just leave me? Why didn't he give me a life?'

The following weekend, Elizabeth set off early, drove a hundred miles south to the big city, then, with Paul and his wife on board, a further two hundred miles south-west to the town they had grown up in. 'There he is,' she said, pointing out the old tramp opposite the gate. The man was staring at them. 'Oh, but she's made a lot of improvements!' Paul's wife said appreciatively. It was the first time she had ever seen the grass of the savannah cut, the path from street to chalet and prison block swept and clean. Seedlings were shooting up in a couple of vegetable plots behind the old house beneath Fyodor's kitchen window. There was an attractively rural look to it all.

Charlotte seemed pleased to see them. She kissed her son effusively. 'You do need a haircut though, my dear.' She had found a new worker, she said, to redo the window frames. A Moroccan boy. The other two good-for-nothings were bothering her about having spent money on materials before paying them, but that was their fault. She would pay soon enough. 'I never broke my word with anyone,' she declared. 'Unlike someone we know. There's a barber's row on Harper Street. You can go tomorrow morning.'

Rather precipitously, over supper, Paul's wife rushed in with their proposal. 'We would like to sell the whole property now, Mrs Marshall, all three properties in fact. Then with the money you could get yourself a nice little apartment, more or less anywhere.' Charlotte stared at her daughter-in-law. The old woman had a fine gaunt face and dyed blond hair.

'Anywhere, where?' she asked.

'Near one of us, we thought.' Elizabeth tried to save the situation.

'I will never live anywhere but here,' the old woman declared.

Paul's wife became condescending, as if speaking to an unreasonable older patient. 'But why would you sell the old house,' she enquired, 'and not the other two? It's just a bluff, isn't it Mrs Marshall, so that we'll offer you some money to do these repairs? But what's the point of trying to repair a place that's had its day?'

In the normal way of things, Paul admired his wife's toughness. But now he felt an old pit opening. 'Mum,' he said.

Charlotte was on her feet. Her old dress was loose on skeletal shoulders. 'Had its day?' she demanded. 'This place has never even been finished. Do you understand? It never began its day!'

'But Mrs Marshall...'

'Get out,' Charlotte shrieked. 'Get out of my house!'

Paul's wife was ready to battle on, but Paul suddenly stumbled to his feet. 'Please, Mary.' The children were to sleep in the chalet. As they left the prison block, Elizabeth was aware of someone stepping back from the window above them. Old Budgen no doubt. Or the supposed whore Sandra. Immediately, Charlotte's light went out behind them, as if she had just been waiting for them to be gone to sit alone in the dark.

There was a moon out. Crossing the unlit savannah, it was hard for the three of them not to remember how Albert Marshall had, so it seemed, dragged himself through the deep grass in the middle of a January night, completely drunk, pulled himself up to knock on her ground-floor window, begged to be allowed to use the phone, been refused, told he had just overeaten again. 'She's a monster,' Mary announced. 'She's going to thwart us on purpose.' Neither brother nor sister responded.

In the chalet, the taps were working, but the floor was still bare cement. Paul and Mary slept in the old double bed in the larger room. Though he was sure he must have told her this before, Paul explained to his wife that the chalet had been built in great haste for his parents, in return for Albert's accepting the shotgun wedding. Then, together with Charlotte's dad, Albert had built the prison block as a speculation – there had been talk of the railway passing nearby – but when the old man died it never got finished. 'Dad travelled so much,' Paul said, 'when we were kids. Actually I'd end up sleeping here a lot of the time. Mum was lonely.' Sensing her man was tense, Mary tried to embrace him, but he would not respond. 'We must do something to stop her,' she said.

In the adjacent room, lying in the bed her father had used for the last years of his life, Elizabeth too was finding it hard to sleep. They were lumpy old mattresses from a different time. She remembered finding him in intensive care in hospital. His face was badly bruised. He was seriously overweight of course. Presumably the heart attack had caused him to fall and bash his head on some piece of furniture, or a step. He didn't want to talk about it. 'Pussycat,' he whispered. It had always been his name for her. 'Don't let that bitch visit me.' Elizabeth had shaken her head: 'She wouldn't even if you wanted her to.' He tried to laugh. Staring at the ceiling, Elizabeth knew her mother had refused to go through those papers for fear of what she might find there. Two days later he was dead.

The following morning, Charlotte was her normal self again, laying out a generous breakfast. Her rages didn't last long. The roof would cost about 15,000, she said, just a few years' worth of rent and pension. The children listened. As soon as she had finished her coffee, Elizabeth walked back across the savannah, past the chalet and out of the gate by the old house. Sure enough the wrinkled man was there, squatting on the opposite side of the road. There was a tobacconist's, a grocery and a small timber-yard. 'I believe you wrote to me.' The man sat on the gravel watching her. 'Show me,' she said.

Meantime, the two workmen contrived to find Paul and Mary as they set out for a walk along the river. Paul hated such encounters. He was a little frightened. In their mid-fifties, the men were thickset and ignorant. Their voices grated.

'We warned that brown boy to steer clear until we've been paid,' they said. 'You owe us the money.'

Fortunately Mary took over. 'We can't honour all the old lady's debts,' she said sensibly, 'otherwise she'll just ask for more and more things she can't pay for.'

'Family is family,' one of the men protested.

'I'll make sure she pays you as soon as she can,' Paul said.

Charlotte was tackling the Greek student. What about if, in return for exemption from rent, he put these tiles down in the chalet? The suppliers would be delivering on Monday. Having no experience, the young man was perplexed. 'I can tell you how,' she said. 'I've watched it being done a hundred times. Albert was a builder, you know.' She put her arm round the young man's shoulders. 'You remind me of Paul when he was young,' she said indulgently. The young man asked her if she would like a fish from the river some time.

Elizabeth found herself in the disused timber-mill half a mile downstream of the house. These old rural industries were all closing down now. The service sector was moving in ahead of the suburbs. They walked through a hole in the fence and across an abandoned courtyard. The main door was boarded up, but the elderly man led her to a side entrance where there was no door at all. In an echoey space, amid disused machines and dirty mattresses, two elderly women were bent over a makeshift table preparing vegetables. The table, Elizabeth realised, was once the door. There was a queer smell. The three of them spoke a moment in another language. One hurried away into a room behind and came back with a bundle. She moved the blanket aside to show the sleeping child's face. There was no obvious likeness, Elizabeth thought. But then the baby was young and there were no family traits she could think of between herself, her father and Paul. 'It could be any baby,' she muttered. 'We can prove it.' From one of a pile of bags in a corner, the old man found a bundle of papers and a photograph. It showed Elizabeth's father in just his underwear with two girls, barely in their teens it seemed, on either side. They were properly clothed, but one had her open hand on his fat chest.

'Let me speak to the mother,' Elizabeth said.

The old man exchanged a word with the women, then said: 'No. Anyway, they are not here now. Your father came very often to see them.'

'Here? He came here?'

The man stared at her, as if she were being stupid. Eventually he said, 'Your father was generous.'

Elizabeth hesitated: 'What do you actually want?' she asked.

'Help,' he said. 'We will bring the child up in our own way.'

'How much help?' The man said nothing. He had a way of chewing when he was not speaking. Or appearing to chew.

Elizabeth turned and walked to the door. The man followed her. They stopped by the breach in the fence. 'He came to see them every day,' the man repeated. Elizabeth looked at him. His few teeth were yellow and broken, his breath powerfully sour. He looked dreadfully shrewd. Finally she said: 'I think, just before my father died, somebody must have beat him up. That's why he had a heart attack. There were bruises all over his face.'

'I know nothing about how he died,' the man said.

'I think I should go to the police,' Elizabeth said quietly.

The old man repeated that he could prove the child was her brother. 'And my great-grandson,' he added. For the first time he smiled. Elizabeth bit her lip. Some statement was expected of her.

'Neither I nor Paul – that's my older brother – can help you. We don't have money. My mother is running up debts repairing the houses. But when she dies, we will sell the property and then perhaps we can help.'

'You give your word,' the man said quickly.

Elizabeth didn't know what to say. 'I suppose,' she managed, 'if you prove it is my brother.'

That evening they sat around the table in Charlotte's living room in the prison block, while from upstairs came the weary 'thump, thump' of the Budgens' little assembly press. Charlotte was pleased her son had cut his hair. Animated by a couple of glasses of wine, she embarked on a series of stories about Albert's mythically bad behaviour over the years. It was hard to tell whether she was delighted by the quality of the anecdotes, or furious with all she had put up with. 'I'm just going into the bank' – she imitated her husband's rather slow, grave voice – 'you pick up the groceries and I'll meet you here in fifteen minutes. "Fifteen minutes!" he said. And when did I next hear of him? Three months later he phones me from Tripoli. He had a job in Libya of all places. While I had two children to feed and an ancient incontinent mother in a house without a proper roof.'

'Poor Mumsy!' Paul reached across the table and took her hand. Elizabeth felt ill.

'I want to be buried in a different graveyard,' Charlotte declared. 'Don't bury me anywhere near him!'

'She really is quite a character,' Mary remarked as once again they crossed the savannah to go to bed. But before leaving the following morning she reminded her mother-in-law that legally she could not make structural repairs to the prison block or the chalet without Paul and Elizabeth's signatures. So what was the point of selling the old house if they wouldn't let her spend the money how she wanted? Charlotte had put her hands over her ears. 'I'll speak to my children,' she said, 'but not to you.'

Driving home in sober mood, Paul said, 'In our house nothing ever gets resolved.' They still had no idea whether mother really meant to sell the old house. They still couldn't be sure that she had understood that she mustn't do any serious work on their properties.

But some three months later, one small matter was resolved. Fyodor Samsich found the old tenant Violet Johnson's corpse in the river where he fished. A small promontory just upstream created a little eddy, and the body, face down, was turning there in the slack water. Convinced it was suicide, her sister explained to the police that, about seven in the evening, Violet had gone downstairs to beg Mrs Marshall not to increase the rent. It was winter and there was fog.

Charlotte admitted that a tearful interview had taken place, but insisted she had backed down. Or, at least, she had promised the old tenant she would reconsider the matter. Though the rent was laughable. In the event, an autopsy showed that Violet had not drowned. There was no water in her lungs. Questioned separately, the two unemployed workers confessed to threatening behaviour towards Mrs Marshall. But how could they possibly have mistaken Violet for their employer, despite the dark, despite her presence at Charlotte's door? 'Mrs Marshall isn't someone you could kill without an argument,' one of the men said. Asked if there was anyone else who might have motives for killing either woman, the two men shrugged their shoulders.

For some weeks, serving cool flowers to customers in her distant northern town, Elizabeth wondered if she should contact the police inspector. It would be impossible, though, she thought, to talk about that photograph without all sorts of other things coming to light. They were best kept hidden. 'I'm too old now.' Elizabeth decided. Sometimes she had fantasies about mothering the boy. In the end, whoever inherited, it was too late to make any difference.

After All I Gave up for Him!

'After all I gave up for him!' Bonnie exclaimed.

'You're telling me,' Charles said. He offered a wry smile across the table.

'And the thing is, I just can't understand why. It's so... humiliating!' For a moment her educated voice rose to a squeal.

Charles waited. He had been curious to see Bonnie again, but no more than curious.

'And I'm a bloody psychiatrist!'

'Right, I suppose that sort of excludes getting professional help.'

She was shaking her head. Bonnie had thick hair, probably dyed. He had forgotten the extravagant perfume, the frilly dresses.

'I just can't see how I could have been more supportive! You know? I did *everything* to make things work out for the best. And now after all that he turns against me. No, not even that, he turns cold on me. It's worse.'

'Of course, I only heard gossip,' Charles said carefully. The whole premise of this reunion, as he saw it, was that she would fill him in on this extraordinary trouble her husband had been through. There had been an article in the papers. But now that they were at table she seemed reluctant.

'He's just icy,' she sighed. 'As if I didn't exist. And you remember I used to complain how stupidly loving he was. I needed space.'

Charles remembered. He coughed. 'It's not that he, er, found out anything, by any chance?'

Bonnie finally laughed. She drained her glass. 'Kevin's the most trusting person in the world. He probably doesn't even think me capable.'

To Charles this seemed unlikely. He had understood from the moment he saw Bonnie what she was capable of. It was the mouth.

'Now it's like he's punishing me. But for something I haven't done.'

'At which point I suppose one has to ask, is there someone else?'

She was trying to catch the waiter's eye. 'What? Oh, don't make me laugh. That was the ridiculous thing about this stupid court case. It was so obviously *not* Kevin.'

'I suppose not.'

'Though in the end I don't think that's got much to do with what's happening now, you know? If anything, it brought us closer, while it lasted. The worry and so on. But the situation now is unbearable. Like a permanent state of undeclared war.'

'Marriage,' Charles sighed. This kind of conversation bored him. After a decent pause, he said: 'Come on, Bonnie, give me the gruesome details, if only so I'll be prepared if it happens to me.'

Rather dourly she said, 'Just don't open the door to fifteen-year-old Romanian girls.'

'Fifteen-year-olds? Me? Charles Stacey?' The most staid man in Staines.

He waited.

'It was too crazy.' She shook out her hair again. 'Look, Charlie, see if you can get hold of this miserable waiter. I need at least one more drink if I'm going to go into all that.'

Charles got to his feet and went to bother the man.

'So, when did we stop seeing each other?' she asked as he sat down again. He had brought the drinks himself. 'Two years ago?'

'Three.'

Their eyes met for a moment. She sighed and picked up her glass. 'Well, we don't want to go over that again, do we? It was hard stopping, but I never regretted it. Anyway, Kevin, I don't know if I told you, had just decided to go freelance. It was a big moment. He was working himself to death. Stuart had left for Durham. Catherine was getting to that teenage stage where they seem to be out all the time, you know? So we had the house pretty much to ourselves at last. And for a while, everything was fine, one of our best periods in fact. Maybe a year. Then one day the police turn up on the doorstep.'

'Just like that?' Charles said.

'How else? It was late afternoon. I'd just got back from the hospital. The doorbell rings and there are these two blokes in uniform saying they want to ask Kevin a few questions.'

'Frightening.'

She sucked her vodka through a straw. 'Of course,

I imagined there had been a break-in or something and they were just making enquiries.'

'You said they wanted to speak to Kevin, though.'

'Right. The older bloke says: "Perhaps Mr Jackson might wish to be interviewed alone."' Bonnie made a half-hearted attempt to mimic a gruff voice trying to be formal. She frowned. 'But Kevin says, "Not at all." So you can see it was quite unexpected to him. We all sit down in the lounge and the other policeman pulls out a sort of notepad and says: "Mr Jackson, we must warn you that a fifteen-year-old girl has accused you of having sex with her for payment. Since the girl is a minor, this is a most serious charge."'

'Christ!' Charles said. 'Every man's nightmare.'

'Kev and I just sort of looked each other in the eyes, and he was so flabbergasted I knew it couldn't be true. I imagined it was some kind of mistake. They'd come to the wrong house, the wrong Jackson.'

'So who was this girl? I mean, what I can't understand is why the police would even arrive at your doorstep before checking that it was serious.'

'You'd think,' Bonnie said drily. Charles remembered this way of speaking she had, as if permanently scandalised by a world of unforgivably bad taste.

'What it seems was happening' – Bonnie was stabbing her straw among ice cubes now – 'was that this man, a certain Mr Gordon Flint, was going around Staines, ostensibly selling insurance. I mean, he really was selling insurance, for some fly-by-night company or other, but he also had this girl in tow,

Romanian, an illegal immigrant or something, and when he found houses with blokes on their own he tried to sell them the young lady's... services. In the comfort of your own front room sort of thing, and for a modest fee. Anyhow, this little slut – she had some improbable, unpronounceable name – claimed that she had given Kevin a *blow job* in our bathroom.'

'You've got to be joking.'

'She made a sworn statement.'

'But why? Why would she do that?'

Suddenly Bonnie's voice was shrill again. 'Our Kevin, can you just imagine? A blow job in the bathroom, with all his church upbringing and always feeling guilty about everything, not to mention never wanting to pay for anything! And all the time this creepy insurance bloke reading *The Daily Mail* on the sofa downstairs! Every time I try to picture it, I don't know whether to laugh or cry.'

'I'm sorry,' Charles protested. 'I don't understand. Why did the girl go to the police if she was a prostitute?'

Bonnie stared. 'No! Of course she didn't. She and her man Flint, the insurance pimp, were arrested. Some wimpy husband had confessed to his wife. The wife phoned the insurance company, they fired their salesman and reported him to the police. Seems the girl was the daughter of some woman he was living with.'

'So the story of them going around selling sex and insurance was true?'

'Oh, yes. Anyway, the police arrested them, and the charming Mr Flint was trying to get his sentence reduced by giving the police the details of all the blokes he had been taking the girl to.'

'I see,' Charles said. He bit his lower lip. 'And Kevin was one of them?'

'It was crazy, of course. I gave them a pretty amazing piece of my mind, I can tell you. The policemen.'

'I can imagine,' Charles said. He had been on the receiving end of Bonnie's indignation on more than one occasion. It hadn't been an easy affair to end.

'But did they have any evidence, I mean, beyond the mere accusation?'

'I told them, if you had any idea at all what kind of man my husband is, you'd know how ridiculous these claims are.'

'Right,' Charles agreed.

'So,' Bonnie frowned, 'this girl claimed she had given the owner of 10 Feltham Way a blow job on three occasions, in the bathroom, and had sex with him once. She didn't even know his name. Just the address.'

'In the bathroom again?'

'Apparently a lover of hygiene. Obviously she didn't know Kevin because even when we were younger he'd never do it anywhere but on a proper double bed. I don't think we ever had sex in the car or outside or anything. He just wasn't like that. And he isn't a blow-job man.'

'You would know,' Charles said carefully. He and Bonnie had made love almost exclusively in cars, or on country paths and once simply lifting her flowery dress against a lamp-post. It was quite a memory.

There was a pause. Then he added: 'Still, it's hard to believe the police would risk bothering you just on the basis of them making these claims. Just their word against his.'

'She said she could describe the bathroom,' Bonnie conceded. 'In fact, they'd brought cameras to photograph it.'

'I beg your pardon?'

'The police, to corroborate her version. It seems she said that since she'd done these blow jobs while he sat on the side of the tub, she remembered that it was green and that there was a long brown stain under the tap.'

Charles was confused. 'So, she had been in the house?'

'Oh yes, Kevin accepted that at once. The guy had come round trying to sell him some sort of cut-price car insurance. Apparently the slut was dressed in a tight skirt with her stomach bare and red panties highly visible. Kevin said she looked at least twenty-five.'

'And the details about the bathroom?'

Bonnie burst out laughing. 'The funny thing was that right when we took the police to look at it, Catherine lets herself in and comes dashing up the stairs – she was still at school then – shouting, "God, if I don't pee right now, I'm going to burst!" and goes flying into the policemen. When I told her they were accusing Dad of having call girls in the tub she nearly wet herself giggling.'

'I bet,' Charles said. It was this alternation of sophisticated propriety and ready crudeness that made Bonnie such an act. Now she dipped her chin into her cleavage to put the straw between her lips, batting long eyelashes.

'But was the Romanian girl right about the bathroom?' he asked.

'Well, of course she was. While her salesman fellow had been describing his policies, she'd asked to go to the loo, and so had all the time in the world to make notes of what it looked like. She might even have had a mobile with a camera in it, for all I know.'

Charles laughed. 'Good job she didn't remember a particular mole in Kev's pubic hair, or something damning like that.'

Bonnie frowned: 'In the unimaginable event of his actually doing anything,' she muttered.

They were both silent for a moment. Carefully, Charles asked, 'Does he have one by the way? I mean some blemish or mole or something you could distinguish him by...'

'His is bigger than yours,' Bonnie said promptly. 'Yours is darker and harder.' She laughed unhappily.

'You're missing the point,' Charles insisted. 'I was just saying that if he had some distinguishing mark and she hadn't noticed it, then as a defence...'

'Oh, do come on!' Bonnie said abruptly. 'Charles!' She sighed. 'Think of poor Kevin. He had just got his first big contract. I don't know, software for building-site management or something. He was working night and day. Really, I saw it as a way I could make things up to him. Show him how loyal I could be. The kids were incredibly supportive too. Stuart was all for suing for damages, psychological stress and so on. Anyway, as soon as the police had gone, I told him not even to think about it, to get right back to work, that very moment sort of thing, that very evening, and I'd call a lawyer and handle everything myself. It was such a crazy story, justice was bound to be done in the end. And of course I was right. Only it took *so long*. Sometimes I wonder if the tension over all those months didn't affect him in some way that's only coming out now with this awful sort of deadness we're going through.'

'Stress is a bugger,' Charles remarked. 'There are days when I find I scarcely have time to squeeze a darkie.'

'I beg your pardon!' Bonnie squealed.

'Spend a penny,' Charles laughed. At that very moment, as if to confirm this image of the busy man, his phone rang. He studied the small screen, tilting his head back to look through the lower part of his bifocals. 'Damn.' He turned it off.

'Margaret?' Bonnie asked.

'Just some idiot about work.'

'You didn't tell her you were going to be seeing me, I hope.'

'Sure I did.'

'And?'

'Well, she was vaguely pissed off of course, but nothing serious.'

'She's very forgiving,' Bonnie said soberly.

'Lots of water under the bridge,' Charles told her lightly. 'Hang on a sec.' He turned his phone on again, waited a moment, tapped out a text message, then turned it off. He smiled. 'Where were we? Actually, if you don't mind me saying, I mean, horrible for you and everything, but a fascinating story.'

'Working in a psychiatric ward,' Bonnie objected dourly, 'I've had it up to here with fascinating stories. There's always someone being masturbated by his grandmother or raping his daughter-in-law. After a while you just wish everybody was boringly mon-ogamous.'

'I hadn't thought of that,' Charles admitted. He remembered that in the first heady weeks of their affair, her first it seemed, they had done nothing but talk of people's sexual adventures. But he also remem-bered how she liked to lure you into one mood then catch you out with a sudden change of tone. He had never figured out quite who she was.

'So?' he asked.

'So, the problem was the others, the other blokes the slut was accusing, I mean. As the lawyer said, there wasn't really enough evidence to convict Kevin. But all the other people she'd named had confessed.'

'Ouch.'

'It was a trick, obviously. The police tell you the others have confessed. They offer a suspended sentence if you'll plead guilty and so, rather than face a trial, you accept. The lawyer even suggested it might be a solution.'

'So what did Kevin say?' Charles was acutely aware of the need to hide his growing curiosity, or at least the kind of curiosity he was now beginning to feel.

'Since he didn't do it, no way he's confessing, I told the lawyer. The bloke was a bit of a wimp, to be honest. If there's one thing you realise being around schizophrenics all day, it's how dangerous it is to lose a grip on reality. I mean, would you confess to being a paedophile just because they tell you you'll be let off?'

'He wasn't being charged with paedophilia, surely?' Charles caught his breath.

'No, for Heaven's sake. I meant, for the sake of argument.'

'Ah. No, I suppose not. But how did Kev respond? I'm trying to understand how he felt about it.'

'Poor Kevin.' Bonnie shook her head. She dropped her chin and picked at a St Christopher that nestled inside her dress. 'He was just overwhelmed. Working all hours, then this as well. He felt the problem was that no one would believe him, in court I mean, with all the others having confessed.'

'How many others?'

'Twenty-something.'

'Woah! Busy girl.'

'Quite. Think how many bathrooms she was having to remember. Quite probably there were five or six with green tubs and a stain under the tap. Green was all the rage when our place was built. And those Seventies enamels always stain.'

'I can almost see Kev's point though,' Charles said. 'If they'd all confessed.'

'Of course, poor thing. Of *course*! He said if it wasn't for the support he was getting from me and Stuart and Cathy he'd just confess and have done. Because of course the jury wouldn't know him from Adam. Not the way we do.'

'Quite. But in the end he pleaded not guilty, you said.'

'The problem as I saw it,' Bonnie insisted, 'was: if you start confessing to things you haven't actually done and didn't even want to do or dream of doing, where will it end? You lose all control of your life, even your sense of who you are. Just go into the witness box and tell the truth, I told him. Which is what he did in the end, and of course the jury found him innocent. But that was almost a year later, and in the meantime poor Kev was reduced to tears a lot of evenings. He just didn't know how to deal with it. I mean, he's a genius at his software and everything, but he's pretty weak when it comes to dealing with real life. He was terrified by the thought they'd find him guilty and give him a prison sentence when these other guys who'd actually fucked the little bitch were all getting off scot-free.'

'I suppose pleading not guilty is always a risk,' Charles said. Watching Bonnie as she talked, he had begun to remember all kinds of things.

'Fortunately, like I said, Stuart and Catherine were fantastic.' Bonnie laughed: 'Cathy kept saying, if they put Dad in prison, she'd camp out at the prison gates the whole time he was there.'

'Good for her,' Charles said. 'And what was the girl like? The Romanian, I mean. Presumably you got to see her at the trial.'

Bonnie hesitated. 'Not what I'd expected, actually. She looked about eighteen, sort of serious school-girlish, glasses, long legs. A bit sly. Quite a bust.'

'Fuckable?' Charles asked brutally.

Bonnie pursed her lips, raised an eyebrow. She burst out laughing. 'Actually, I wouldn't have minded myself.'

Impulsively, Charles leant across the table and squeezed her hand. 'Still an obsession?'

'I've promised myself I will one day.'

'When it happens, let me come and watch.'

'Charlie!' she shrilled, then shook her head. 'You awful old roué! Anyway, it's all over now.' She withdrew her hand. 'Looking back, it even seems like a happy time. We were close, even if we didn't make love very often. Now it's just death, death death death, for months on end.'

Charles tried to be generous: 'You still haven't explained exactly how. I mean, it's hard for me to say anything useful.' He looked across the bar at a group of youngsters taking their seats.

Bonnie bit the inside of her mouth. 'There are no details, no story.' Her face clouded. For a moment he thought she would burst into tears. Then she recovered: 'If somebody described it to me when I had my professional hat on, I'd say autism, a mild form of autism... if onset were possible in adult life.'

Charles had nothing to say to this.

'But you must speak to each other,' he eventually suggested.

'Of course, all the routine exchanges, but it's as if he's not there, somehow. He's withdrawn himself, shut himself away. And he's doing it on purpose to hurt me. When I suggest he might want to see someone, an analyst, a counsellor, he just denies there's any problem.'

'No problem, no solution,' Charles observed. The remark seemed to have put an end to their conversation. A few moments later they were standing up to leave. The reunion was over.

But no. No sooner were they outside on the pavement than it came over them to make love. This was unexpected and even unwanted. The evening was mild. Someone somewhere had mowed a lawn. As they embraced to say a goodbye, Bonnie held him a fraction longer than was necessary, her perfumed cheek was against his mouth and only seconds afterwards it was, 'Let's… Where? Your car or mine?'

'I love the look on your face,' she told him as he drove swiftly down to the river.

'What look?'

'Purposeful, determined.'

'I've put on weight,' he pointed out.

'The better to fuck me with.'

It was uncanny how swiftly they could fall into old ways, as if, despite the three-year interruption, this secret side of their lives had always been going on.

'I'll give you bigger,' he whispered later when they were parked among the trees. The river was slow and brown here, its muddy smell drifting in through the crack of window she had opened.

'Do, do,' she sighed.

Afterwards Bonnie stared out over the river. 'No, I've given up,' she told him, when he remarked on her not lighting a cigarette. 'It was part of the new me when we stopped, you know. Kevin always hated me smoking. It was part of deciding to be a good girl and stay home.' A moment later, she said: 'I just can't believe how unhappy I am. You know? I can't believe this could happen to me. Such unhappiness.'

They drove through the quiet streets back to her car.

'When you get home,' Charles eventually said – the car was waiting at a traffic light – 'why not tell him you just fucked an old friend in a car by the river? Tell him.'

'Charles! For Christ's sake!' She sat up. 'Don't even joke about such things.'

'I'm serious,' he said.

'Well, thanks a lot. Weren't you the guy who always said: "Deny everything"?'

'Of course,' he turned from the road to smile. 'But I've been caught so often, haven't I?'

She looked at him in consternation. 'But what would be the point? I couldn't.'

'You're the psychiatrist,' he remarked. 'I just count pennies.'

'I'm sorry, but I really can't see the point. I mean, this evening is just a complete one-off. You know that. We're not about to start again. If I wanted to confess something I should have done it years ago.'

'Shit.' Charles suddenly pulled the car over to the kerb and stopped. He rummaged in his coat for his mobile, turned it on, waited, tapped out a message and turned it off again.

'Keeping Margaret happy?' Bonnie was sardonic. Charles turned and looked hard at her.

'No, a girlfriend,' he said.

'Charlie!'

'I'd told her I might be able to see her later on. I didn't think we'd talk so long.'

She thought about this for a moment. 'And you made love to me while you've got someone else on the go?'

'Looks like it.'

'You're disgraceful!'

It was hard to understand whether she spoke in anger or mockery. Perhaps she herself wasn't sure.

'It's disgusting,' she insisted.

'Bonnie?' He smiled. Then he decided. There had always been something about the woman that eluded him. 'Bonnie, I'm going to tell you something.'

Her eyes narrowed. 'Not if it's unpleasant, please.'

'Not at all.'

'Go on, then.'

'While I was with you, Bonnie, I had three or four other girls.'

They were facing each other in the strained light of the dashboard. Teeth clenched, she sucked in air through her nose. For a moment it seemed she would hit him. He could sense the tension in her jaw, the breath held, the skin alert. It wouldn't have been the first time.

'In fact, when I told you Margaret had found out about us, it was actually someone else she found out about.'

There was a long silence in the car. They were parked in a perfectly anonymous side street on a breezy spring evening. Twenty yards away a man in an overcoat was tugging at a dog's lead.

'Well, how nice of you, Charles Stacey,' Bonnie eventually said. Her voice was cold and distant. 'Thank you so much. No, that wasn't unpleasant news at all. You've only ruined what I thought was the one great passion of my life.'

Charles scratched the hair on the back of his neck. 'Nothing's changed, though, Bonnie, I mean if you think about it, I'm still exactly the person I always was. The times we had were exactly what they were.'

'Not for me,' she said sharply.

He sighed.

'Listen, don't you see what I'm trying to say?'

'Actually, no. And please don't try to explain. Take me back to my car.'

'Bonnie, it *was* a great passion, for me too, it *was*, but...'

'I said, take me back to my car.'

He drove. It was hard for him to frame the intuition he had had. Certainly, it was because they had made love, because he loved her in a way, that he had wanted to help. He had put himself out.

'Bonnie,' he eventually tried, 'let me just say this: one of the reasons I'm still with Margaret, I think, is that she's suspicious, you know?'

'Oh, regressive Mr Stacey needs a mummy figure, does he, who will check up on him when he's been a naughty boy?' She spoke in a dismissive sing-song.

'She doesn't check up on me, Bonnie. But I'd feel pretty humiliated if she didn't think I was capable. I'm sure *she* is.'

'I would never have married someone like you,' Bonnie said. 'You make me feel filthy.'

As the car slowed to a stop at another light, the woman suddenly pushed open the door. 'Bonnie!' She stepped out and started to walk.

'Bonnie, Bonnie!' Charles was still shouting. He buzzed down the window. 'Listen...'

'They'll arrest you for kerb crawling,' she said. 'Go and see your little slut.'

Bonnie walked for about twenty minutes. Her mind appeared to have switched off. She thought of nothing. She was outraged, but somehow satisfied too. She couldn't have said how she felt. Then she was climbing into her car and driving. It was only a few minutes to Feltham Way. She drove, as she always did, sensibly, calmly, with a slight frown on pursed lips. It was a residential street with plenty of parking space. The plane trees were putting out leaves. Number 10 was solid behind its tidy hedge, its rhododendron. The Romanian girl knew the address, she had told the jury, because Mr Flint kept records of the houses he visited about insurance.

Bonnie stared at her home. A pale yellow street light held the dark façade in its suburban spell. All the curtains were drawn. It was quite quiet. Both children were away. Her husband went to bed early and would be at work before seven. She had half climbed out of the car when she changed her mind, closed the door, and turned the ignition key again. She was driving to the hospital, to work. 'Well,' she thought, 'I'm the chief consultant, aren't I? I can go to hospital any time I want.'

It was almost midnight. She took the lift to the sixth floor. The corridors were deserted. The ward door was locked and she had to ring for the night nurse. 'Doctor Baldwin is sleeping,' the young woman said. She seemed anxious, as if Bonnie might be trying to catch her out, turning up unexpectedly like this. 'Something I left in my office,' Bonnie lied.

'There was an admission a couple of hours ago,' the nurse went on. 'A young bloke. He's sedated, in room four.'

'I'm just in and out,' Bonnie said. She unlocked the door to her office and sat down behind the big desk. 'I came to get drugs,' she thought. 'Because I knew I wouldn't sleep.' But now she changed her mind. The room gave her a reassuring sense of usefulness and power. She breathed more evenly.

As if she were starting a regular working day, Bonnie picked up the admissions file. The new patient was twenty years old. He had locked himself in his room at college for a week. Fellow students forced the door. The room had been painted black and the walls smeared with shit. No resistance had been offered, but the young man was extremely agitated. A number of superficial, self-inflicted wounds on his genitals had been medicated.

Bonnie glanced through the drugs that had been administered. It was all in order, run-of-the-mill. There were ten rooms on the ward. All the doors were locked for the night. All the patients were locked in themselves. They didn't mind the key turning. Not such a sad place when you got used to it. 'I feel more sane among the mad,' Bonnie decided.

She put down the file. 'Why did Charles tell me that? It was horrible, mad.' She pulled out her mobile and rang his number. Bonnie herself had had casual flings with two other men during their relationship, but she would never have told him. 'Why?' The phone was turned off. 'Damn!' Suddenly her eyes filled with tears. 'Oh God. Why do I feel like this? So vulnerable, so angry?' She breathed deeply. She put the palms of her hands flat on the big desktop. 'It had been good to make love in the car,' she thought, 'I needed that, but afterwards the sadness had flooded back. Waters closing over my head. This constant feeling that I'm about to cry. Perhaps I'm clinically depressed.' And Charles had seen she was sad, he had seen, and what had he done? He had told her something horrible: 'While I was with you, Bonnie, I had three or four other girls.' 'Why, why why?' He couldn't even remember how many, the bastard. 'Damn!' For perhaps two or three minutes she sat with her lips twisted into an unpleasant grimace, breathing deeply through her nose, shaking her head rhythmically from side to side. She felt the control coming back now. On reflection it hadn't really changed her opinion of him, though. He was right there. She knew who he was. 'Perhaps I always knew that,' she found herself whispering. It was strange.

'Goodnight,' Bonnie called to the nurse. 'Keep an eye on room four.' The girl was watching television. 'Goodnight, Doctor Jackson.'

Bonnie drove home. She let herself in and entered the code for the alarm system. Would the sharp little beeps wake her husband? Kevin is a light sleeper. The staircase seemed longer and higher tonight.

'A mountain to climb,' she muttered. 'Shrouded in cloud,' she thought on the landing. In the bathroom, as she cleaned her teeth, she studied the green tub, the orange stain. 'Brown', the girl had said. Bonnie didn't shower. 'I'm damned if I'm showering.'

'Are you asleep?' she whispered, undressing by the bed. She never knew if he was pretending or not. She threw her clothes over the back of a chair. 'Don't you want to know where I've been? Kevin?' There was no reply, perhaps a faint disturbance in the breathing. 'Can one fake such things?' she wondered. 'Is there anything one cannot fake?'

Bonnie lay down beside her husband. The room was very quiet, and dusty. Through lace curtains the headlights of a passing car slid over posters hung years ago. 'You've made your bed, now sleep in it.' Bonnie began to cry.